Everran's
BANE

Everran's
BANE

Sylvia Kelso

Five Star • Waterville, Maine

First Edition, Second Printing

Published in 2005 in conjunction with
Tekno Books and Ed Gorman.

Set in 11 pt. Plantin.

Printed in the United States on permanent paper.

Library of Congress Cataloging-in-Publication Data

Kelso, Sylvia.
    Everran's bane / by Sylvia Kelso.
        p. cm.
    ISBN 1-59414-353-6 (hc : alk. paper)
    1st ed.   I. Title.
PS3611.E475E94 2005
    813'.6 22   2005004991

For
The Four Wise Women
eluki bes shahar
Lois McMaster Bujold
Pat Anthony
And now
Lillian Stewart Carl

sine qua non

Acknowledgements

With thanks to Gordon Aalborg especially for his speedy and patient editing and for playing Virgil through the first publishing *bolgia,* and to John Helfers for his equally patient help and speedy responses throughout.

And to the family members who read this book in progress and wanted more.

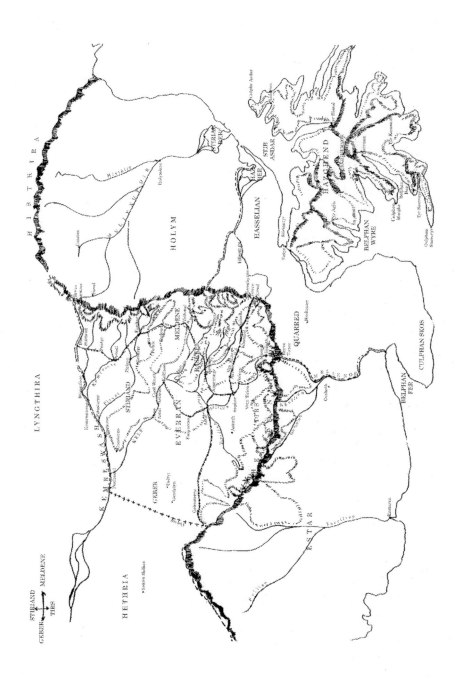

I

Where the dragon came from, nobody knows. It may have flown down from the torrid north, up from the icy south, east across the endless red deserts of Hethria, or west over the bulging blue eyeball of Nerrys'yr, the Peaceful Ocean. Whatever its origins, most people were sorry that it fell upon Everran, which was not only a small kingdom but prosperous, and not only a prosperous land but a contented one. They may have felt such a place should be dragon-proof as well as extraordinary.

As dragons go it was quite ordinary. That is, it was longer than an ocean-going ship, black, mail-clad, claw-toed, fire-breathing, winged, and ravenous. Or silver, fire-breathing, crested with stings, bearing a scorpion's tail, and ravenous. Or molten gold, crocodile-legged, fire-breathing, winged, clawed, possessing eyes that spellbound its prey before the teeth dismembered him. And ravenous. Always ravenous.

These descriptions come from eyewitnesses, or, at least, those who left at speed from a safe distance. No one close enough for accuracy survived.

Which brings me into this song: my name is Harran, and for three years before the dragon came I was hearthbard to the Everran kings. Being hearthbard, I am naturally a harper, which as naturally means, lore-keeper: the guardian of past and present, to whom truth is a sacred trust. I shall have cause to remember that, before this song ends. But I pledged myself to make it, and the holder of that pledge shall have truth entire and unbroken, however discreditable it proves to me.

My own origins are not a mystery. I come from Meldene, those high western hills where the winds riot and the yeldtar bloom crimson amid the gray rocks and gray hethel trees. People call it a hard country, grudging, dull: but if you pause to watch the sun slide on the hethellin groves, or try to number the subtle shades of gray that play amid the leaves in their twinkling galaxies, you may never crave bright colors again.

Perhaps that vision, like the memory of my parents' tall, narrow house above the gate in Vethmel, is biased by time as well as miles. After all, it is eleven years since I left for Saphar with a harp under my elbow and a most noble ambition to be the crower of the age, eleven years that have brought me from the carriers' taverns to the houses of the carriers' masters, thence to the hethel oil and vineyard owners' halls, and on to the marble floors and rosewood ceilings of the palace itself. It is a fine palace, despite its oddity. It overlooks Saphar as Saphar overlooks Everran: a thin angular heap of towers and sun-rooms and open audience halls, straggling along the thin high cinnabar scarp from which Saphar falls in rucks of red tile and golden thatch and whitewash to the loop of Azilien, whose clear blue currents girdle the city like a gemstone in a ring.

Curiously for a capital, Saphar itself was a happy town. There were few beggars, except those too lazy to work, and Everran has plenty of work. The soil of Gebria and Tirs and Meldene is too poor for our neighbors to covet, but the vineyards of Stiriand and Saphar and the hethel groves of Meldene demand much labor, and repay in kind. Hethel oil has underwritten half our aristocrats, and our wine is counted the best in the Confederacy. Since our people are too canny to breed big, expensive families, we need not export men, and our lords learnt three generations back to keep their place in things. There were cobbles in the streets, good engineers had arranged the water supply to the many fountains, and the houses rarely fell down, causing lawsuits more often than funerals when they did.

I knew little of that when I looked up that first time, pausing on the bridge over Azilien. It was a clear sunset, with a sky like a vast azure bell, making the crimson-shot bulk of the Helkent ranges a mere backdrop for the city beneath. In the elbow-crook of river and range it rose upon its knoll in cornice after cornice of golden light, glossed blue with smoke, edged bright with sunset gilt, buzzing and ringing like a happy human hive. Close by came a cheerful racket from a wayside inn. Higher, a harper was playing in some wine-lord's feast. Highest of all, silver bells rang out from Asterne's lookout post, a sweet wind out of the autumn sky. I shifted my father's harp in its old leather sling, and thought: *I shall be a song-king. Here is my inheritance.*

If there may be more than one kind of king, there was only one king in Saphar, as Beryx taught me the first time I played for him. It was in the great audience hall, at the feast on Fire's day. My patron was a high lord, since I was well up my peak by then, and he took me as others took their jesters or jugglers or fire-swallowers: to amuse Beryx, after the lord Iahn had been pledged on His hearth, and the real drinking of the night began.

In such a small capital royalty is not remote. Beryx had crossed my path a score of times, riding out with hawk or hound or border cavalry, banqueting in guildhalls, dispensing justice or inspecting half-built porticoes, overseeing the wine and oil weighed in market when the Confederate traders came. That night in the palace still seems my first real sight of him.

Red light from burning tarsal wood and golden light

from pendant hethel lamps overflowed the hall, cascading through open arches into the sky where Valinhynga, the evening's herald, loveliest of planets, was just pricking through. In Saphar, men dress their halls in air and dress to allow for it. All down the table the lords wore fur-lined jackets and trousers of creamy Quarred wool, with gold chains of office shining over everything. They answered the silver tableware, the ruby glow of wine, the glitter of gems on the ceremonial sword sheaths propped against each chair. But at the table's head Beryx leant a little aside, chin in palm, elbow on the arm of the king's seat, and all the light of the hall seemed to gather on his royal crimson cloak, his raven hair, and his long, lazy, twinkling green eyes, that saw so much and made such a joke of it all.

Sea-eyes, the name means, so it was of sea I sang: not Nerrys'yr, the wide blue ocean, but Berfing, the green southern sea where the whalers of Hazghend stain the ice-floes red with blood. Everyone knows that in boyhood he ran away to ship with them. As I sang I could see the royal brooch, a huge circlet of whale-tooth ivory, rich cream upon his crimson cloak.

The lords clapped at the end, in more than courtesy. It made my patron flush. He was high in his clique, and ambitious of climbing higher, and had seen me as a chancy ladder rung. He called to Beryx, "Is he not a prince of harpers, lord?"

Beryx nodded. Then the corners of his long mouth went up, and he drawled, "A prince of harpers, Vellan. But not—yet—a king."

Though Vellan was a ruddy man I saw his color fade. It was a mere moment, a tiny aside. Yet I, too, saw those eyes were the color of an iceberg's shadow, and I, too, understood.

Then Beryx looked back to me and smiled, a real smile

this time. "Harpers are long-minded in Meldene," he said. "So, you will find, are kings."

So I went back to the lords' halls, and I wrought with my art as vinegrowers do with weeds. And two years later, when the corsairs ravaged Quarred and Beryx took his soldiers down to a great cleansing by the sea, I made a song about newer deeds.

When I finished, he leant back in the high seat and nodded toward the right side of the fire, the place of a hearthbard, which had been empty since his father's harper Quennis died.

"Bring a seat for the harper, Kyvan," he told his chamberlain. "He has been standing long enough."

The king's hearthbard is expected to entertain at every banquet, with an endless fund of songs and a fine tact in their choice. He also adorns household ceremonies, from Lords' days to chambermaids' betrothals, creates memorable lore from mundanities, and commemorates both his lord's judgments and his nobility. I had my rank, my bardic lodging, my robes and role to fill. The one flat in the strings, and that an ungrateful one, was within me. Beryx was easy to serve and easier to compliment: in three years I never had to hide one shabby deed. But in those three years I was never more or less to him than a hearthbard, and he was never more or less to me than a king.

Nevertheless, it was as hearthbard that I had attended audience, on that chill spring morning when the first news came. Counselors, messengers, plaintiffs had all come muffled to the eyebrows: I relished the fire near my own ribs. Vast blue gulfs of air spread below us over the slopes of Saphar Resh, which were all that most delicate green of newly burgeoned vines. Trying to catch it in a couple of phrases, I hardly heeded the messenger, till the silence round him made my fumblings over-clear.

". . . from Pentyr, lord." A farmer, an ordinary pharr'az, dirty breeches, wide straw hat, wide red face. But the cheeks were drawn in, and shiny with sweat. "Couldn't find a mirror-signaler nowhere, we thought best to send . . . There's half a deme of vineyards scorched to ash. 'N steadings burnt. My neighbor Varn." He swallowed noisily. "We heard the screams. 'N Pensal's gone, lord. That self-same night. Fire high as the stars . . . Burning. We smelt it on the wind."

I saw general Inyx's hand clench upon his sword. He had gone against the corsairs. He knew what such burning meant.

Counselors clucked like hawk-scared fowls. In the high seat, Beryx's face was hidden from me, but Inyx stiffened when he spoke.

"Pentyr deme burnt. Pensal razed. Where was my lieutenant in the north?"

The farmer rolled his eyes up. Appalled, I saw he had begun to weep.

"Marched out, lord. All t'garrison of Pirlase, 'n Lyvar at their head. When I left 'twas three days—three days quiet. 'N never a man of 'em come back."

Inyx's sword rasped, half-drawn, then driven home into the sheath. Beryx said, "Thank you." Then, to the chamberlain, "Kyvan, attend this messenger. Counselors, good day."

Counselors' mouths opened. Shut. Out they went, and the rest with them. Only Inyx stood his ground.

Beryx left his high seat and paced about. Harper and general, we watched him as he walked, wind fluting the crimson cloak, across the hall and back across, blazing, dulling, from arch to sunlit arch. Tall, and straight as a spearhaft: a kingly king.

Halting, he looked at Inyx: squat, black, gnarled as an aged hethel tree, his calling in his face. Their eyes spoke, an old comradeship.

Beryx said, "Pentyr deme. Half Stiriand Resh."

I remember finding it odd that Inyx, usually so definite, should seem hesitant, indeed reluctant to speak.

"Lyngthirans," he growled at last.

Beryx shook his head. "There'd have been some alarm."

"Quarred, then."

"Too early. And too far north."

When Inyx said nothing, he went on, "Pensal sacked. A whole deme burnt in a night. Not an entire army could do that."

Inyx growled in his throat. Beryx said, "And the Pirlase garrison clean gone. If it were raiders, someone would have got back."

Not raiders? What else on earth could it be? I looked at Inyx, still mute. Beryx looked too.

Then he said, "You think it is."

If Inyx did not want to listen, nor did he like what he heard. He shook his head about. Then he burst out, "Why should it be? What's to say it's that at all? It could be—"

"It could be what?" He waited. "It could be what, old lad?"

Inyx growled under his breath and tossed up both hands in a surrender long since become habitual. "The Phathos?"

"The Phathos," Beryx agreed, "first."

So messengers went to the observatory of the Phathos, the seer of Now, Then, and Soon. And the Phathos, sitting in the high seat with his claw fingers on the carven chair arms and his thin white beard tumbling over the blue velvet gown that hid his thin old knees, closed his eyes and said in his thin high voice, "It is a Skybane. Its name is Hawge."

Any question of Whence or Why it came or How it might be removed, he declined to hear.

Since the hearthbard is also made free of the king's presence chamber, I too received that messenger. After he left, Beryx set a foot on the hearth-curb and stared down into the core of the fire.

"A Skybane," he said.

On the hearth the coals glared, red as the aura of that word. A Skybane: known in lore if not in living memory, and through that lore they move like baleful meteors. Small matter indeed if it had come down from the torrid north, up from the icy south, east across Hethria, or west over the Peaceful Ocean. It was here. Fabulous, legendary. Crown of scourges, king of catastrophes.

Slowly my training reasserted itself. Harpers are men's judges as well as their memorials. It was for Beryx to deal with this. It was my part to gauge how he dealt. But within the common urge to refuge with our betters from disaster, within the harper's scrutiny, rose a small sharp personal interest: now, at last, I would plumb the man under the crown.

He was still gazing into the heart of the fire. The green eyes were cold, but to my astonishment, full of an intransigent mirth. Then his mouth corners went up.

"A dragon," he drawled. "And in our time. Sad luck—for us."

"Sad *luck?*" The last thing I had looked for was frivolity.

He gave me the tail of an eye. Then he said wryly, "Prophets are seldom so . . . concise."

I gave my opinion of the unhelpful Phathos on my harp. Beryx laughed.

"And its name," he said, "is Hawge." His brows knit. "Is there value in knowing that?" Of a sudden he thrust out a foot to hook round a chair and swung himself astride it with elbows on the back as any carrier in a tavern might. Kingship was in his blood. Kingliness he could shed like a cloak.

"What does the lore tell of dragons?" he said.

"There are many songs," I began.

"Sing them," he said.

The shadows reversed from east to west while he listened, chin in palms, eyes unwavering upon my face. I sang of the goldsmith who became a dragon when he fell in love with his hoard, and his brother whose greed brought a youth to slay his bloodkin on that golden bed. Of the sea-dragon who ate maidens chained to a rock, slain by the head of a woman whose face turned her beholders into stone. Of the lion-hero who slew the dragon guard upon a tree of golden apples at the Other End of the World, of the fire-breathing monster whose slayer was obliged to ride upon a winged horse. Of the sage who mastered a dragon simply by speaking its name, and the dragon who from vanity showed a spy in its lair, its only chink. Of the bowman who found that chink.

When I finished, Beryx said, "Go on."

I looked at him. He said, "You know you haven't sung it yet."

So I sang of the old king who went out, with nothing but mortal might and valor, to slay a fire-drake and save his land: how the dragon seared his flesh and melted his armor, his horse died, his company fled, and he himself, sore scathed, gave the dragon its death wound and took his own.

I made a cacophony of the final chord. Beryx paid no heed. As the jangle died away, he murmured, "But he saved the land. In the end."

17

Then he sat up and began to number briskly on his fingers, showing me how a harper's vision differs from a king's.

"Dragons breathe fire and fly. They are so armed and armored, it is an ill march going against them without some great weapon. Of knowledge—or of magic. Which we lack. Or unless you are a hero-god. Which we are not. Their stomachs are bottomless, but they hoard gold: I must visit the Treasury. You can parley with them. We must wait till it lairs for that. They may be mastered by a wizard. Which we also lack. Or . . . by courage alone."

"What may be done by courage alone?" asked Sellithar the queen, entering from the garden with a swish of silk and a timbre of laughter in her voice.

Sellithar is tall, and fair as Beryx is dark, and comely as women go: but her deep, pure voice is resonant as human harpsong, which is why I have been in love with her since the first word I heard her speak.

"What may be done?" she repeated as we rose. She was smiling, yet her wide blue eyes held a sort of timidness.

"A dragonslaying," Beryx told her, smiling also, "as demonstrated by the king of the Geats."

She caught her breath. Her hand caught the band of sapphires at her throat. Faintly, she said, "Oh, no."

"No?" He was still smiling. "Why not?"

Her pupils widened till her eyes seemed almost black. "You," she sounded breathless, "are the king."

Then, at last, I saw the fullness of the threat. Climbing to my eminence, I had never paused to wonder what upheld the world for me to climb, never pondered the nuances of that word "king." Never thought past the lucky wanderer, the dashing soldier, to the years of trading, building, dealing justice, managing lords and guilds, guarding borders, keeping the Confederacy in tune. Yet each dull daily decision asked as much skill and foresight as that cold glance which had quenched Vellan's uprising with a look. How often had I heard it, at some insoluble debate in market or quarry or guildhall? "Take it to the king." It was upon this Everran rested, as upon the harp's firm arms the fragile strings.

"Starflower," he was saying, light as ever, "you and my harper are a pair. He's sung all morning round what any ditch-digger would tell me. And you won't even think of it."

When she did not reply, he spoke at last those words I had so sedulously avoided: the first words in dragon-lore.

"A dragon's coming is a curse upon a land. Unforeseen, but not unearned."

She looked down on Everran: lovely, carefree, and prosperous. "What has Everran done, to earn a curse?"

He turned his hand out. "You know the saying."

"Not in Tirs." She is from Maer Selloth, citadel of Tirs, our southern Resh. The Resh-lord's daughter. Wed, perhaps, to secure all three.

"Liar." He was laughing still. *"Skybane, king-bane. King-summoned, king-slain."*

Frightened out of respect, I snapped, "If the king is an idiot."

"Master harper," he remarked, while I sat gagged by my insolence. He did not seem offended. He was studying the rich, dark beams of the rosewood roof. "Master harper, what do you suppose the Findarre and Kelflase garrisons will say if I send them after Lyvar's men—alone?"

I retorted with spirit, "That you are a wise general as well as a king."

He shook his head. "That's no road for a king."

"Better," I lost all prudence, "to fry nobly and leave

19

Everran to the dragon—and to Vellan's kind?"

He was looking at me as he had at Vellan. He had not moved a muscle, but his pupils had dilated. It was like hurtling headfirst into two black, deadly, sentient wells.

"Harran is right," Sellithar, invisible, sounded more breathless than ever. "Beryx, he's right. If you were—what would Everran do?"

My sight returned. The king had looked away. He strode to his high seat and whipped around, fingers white on Everran's carven crest of the shield and vine.

"This time," he said balefully, "*I* shall quote some lore." He jerked a thumb at Saphar. "Nine kings ago, our founder Berrian turned that from a pit of brigands to a country's capital. Eight kings ago, his son threw the Hethox out of Gebria and built a wall to keep them out. Seven kings ago, my forefather Berghend ransomed Meldene when he leapt onto the Hazghend spears. Six kings ago, his son met the Lyngthirans in Stiriand and drove them north of the Kemreswash for good. Five kings ago, his son Berazos founded the Confederacy. Four kings ago, his son brought it through the plague. Three kings ago, my longfather taught the Everran lords that a king is not a corsair's figurehead. Two kings ago, my grandfather built this palace," his eye softened, glancing up, "after he led Quarred and Estar to burn the corsairs in their ships. One king ago, my father rebuilt Saphar to match, after he steered us through the five-year drought." His hand clenched on the crest. "Now comes a Skybane. The king of plagues. Up there," his hand shot north, "are wasted lands, burnt steadings, razed towns. Dead men. Soldiers. And helpless, innocent folk. That is my land! My forefathers' trust! Do you think that I, a Berheage, will sit like an Estar shophet and watch it butchered before my eyes!"

From the palace garden a black and white eygnor sang liquidly, limpidly, in the hush behind his steps. Then Sellithar said, between tears and laughter, "He always goes where he wants. And you would have to fight, if you did get there first."

My only answer was in the harp. It grasped a child's phrase, summoning the apple-buds to Tirs. Sellithar caught her breath. Said, "Help him, Harran," and went.

A fine parting chord. But how was I to follow it? A harper preserves lore, graces banquets, and soothes unquiet breasts: he does not change the key of kings. But she had asked for Beryx. And it was Sellithar who asked.

The king was in council. I duetted with an eygnor in the sketchy shade of hellien trees where palace garden meets gatehouse bastion, until green gowns filled the gate beneath.

Inyx was making for the armory and merely nodded when I fell into step. He was in haste. I asked, "What does the king plan?" He answered as soldier to soldier: quick, curt, and frank.

"Scouts. Evacuate. Raise the Confederacy. Levy. March."

"March where?"

His sharp black glance was wholly incredulous. "Stiriand!"

"The king goes himself?"

I got both eyes that time. "What would you think?"

We strode down the walkway past the Stiriann watchtower, Gebrian and Meldener, short and tall, thick and thin. Looking down on those wide, solid, desert-fighter's shoulders, I decided to take a chance. "I think—surely, that is general's work?"

He swung and stopped. He stood four-square, a fire of haste frozen by soldier's discipline. I half expected a challenge for imputing cowardice, but with same clipped gruffness he said, "Laid me five to one in gold rhodellin you'll find a prophecy to keep him home."

I threw up both hands. "If I could!"

He altered neither look nor posture: but his words announced the ally I sought.

"Told him, it's running the whole phalanx into forceps before he's set skirmishers. Like his father. If they don't want to listen—chut!"

"But surely . . ."

"He's a Berheage. They're not much at leading from behind."

He was off again. Keeping pace, I asked, "Inyx—what will it be like?"

His face lost all expression. "You'd know better than me."

I thought of what I knew. "But—Lords of the Sky, he'll not take levies against that! Untrained levies—raw Everran farmers—!"

Inyx gave a short grim snort. "Levies are for Saphar. He's taking volunteers. Three hundred picked volunteers. From the Guard." I gulped. "Phalanxmen that can ride. I'd be luckier finding teeth on a chicken. But they'll ride for him."

There was feeling now: not envy but the rawness of anticipated grief. The thousand Guardsmen, core of Everran's army, trained, tried, tempered to a single sword-arm, were the pride of Inyx's heart.

"But surely Estar . . . Hazghend . . ."

"Seen a dragon lately? Their champions'll be raw as ours."

"Oh, Four!"

Another snort. "Fine sight we'll be. No mail, he says. Iron'll fry you alive. Leather, he says. Bull-hide from toe to

22

crown and round the sarissa hafts. Set of grannies waving fifteen-foot spindles. And archers. In a phalanx. Never led such an abortion in m' life." His stride quickened. " 'March in three days,' he says. I must get on—"

Next morning, down in the marketplace before all Saphar, I watched Beryx seek his volunteers.

The Guard marched in with that concerted thump and ring of perfect unison which only the best troops can achieve: tall stalwart Meldeners, tough lithe Tirianns, squat massive Gebrians, wrestler-built Stirianns, all the weight and muscle and endurance the phalanx demands, a two-hundred-and-fifty file, quadruple column, of shining greaves and mail hauberks and wide-brimmed helmets, their big round shields bearing Everran's crest. And rippling above like the quills of a deadly porcupine, the sheeny heads and fifteen-foot hafts of the sarissas, the phalanx spears.

Inyx bellowed. Two thousand iron-shod boot-heels crashed. Crashed again. With a halt and half-turn they formed a semi-circle about the auctioneer's rostrum, just as Beryx ran lightly up its steps.

"You all know," his voice, barely raised, was clear and carrying as a trumpet call, "there is a dragon loose in Stiriand. Our folk are dying up there. This is not a matter for orders." A sudden elfish smile. "This is a matter for companions. I am going to meet the dragon. I ask for three hundred volunteers."

The ranks rippled sharply, once. For an instant I wanted to cover my eyes, not to see his shame. Then I realized the front rank had shrunk their shoulders as if overcrowded, heard the hiss from behind—"Isyk, you great oaf, lemme *through!*"—and understood.

There were a thousand volunteers.

★ ★ ★ ★ ★

Slowly I climbed away from the scattering crowd, the carriers' taverns, the lords' mansions, the huge spouting serpents of the gate-square fountain, up the zigzag way whose every turn brings your right, unshielded side to the bastions above. Under the massive gate arch built by Berrian, cut with his personal crest: a wide, unblinking, huge-pupiled eye. Up the gatehouse steps. Past the barracks and retainers' houses, the watch and fighting towers, the armory, halls, garden, royal apartments. Still that unblinking stone stare was on my back. I am a harper, I told it. My task is to preserve lore. To make it is heroes' work.

The eye did not blink.

I descended the Meldene walkway. The hearthbard's tower looks to those gray hills from the citadel's brink: a nice touch, I had always thought. The door opened on my harp, hung in its new cover, marehide stitched with beryl stones to outline the vine and shield in scintillant green fire. Beyond was the great Quarred hanging, miniature gods and heroes in a verdant paradise beneath the smoky-lavender clouds of terrian trees in bloom: my last year's Fire-feast gift. On the sideboard stood the silver jug and goblets he gave me for that corsair song. The set of ivory tuning keys, the inlaid Hazyk armring, the riot of seven colors in the hearthbard's ceremonial robe— Enough! I cried, whirling to the window. Sellithar was sitting with her maidens in the tiny pleasance just beneath.

Very clearly, as the door closed, I could recall the flower hues of their dresses, the twinkle of needle and ring, the crisp eucalypt tang of the helliens whose thin shade splashed Sellithar's hair. She was wearing a coronal for which I once made a song: a play on, "gold and lesser gold, the lesser crowning more." It ran in my head as I went, searching for the king.

24

The Treasury is a place I love, not for avarice but because the play of light on precious things is the music of light itself. Everran had its share in those days: gold, silver, gems; gifted, won, inherited. The king stood facing the barred window, the Treasurer at his elbow, and as he turned I recognized what he held.

If nobody remembers Maerdrigg, all Everran knew his maerian. Berrian brought it, to be the pride—some say, the luck—of his house. It is oval, a palm wide, an inch thick at the center, the color of translucent milk: but move it, and the depths prickle into shifting, arrowy, red and golden fire. They say men were and are and will be ready to kill for it. It was also the only gem in Everran's treasury I had never been able to like.

Beryx had been handling it with something like my own fascinated repulsion, but as he glanced up it vanished in a glint of mirth.

"Master harper." He acknowledged my bow. His mouth corners puckered. "Have you come to reveal a prophecy, by any chance?"

"Alas, lord," I answered blandly. "You have lost your bet."

He laughed outright. "So my old Lockjaw talked at last! What is it, then?"

"It is a favor, lord." My own voice: why did it sound so strange? "I have come to ask for a horse."

He grew very still. The quiet of masked regret. Even, possibly, grief. "And, master harper, where do you wish to ride?"

"To Stiriand," I said.

The Treasurer opened his rheumy old eyes and stretched his tortoise neck. Beryx looked taken aback. Then he said rather hurriedly, "Master harper, I will not hazard you. This is no harper's work."

25

"Permit me a confession, lord." I kept my tone light. "There is another lore-word I omitted. When the war-lords meet, it says, 'The bards of the world appraise the men of valor.' Such a meeting as this, then, is surely harper's work?"

His eyes narrowed. Then they altered. He handed the maerian away without looking where. "Harran," he said a little thickly, "you shall have your horse."

And I went out feeling absurdly pleased for one who has just contracted to commit suicide, because he had never before called me by my name.

From then on Beryx most resembled a whirlwind set on legs: you cannot simply walk out of a kingdom and clap to the door. Message after message went out to call up levies in Gebria, Tirs, and Meldene; to ask help from the Confederacy in Quarred, Estar, Hazghend, and Holym; to summon his uncle as Regent from Aslash; to order urgent evacuation of Stiriand. Nothing mobile would stay in the dragon's reach. And north, too, went the scouts and mirror-signal relayers who would direct our march.

I had my own kingdom to arrange. My one body servant, used to bards, said calmly, "To meet the dragon. Yes. Will you be taking the great robe?" But there was also my treasury of lore, more precious, more jealously warded than my blood. I spent the next two days feverishly rehearsing my apprentice in the Ystanyrx, the Great Tales, inwardly crying, Why did I do so little? Why did I start so late?

When he was saturated, I said, "Tomorrow, then." He rose from the window seat, carefully wrapping his harp, a slender, serious lad with deep brown eyes. Almost desperately I said, "Zarrar, you will remember?" And his face broke into its rare, impish smile.

"Have no fear, lord," he said. "Whatever befalls you, the songs will be sung."

I was so wrapped in my own affairs that it came as a surprise when the queen's steward asked me, next morning, to play for her at Ilien's festival.

Everran honors the Four Sky-Lords without ostentation: people go in their own way and their own time, up to fly Air's huge gaudy kites atop Asterne's thousand steps, out on the roads with the saplings to plant for Earth, off to Hazar's little green plain where bonfires seed the dark for Iahn's day, and down to the river for Ilien. Descending through the city, Sellithar and her maidens and I swelled a steady stream of families and households, each with the wine-pitcher and the toy boat piled high with Water's beloved smoky-lavender terrian flowers.

Below us the long narrow parks along the river margin were moving flower beds, and Azilien's bosom wore a drift of smoke-blue petals and tiny white sails, their progress followed with cries of tension and delight and cheerful woe. If your boat reaches the bridge safe, says Saphar, your wish will return in the coming year. Sellithar's maidens were merry already. Sellithar, in a smoke-blue smoke-thin gown that honored the Water-lord and made her eyes rival Azilien, was quiet.

As we crossed the springy new grass, she said abruptly, "Beryx was too busy. It's the first time I've been—alone— for Ilien's day."

"I remember," was all I could manage. Being near Sellithar always clogs my tongue.

She glanced east. In the river's bight, a stand of silver-green morgas trees cupped the white head of the Phathos' tower.

"Was the Phathos," she said with the same strained abruptness, "no use?"

"All he told us," I answered ruefully, "was the dragon's name."

"Its name?" Something near horror dilated her eyes. The coronal's freestanding golden terrian sprays shook above her golden coils of hair, and something squeezed my heart.

"Lady . . . Sellithar." I hoped she would not catch the interval. "It will never reach Saphar. And if it did . . . the king would have you away long before. He would never risk such a—"

Treasure. What can you say, when every word turns to revelation, or to fulsomeness?

Her hand twitched and jumped on her sapphire collar. She was distressed for some hidden thing, and I knew it. And it was not my place to comfort her.

"Lady," I said, "shall we trust it to Ilien?"

So at the water's brink I sang the slow, sinuous Ilien'nor, while Yvalla poured the wine, slowly, gracefully, its red thinning and coiling away into the pellucid stream. Then, more graceful than the falling wine, Sellithar knelt to launch the boat.

The water cradled it: a propitious breath of westerly plumped the sail. It glided away. At such times a ninety-year-old can be only nine. Yvalla and her fellows jumped squeaking up and down, gasped, cheered in relief, and so did I. Sellithar stood rigid, eyes fixed painfully on the dwindling shape.

It neared the bridge, one among a flotilla converging on the pier eddy, Yvalla was running deer-like for a closer lookout—and the wind changed.

Like a slap it backed to the north: a vicious gust scourged the river-face. The tiny sails jerked aback, entangled, capsized. As the gust fled away, the bridge-arch swallowed a drift of pathetic debris and a trail of drowning flowers.

Sellithar went so white I almost dared to catch her arm. "No," she said faintly. "I am well. Thank you, Harran. No. I can walk alone. Only . . . only . . . I think we will go home now."

Ilien's day falls on a full moon, which left the eygnors wakeful as I. I tracked the lattice shadow, dismembered the bed: hated birds' effortless mastery. Then surrendered, took harp and cloak and went out into the noon of night.

South-east of my tower a tongue of garden slants down from the royal apartments to the deep-cut stair of an ancient postern gate. The garden was afloat, ethereal, the loftiest terrians reduced to pure line and shadow, a painter's sketch in an unpaintable light, but the air was rich. Dewy grass, tang of helliens, honey breaths of norgal tree blossoms, mingled with a drift of pure wizard's spice: a rivannon tree, thick with sprays of brown and yellow flowers. In its shadow I sat down, tuned, and waited for music's release. But the spell was never realized.

Someone was trying to take a mule through the postern gate.

I heard the obstinate clatter and snort. Breathless mutters: a muffled clang as the iron wicket swung shut. Moonlight showed me the tall ears, the obstinately humped quarters: a swathed head, skirts.

"You really should know better," I said, coming along the wall, "than to try that with a mule. Especially at night."

The mule cracked its nostrils, the driver choked a shriek. I just caught the halter in time to prevent a bolt. The mule skittered, trembling. The woman faltered, "I could not—there was no other way." There was no way of disguising that harpsong voice.

"Sel—Lady," I said. "Where—why—what in the Four's

name are you doing here," I took in her coarse clothing, "like this?"

The over-tuned string broke. Dropping back against the wall, she buried her face in her hands and burst into such a spasm of sobs as almost tore me apart. I could not release the mule, I dared not embrace the queen. Another rescued us both.

"Sellithar."

The mule's ears flickered and relaxed. The queen fell forward to that quiet, all-sufficient voice.

"What is it, clythx?"

It means, Heart. And he said it with such tenderness.

The sobs died away. The queen rested in his arms as in sanctuary: but the note in that pure voice was defeat.

"I was going away. To Stiriand."

Beryx did not stiffen. And only I could see his face.

"But clythx . . . why?"

"Because," another stifled sob, "I asked Ilien . . . and the ship sank. Before the bridge."

I would have cried, Will you augur from such child's omens as that? Beryx knew better. Kindly, gravely, he persisted, "But clythx—why Stiriand?"

I made to shift the mule. He gave his head a violent shake. Within his arms, that pure voice spoke with a rending despair.

"To find the dragon," it said.

I think I froze. Certainly, I could not believe my ears. Beryx sounded carefully casual.

"Surely, clythx, a king and three hundred guardsmen can deal with that?"

"But the curse is my fault," said the hidden voice. "It has been my fault these last five years."

The eygnors caroled on, heart-whole, oblivious. The

mule hove a bored sigh. Very slowly Beryx freed a hand, cupped her chin, and lifted her face to his.

"Clythx?" The quiet had changed. Now it chilled my spine. "Who has made you think a queen must breed like a carrier's mare?"

She merely shook her head.

I saw his shoulders straighten. When he spoke, his voice had changed again. Steady. Deliberate. Accepting more than the role of comforter.

"Clythx . . . remember the lore. If it *was* that which—brought the curse—a dragon is summoned by the king."

I must have jerked the lead-rope, for the mule flung its head up and his voice changed in a flash.

"Now Harran shall stable your nag and you can take off those abominable clothes and we'll all forget this," I felt his eye on me, "and go where we ought to be: home in bed."

He turned her about in his arm, and they walked away, her head against his shoulder, his arm tight about her waist. Left with the mule and the moonlight, I tried to feel thankful, and could find only an ache that overrode the too explicable dread. For we both needed comfort, and she had taken it: but the comfort she had taken was not mine.

II

We marched from Saphar with the Helkent pinnacles black on a tiger's eye streak of cloud. Torches lit the marketplace tangle of skittish horses, clumsy riders and swearing, laughing grooms, and all Saphar had come to see us off. Hooded market-women jostled lords untimely out of bed, urchins dived among wives anxiously watching their men cling to reins and manes, or counselors disordered by reversing rumps. Sellithar had not come, but a bright yellow square of window marked the queen's tower, high in the gloomy sky. There were no cheers, no thrown flowers: just a great many quick, quiet embraces, some bleats from the Regent, and a few heartfelt cries of, "Luck!"

After things settled, I found myself riding close behind the banner, the trumpeter, the general, and the king. Inyx, top-heavy in mail on a shaggy mountain pony, resembled a bandit off on a raid. Beryx, resplendent with crimson cloak, damascened corselet, and plumed helmet, sat his big brown blood-horse like the pattern of a cavalryman. As the bumping, grumbling, jeering tangle unwound behind us, hide armor bundled on horses' rumps and sarissas waving all ways to imperil neighbors' heads, he glanced round and grinned. "Thank the Four," he remarked, "they'll be earthborne before we charge."

It was my first true acquaintance with flesh and blood warriors. They may be gallant and lordly in combat, but beforehand they grumble, quarrel, get drunk, lose their gear, their money, their horses and themselves, make lewd jests, sing lewder songs, and need more shepherding than all Quarred's flocks. Nor do they relish civilian company.

At first the horses kept them humble, but the second night Beryx and Inyx took me along with trumpeter, banner, and armor-bearers when, as usual, they joined the circle at the nearest fire. Beryx too had noted some surly looks. The moment we settled, he called across, "Harran, will you give us a song?"

Soldiers have their own bards: they have poets as well. Some of this doggerel had been running in my head, mixed with the rhythms of our going, the broken clop and crunch of hooves, the jingle of scabbard and bridle, the gusts of talk, the heavy flap-flap of the long green banner on its haft. I patterned the rhythms and married in the rhymes, adding a few of my own. What emerged was a marching song, scurrilous as always, deriding everything from the dragon, "that flame-throwing lizard," to the king's helmet plume, "tall enough to tickle the dragon's—"

I had begun in dour silence. I progressed in stunned quiet that broke in a roar of delight. A little unsure how Beryx would take it, I glanced across, and he shook his fist at me, laughing with the rest. Then a huge Gebrian's friendly pat almost snapped my collarbone, his neighbor soused me with a battered tin bucket of wine, and next day I had to ride with the first squadron, who all wanted to sing, but could not quite recollect the chorus of my song.

All those days are merry, when I look back. We were on the road, an enlargement in itself: riding in the effervescent spring weather, and it was fine. Meeting a new challenge, and in my case, finding a new fellowship. And crossing the uplands of Saphar Resh, Everran's heart, with its trim whitewashed villages, its endless rolling green vines, its cultivated trees at every well and roadside, its cheerful, prosperous people to feed and stable and wish us on our way.

Beryx too was merry. He had become a soldier, no more than first among equals, and he had the soldier's gift of living now, shutting out before and behind. Often he made me think of the boy who shipped with the whalers those fifteen years ago—until the mirror signal came.

We were nearing the rust-red, deep-cloven uplands of Raskelf, where the Kelf river springs and Quarred summers its flocks. Against the Helkents' embery flanks the signal made a white stutter of light in the early dawn, bringing the column to an instant spontaneous halt. Inyx leapt from his pony, whipped round his little polished cavalry shield, and flashed an acknowledgement. Around me men leant forward: many of the phalanx veterans could read mirror signals too.

"Findtar . . ." someone muttered at my shoulder, ". . . burnt. Oof! Garrison . . . east. Evacuation . . . what in the Four is—?"

"Dislocated," rapped another voice. "Sarras—" "He runs Gesarre—" ". . . fallen back on Kelflase. Fire reported—to his . . . south!"

"Four!—" "Shut up!—" "Scouts lost . . . delayed . . . last report—"

"Smoke in the . . . Perfumed Vale. Finish. Luck."

In the deep dull hush, someone else muttered, "Thanks."

Beryx had been sitting utterly still, a carven cavalryman on a carven horse. Now he turned his head. He and Inyx exchanged a half-dozen staccato sentences and he wheeled his horse. The merriment was gone. His face was as honed and planed as a sword bared for the thrust.

"Forced march." His voice matched his face. "Squadrons close up. At the trot." And swinging his mount from the paven roadway, he jumped the ditch and headed in a bee-line for the north-east.

"Ain't the pace—worries me," panted a tall Stiriann, as we towed our grunting horses over yet another limestone scarp. "Beryx always—gets along. It's these four-footed bladder-bags—we gotta tow behind. Here, harper. Give's its head. Now belt it, Asc!"

My horse came up with a bound, my Gebrian acquaintance lumbered after it, and we slid slantwise down a scree fit to capsize goats. In the ravine bottom, the banner-bearer was girth-deep in stones and foam. On the further brink Inyx's pony reappeared, black with sweat but tossing its head in a clear question, What's keeping you? As Beryx put his horse to the climb, I could not help asking, "Surely the road would have been quicker?" which brought a snort from Asc.

"General's playing scout. We'll be headed for the Perfumed Vale quick as morvallin fly."

We ate noonday bread and cheese on the march, watered in mid-afternoon at a river Asc called the Velketh, and biv-ouacked on the northern side of a valley paved with the world's hardest stones, amid the glorious confusion of our first picket lines. I was almost too weary to walk. Beryx was everywhere: adjusting hobbles, hammering halter stakes, checking head-ropes, hooves, and backs, all with a crisp ur-gency worlds from his former merriment. The men did not seem to mind. They leapt to obey his orders. They even leapt with alacrity when the trumpet sounded before Valinhynga brought up the dawn.

That day was easier, since instead of running athwart the Raskelf we angled down the Pirvel valley's wooded river-flats, often moving at the trot. "Four send we find this lizard," growled Asc, rubbing his backside as we walked at noon, "before my rump wears out." The horses, hard-ridden by inexperienced men, were white with salt and beginning to flag, yet Beryx still pressed the pace. Errith the Stiriann, also unconcerned, predicted, "Drop these clumpers soon."

The valley widened, a long vista of a green and silver-gray north, with Kelflase somewhere in its folds, but our mirror signals brought no response. Then the slopes of Saeverran Slief began to rise on our left, pale blonde upland grasses that the Stirianns named with nostalgia as they bumped: but that too was devoid of life. In mid-afternoon we struck the Saeverran road. As we swung onto its deeply rutted wagon tracks, Beryx reined up.

"General!" he called. "Do you smell smoke?"

A hundred yards in front, Inyx wheeled his horse. I heard his wide-nostrilled Snff! And as the weary column slowed, a northern air drew it over us: a vile, choking waft of charred thatch, smoldering timber, carrion, and half-burnt flesh.

Inyx looked at the king. "Ah," he said.

Beryx glanced round. Behind the helmet nasal his brows almost met. "Volunteers?" he said. "Scout?"

The first squadron's surge carried along my horse. Beryx said swiftly, "Asc, you've a good eye, Errith, Iphas, Thrim—Harran?"

"When my horse volunteers, lord," I said, "I can hardly retreat."

Asc and Errith laughed. Beryx gave me one glance cut razor-edged down between mirth and irritation and said, "Go on."

Berating my idiocy, I walked my horse forward with the rest. We could all see the smoke now. It was rising from just over the ridge, a thin, languid coil of black upon seraphic horizon sky.

The soldiers fanned out. Asc growled, "Come behind me, harper. Cover you with this bladder-bag," and brought his sarissa to the port. Errith rose in his stirrups. Over Asc's massive shoulder I saw a winged black cloud whirl up, heard a raucous, indignant yark, and then Thrim's growl in his throat. "Morvallin. The black sods."

It was an ordinary upland farm: a stone-gabled house, byres and barns forming three sides of a square whose fourth side opened to the road. Something had struck the house—

No. "Struck," is not the word. From central door to gable, the wall was gone. The king-beam had snapped. The gable itself was a heap of tumbled stone. A fire had been burning inside. Wisps of smoke still rose amid the blackened remnants of wall-timber, furniture, family possessions, and charred stems of fallen thatch.

"Ah," said Asc, deep in his throat. He checked his horse, and sat looking round in the eerie, unnatural quiet.

The white-washed barn door was open, an ox-cart propped in a corner of the yard. Trampled flesh-red soil brought up the gray-green foliage of helliens rustling beyond the house. At the yard's center was a cattle trough, a hollowed tree-trunk that held a glitter of white. Beyond lay a bundle of discarded sacks. They were red-stained. A white bone was sticking out . . .

"Best get off, harper." Errith gripped my arm without looking round. "Don't mind us. First time, most throw up."

As I straightened, he spoke to Asc. "Feeding cattle. That's salt."

"Ah," Asc repeated, that subterranean rumble quite expressionless.

Thrim put in, "Cattle rushed. See t'fence?" It was a post and rail: two posts leant drunkenly, rails hanging from their mortises in splintered stubs. "Went out there."

All the heads turned, in that slow, hair-trigger scrutiny, to the slope behind the barn.

The cattle had run uphill, scattering as they went. The first was a young red heifer. On her back, all four legs straight up, belly torn open from udder to dewlap, intestines strewn around. Asc spat with a disgusted hawk. Next was a calf. Its head had been torn off. Then a cow, ribs stove into the bloated trunk. The next was a bull.

"Four," said Errith under his breath. He had no need to finish, we were all thinking it: what sort of claw can rip out ribs and gouge the spine from a full-grown bull as a falcon does with a mouse?

"Best go back," Thrim said in that wooden voice. The horses were snorting, beginning to crouch and sidle; soon they would be out of hand.

"Ah," said Asc again, eyes on the slope.

Silently we looked with him at a thirty-foot black swathe of grass burnt off at the roots. Then with a speed that nearly shot my heart through my teeth, he swung off and thrust his reins at Iphas. "Hold that."

No one spoke as he came back. He was walking slowly, head bowed, cradling his burden with incongruous tenderness for such a big, burly man. "Back," he said, walking past without a look at us. "Report."

"Playing up hill, I reckon," Errith commented in that empty, controlled tone, as Asc delicately, tenderly, laid her in the road before the king. She could not have been ten, and she had been pretty, once. The slender sun-browned arms, the wisps of silky blonde child's hair, and the long fine legs were pretty still.

"Day . . . Day and a half." Asc, too, used that flat, empty speech. "House smashed. Farmer dead in yard. Cattle killed. But only morvallin've touched. Didn't feed." A thread of deep, savage hatred entered his voice. "Sheer—wantonness."

Beryx was looking at the child. I saw his nostril-rims turn white and his jaw muscles bunch and heard that furious, protective cry in the presence room. "That is my land! My charge and trust!" But his voice was empty too.

"Inyx, fall out the column. Set outposts. You men, come with me. Bury her, Asc."

We rode away in that same unnatural quiet which had lapped the farm and, looking at the men around me, I saw that red-hot, protector's vengefulness in every face.

We struck up over the Slief, far north of Saeverran town, riding in a fringe of scouts and presently, into a sunset that was a silent hymn to Fire. On our right, the slopes from the distant Helkents were a tide-race of fiery gloom and bloodily glowing crests, on our left the Slief climbed in sheets of scarlet and deepest crimson to a cloudless, wine-flushed sky. But in the north the light rose vertically up an enormous cloud bank whose buttresses of molten copper and alexandrite thrust out between rose-black canyons, burning without combustion in the vacant air. A little warm wet wind arose: a northerly. I sniffed the stink of foul conflagrations, but also the tickle of rain on dried-out earth.

Asc grunted. Thrim said, "Just so it wets that sod as well."

Around the fires they regained some spirit, but now there was real malice in the boasts and savagery in the jests, and the dragon was the only butt. Presently rose a cry of, "Harper! Where's harper? C'mon, harper, give us a song." Rubbing his calves, Errith added, "Take m'mind off these galls."

39

My own choice was for something gentle, to erase those still-too-present memories. But a harper must know listeners as well as lore, and escape was clearly the last thing in their heads. Moreover, Beryx would not have thanked me for sapping their courage if it were.

In the end I dredged up a thing I dislike and seldom sing, an ancient vendetta chant of Meldene: a tribesman hunting human blood. It brought a hot, eager roar. As Beryx rose, sounding the unofficial turn-in, Asc rumbled, "Come'n check cloppers, harper. You've done me a power of good."

We lurched off amid the manure piles and hidden stakes and horses luckily too tired to play the fool. A stumble and a clipped, "Uh!" announced Inyx on the same errand, and by common consent we paused at the line end, staring into the starless north.

Asc sniffed. Inyx said, "Ah."

Asc said, "Reckon it's there?" And Inyx growled in his throat.

"Scouting. Flew a circle round Kelflase and back. It's there."

Asc's deep voice was musing when he spoke again. "Ever see the Perfumed Vale, harper?"

"I have heard the songs," I said.

"Ah." More silence. Then, "I don't have the words. But I reckon songs'd miss the gold, for that."

He paused. We moved to turn away. And then all three of us froze in our tracks.

A sound was drifting out of the north: tenuous, bodiless, the very emanation of night. It began on a high note, a thin, tremulous wail: wavered, rose to an eldritch howl, hung at its climax till my teeth hurt. Dropped, ending as if slashed. Inyx exclaimed, quick and incoherent, under his breath. I felt the hair rise on my scalp.

It came again, a chorus this time: a quavering, soprano cadenza, a choir's mourning voice. But from no human throat.

The fires' comfortable hubbub was dead. The silence was complete. The very horses must have been holding their breaths.

Once more that shrill, eerie keening wavered up into the dark: trembled, faded, died to a dissonant finale, and was lost. Then the night pressed down on us until I felt myself suffocating. I let out my breath.

Asc backed straight into me like a panicky horse. I never thought such a man could so disintegrate. "Not me," he was moaning, "I didn't, I never meant, I'm not ready to—" And, as if ungagged, Inyx snarled, "Shut up!"

"Si'sta," he went on fiercely; he must have been shaken too. I had never before heard him lapse into dialect. "Si'sta, this is Stiriand. And th'art a Gebrian, tha great stupid lump!"

Asc was still quaking. I managed to say, "What was it . . . anyway?"

"Ulfann," answered a quiet, cool voice in the dark. "A big pack, by the sound." And the night was only darkness, the ghosts' sobbing the call of feral dogs. "Don't worry, Asc." For a moment the coolness held contained, deadly rage. "If they're hunting anything, it'll be the dragon's scraps."

Inyx came in at once, in something very like relief. "Horse here you should see. Staked in the coronet."

The king moved away. I heard that steely reassurance applied at another fire. Asc did not move. When I thought he could take it, I murmured, "What did you think it was?"

He did not answer for a long time. When he spoke, the

abruptness said his courage had not yet healed. He said, "Lossian's hounds."

"Oh." There are scores of songs, reserved for the evening's end, about the Stiriann Hunter and his bloodless pack that course men's souls. They say that a Stiriann who hears them calling is doomed to join their quarry before the next new moon.

"But," I tried to steady him, "the general was right. You're from Gebria. They hunt Stirianns." He gave a one-shouldered shrug. "Why should they call for you before—anyone else?"

Asc turned away, bringing his face to the distant firelight. It was calm now, composure regained. A man looking open-eyed upon his fate.

"Not me," he said very quietly. "All of us."

We saddled up in a drizzle coming down in slow gray showers from the north, dulling the Slief, shining thinly on horse-rumps and helmets, oiling sarissa blades, blanching everything. Only Beryx's green eyes seemed to brighten in that pallid light. When I rode up to the banner, they shone beneath his sodden plume, and he gave me a hunter's smile. "Just," he said, shaking off a shower of raindrops, "what we want."

The rain shortened horizons. The sky was low too, hiding any trace of smoke or change in light. Almost without warning, the Slief ended and we were on the brink of a precipice, with the Perfumed Vale at our feet.

Deve Astar is a gorge, little longer than a mile, where the Kelf drops from the uplands into Gebria's arid plains and flows to join the manifold channels of Kemreswash, thence to vanish in the insatiable Hethrian sands. The water comes down in a cascade famed for its roof of rainbows and the dazzling white of its froth against the luxuriant greens below, a vision to match the beauty of Deve Astar's air, an invisible paradise.

The forest is artificial, lovingly planted and tended, with every scented tree in Everran among its stock. The topmost terraces bear flowering helliens, with white, orange, scarlet, and magenta blossoms whose honey inebriates birds. Next come the keerphars, orchid-shaped pink and purple blossoms whose dry, delicate perfume enhances the helliens' sweet. Below are twisted rust-red yeltaths, shrubby cennaphars, and norgals whose long green leaves droop about papery white trunks, all mingling honey scents with the torch-pines' aromatic white flowers. At the waterside, the sellothahr's snow-white, gold-hearted blossoms spread their spring morning smell, and along the gorge flanks stand acre upon acre of rivannons whose fragile brown and yellow sprays breathe an incense to ravish Air himself.

Tucked in coigns of the terraces lie foresters' huts and perfumeries, innumerable beehives, and cabins for travelers who come from as far as Estar, less to see than to breathe. The most famous song of the great harper Norhis calls Deve Astar a giant agate: outside are the rust-and-honey bands of the cliffs, then the forest's variegated greens, deepening to the seam of marble-white froth at the gorge's heart.

A shower was passing as we reached the crest. The distant rumor of the cascade, a breath of diluted perfume, floated up. Slowly the farther scarp emerged, glistening sleekly, bay and russet from the wet. Then the rain's wings lifted from the Vale beneath.

Inyx stiffened as if struck. Errith let out a winded grunt. Thrim's was more like a moan. I heard it travel down the column behind us as one by one they reached the prospect of the brink.

Almost from our feet a lane of felled trunks and broken limbs and dying leaves ran away downhill, scored clean across the vale as if some brutal engineer had been clearing a road. The river was choked: as the cascade poured down, heedless, insentient, the water had backed up to inundate the vale below. We could see its cold, turbid glint up where no water should be, but downstream from the dam was worse.

Fire had been kindled there. It had been lashed across the forest like a whip, and the trees had burnt behind it, for most of our scented trees are rich in oil. Huge, charred weals ran hither and thither, with pitiful half-stripped skeletons upright in their desolation, some still smoking, some with a few rags of brown leaf or a couple of heart-breaking withered flowers. The helliens had suffered worst: along the upper terraces the fire had run from treetop to treetop, leaving unbroken courses of destruction: leafless, black. But burning helliens had fallen down upon the keerphars, and the keerphars had collapsed onto the norgals, whose papery bark had fired like candles, spreading the blaze to the yeltaths and the ardent cennaphars, thence to the rivannons, which had disintegrated upon the sappy sellothahr, breaking what would not burn. The subtle spectrum of greens, the soft flower tapestry, was all gone.

A wind moved, and a sickening stink enveloped us: perfumes corroded by the reek of green burning wood and oil-bearing leaves, and the fetor of that burning untimely quenched.

I found my vision had blurred. My throat was thick with tears. I too had cherished the Perfumed Vale, if only in others' songs. One day, I had promised myself, I would come there and make a song of my own. When I was at the height of my powers.

When my hearing returned, men were swearing and mourning all round me. Not loudly, but with the anguish of a hurt too deep for noise. Then, as the first brunt of the blow passed, it became fuel for rage. Everywhere they gathered their reins, clenched their sarissa butts, and looked toward the king.

So far as I remember, Beryx had not made a sound. I do not think he so much as clenched a fist. He was sitting quite motionless. Except that his head was turning, a slight, deadly movement, as his eyes quartered the vale. This, I remember thinking, is a king. No raving, no lamentation: all feeling kept to power the revenge.

Then he turned his head.

His eyes were quite black. The pupils must have dilated until the irises completely vanished, and as he looked at me I covered my own eyes, for that blackness was more blinding than the sun.

When my sight cleared, he was speaking to Inyx, in a soft, impersonal, terrifying voice I had never heard before.

"There is nothing to eat. Nowhere to lair. It will not have stayed. How far to Astarien?" Inyx, looking almost scared, jerked his chin upstream and muttered, "Ten miles." Pulling his horse round, Beryx said with the same glacial ferocity, "Come on, then, you clodhoppers. Ride."

The way to Astarien is mostly footpaths, which was fortunate for the horses, for otherwise Beryx would have foundered them. As it was, we slid and swore and skidded along in peril of our necks, with the king up and down the column like quicksilver: saying little, but making that little cut deep as a knife.

Around noon we toiled up a last ridge, and cross-wise beneath us opened a wide valley whose mouth was shut by the thick green band of timber along the Kelf. Stands of silver-gray tarsal and black-barked elonds scattered the valley undulations, folding up to a silver bezel set above a gray ring-wall. Astarien's lookout tower.

Beryx let out his breath. Inyx let out a grunt.

The valley was thick with trails of ants. From all ways they converged upon Astarien, gray, brown, and colored ants, with the blobs of cattle, horses, oxcarts, and every other sort of conveyance from palanquins to wheelbarrows in their midst. Inyx said tersely, "Evacuation. Town'll be out of its head." Beryx retorted, "There's a governor," and started his horse.

But half a mile from the town he too was riding at a walk, and on the rise to the gates he had to admit defeat. "Inyx!" he bellowed above the bawling, yelling, squawking, and yammering as a mob of cattle engulfed us, inextricably tangled with a flock of irate geese. "Halt—column!" He raised his voice a notch. "First pentarchy . . . follow me!"

Astarien was worse. The gates were jammed with stray stock and fugitives' paraphernalia, while citizens, refugees, and a frantic garrison churned wildly through the streets, and when Asc and Errith literally fought our way into the governor's residence, we found a plump bald provincial on the brink of lunacy.

"No-no-no!" he shrieked as Beryx knocked the door open upon a snowstorm of papers and hysterical suppliants. "No more! Throw them out!" And wheeling to repel the door guard, I was struck dumb to find the king consumed with mirth.

"Really, Gerrar!" his clear voice cut the racket, crisp, winged with authority, intensely amused. "Including me?"

Gerrar gaped. Then he gasped, gulped, and nearly burst into tears. Beryx held up an embrace aimed somewhere about his knees.

"I never thought," he remarked as Gerrar subsided, "when I ordered an evacuation, that it would prove quite so . . . turbulent."

Gerrar clawed the air for words. "Lord, lord, if you only knew—seven days it's gone on and nowhere to put them and we can't raise Kelflase and Sarras said the dragon was headed here and I've nothing to fight it with and—I can't stop them, I can't house them, I can't even feed them and now the dragon's in my Resh and—and—and I don't know what to *do!*"

"First, sit down." Beryx backed him to a chair. "Then forget the refugees. Then think about the dragon. Is it this side the Kelf?"

Flopping into the chair, Gerrar mopped at his brow, and presently assembled a reply.

"Last word was this morning. Coed Wrock. Saw the neighbor's steading burn and ran for their lives. Coed Wrock—" his face knotted with the struggle to recall knowledge basic as his name. "Coed Wrock is . . . just across the Kelf."

"Good." Astounded, I saw Beryx was smiling again: a blade-like smile worlds away from mirth. As Gerrar's jaw dropped, he put a hand on the plump shoulder. "Now forget the dragon too. Just think of someone smart enough to take the king's authority and picket three hundred horses. And then tell me his name."

It proved to be the garrison lieutenant. He had no fresh news, but once extricated and undistracted he collared some farmers and fairly ran them out to the task. As we rode up to our beleaguered column, Beryx gave a little sigh, and there was a kind of gaiety in his eyes.

"Right, lads!" he called, shouldering past a wheelbarrow load of fowls and two collided ox-carts. "You can get dressed. We're off!"

★ ★ ★ ★ ★

The men marched in a mood wild as Beryx's. As they forged through the refugees still clogging our track there were extravagant jests at escape from the horses, extravagant grumbles at the bull-hide armor's weight, extravagant boasts of the dragon's doom. Beryx made them soak each other in the Kelf's shallow fords, which doubled the complaints. Then he formed them in a hollow square with archers and banner in the midst, and after that, to me, the jests rang jarringly false. For as he called the Advance, I saw the high tawny skyline of Astarien's Slief was limned not against gray rain clouds, but on a bleak blue sky rimed with smoke.

I reassessed the men around me. They moved solidly, ponderously, thick bone and muscle cased in each sodden carapace, the sarissas swinging with the even ripple of a long distance march: yet now I could read the tension in each familiar face. Perhaps, I thought, the joking was a thing they could not help.

Beryx alone had retained his horse. Presently he called back, "Harran! Why don't you help these clumpers along?"

So it was the rhythm of an old marching song, older perhaps than Berrian, which swung us up the rutted track to the water-blackened, dust-yellow rock divide that names Coed Wrock. Watershed Farm. And it was upon that rhythm that we topped the crest, and a wide bowl of devastation opened beneath us about two fountains of strong black smoke.

Beryx called the Halt. Inyx went forward to his horse. I heard scraps of talk. "New smoke" . . . "must be here" . . . "Where is it, then?"

The valley was wide, strewn with outcrops of house-sized granite boulders, scattered with thick stands of whippy upland norgal and writhen black ensal trees among acres and acres of scorched, smoldering grass. In all that desolation only the smoke and a black cloud of morvallin moved.

Inyx was still talking. Beryx shrugged. Inyx's voice rose. ". . . daft, I tell you—dismount them and not yourself! For the Lords' love—" Beryx's jerk of the chin superseded words.

He came riding back, calm now, but with a mad, dancing brightness in his eye. "Ready, lads?" Perfect confidence in the smile. "Harper, take cover here. You can't 'appraise the men of valor' with their sarissa butts knocking you in the teeth."

I opened my mouth, but he had already looked away. It was a command, not open to dispute.

The ranks parted for me. Iphas gave me a tight grin. Thrim said, "Keep t'head down, harper." Asc gripped my arm and said nothing at all.

The Advance was passed. The square began to move. I sat up on a rock and watched, defiant, desolate. They reached the burnt ground. Black ash puffed up, I caught the muffled thump of boots, a cough, squeak of wet hide, clink of belts. Then, high, clear, merrily taunting, the trumpet sounded. Not a war-call. Beryx had offered the ultimate impudence: it was the hunter's View Halloo.

I waited, feeling my stomach squirm. The square was well distant now, on an open slope down to the gullies that veined the valley center, swaying and twisting as they held rank over the broken ground. Glaring round, I thought, almost desperately, Damn you, come out.

The ridge-top beyond me moved. Ten or twelve boulders shifted like a rousing snake. A knoll rippled, surged, became a crest of tree-length spines, a spur toppled into a fore-arm, a shoulder, a foot the size of a horse's trunk, with nails and spurs longer than scythes. Then the whole rock line beyond left the ground and swung slowly, drowsily, sideways in midair. Hawge had lifted its head.

Out in the valley came the small urgent ring of commands. The square stopped, shifting as the ranks faced outward on each side. The front line knelt, and the men behind them planted sarissa butts in the ground. It was a hedgehog, crouched for offensive defense.

Languidly, Hawge lumbered afoot. Its back was to me, so I saw the scorpion sting on the dragging tail. The legs sprang lizard-like up from below the trunk and angled down again to the foot, which moved clumsily, hampered by its frightful claws, but the thighs were huge as trees. The back curved up under its crest of spines, as yet lying half erect, dipped to the serpentine neck, and rose again to the head. I still see that in my dreams.

I suppose it most resembled a gigantic earless, hairless horse. The nostrils were monstrously oversized, and the orbital bones exaggerated so the eyes bulged out far beyond the head: pupilless eyes, multi-facetted, twirling like a fly's. What struck me hardest was their color. Because like Beryx's, they were green.

It took a step, and the membranous wings rattled on its sides. It was mailed, as the lore says, iridescent black, gold, silver when it moved, glinting on its lean greyhound flanks. The tail twitched. Then, slothfully, with a volcano's insolence, it yawned.

The jaws seemed to open forever, clean back to the eyes, the lower one pointed and reptilian, both snagged with curving white fangs, clear against black stains on the serrated canine lips, the immense red tongue, and the gullet like a well. It sighed: a forge-like roar. A small jet of fire shot from its nostrils, and I caught the opened-grave stench of its breath.

It seemed half-minded to lie down again, for the head swayed, low to the ground. The eyes revolved torpidly, a green corpse-light against the leathery skull. Then the trumpet rang again.

Hawge sighed in answer, unfurled its wings, black leather mainsails, and leapt up into the air.

The image of those massive flanks and shoulders' wave-like ripple blinded me. I next saw it circling the valley, flying with a vulture's labored indolence, twirling its eyes to study the men below.

Whatever Beryx said, the words were inaudible. The huge burst of laughter which followed them was clear enough, and enough, it seemed, to pierce a dragon's hide. Hawge dropped from its patrol and angled in at them, the mighty wings rowing lazily, the head almost skimming the ground.

Nor did I know Beryx's battle plan. I merely saw the sarissas on that side swing apart, heard Inyx's whiplash, "Fire!" and Beryx yelling above him, "Take its eyes!"

A flight of arrows flashed up and over with a second flight so close that it looked continuous. They were the Tiriann clothyard shafts that can pierce a shield and go on to kill an armored man, and for all its armed and armored might Hawge lifted over the square like a huge black morval that has mistaken its prey. A yell of, "Everran!" followed it from three hundred throats.

The dragon snorted in reply. Fire shot out ahead and wreathed back along it sides. It flicked over on a wing, turned in its length with a breath-stopping agility, and this time there was no indolence in its flight.

Inyx bellowed again. The sarissa points swung out and

down as they do for the charge, and the ranks braced their shoulders for the shock.

Hawge leveled out with tail brushing the ground. Just beyond spear length it reared up as a fighting cock does to use its spurs, beat the huge wings once to give the blow full impulse, and flung itself upon the spears.

Sarissas broke like sticks, men tumbled head over heels, the square side collapsed like a broken dam. But with a scream of pain and wrath that nearly burst my eardrums, Hawge hurtled past the banner and sought refuge in the higher air.

I vaguely recall them pulling each other upright, grabbing for weapons, laughing as they scrambled back into line amid Inyx's brazen roars. I was myself leaping up and down in a manner most unbardlike, yelling taunts to the dragon that now circled fast and furiously, spouting fire as it stoked its rage. Great gouts of flame hung like lurid puffballs in the sky. Beryx was yelling as ferociously as Hawge had, while his horse plunged and gyrated, utterly terrified.

The square had barely reformed when Hawge banked, folded its wings, and catapulted into a dive. It plummeted down like a monstrous misshapen falcon stooping straight on the square's center and so fast I thought it would break its own neck as well as theirs.

The sarissas shot up. I looked to see them all crushed bodily, no steel sting could repulse such a charge. Then the wings backed with a slam like thunder; the dragon braked impossibly and unleashed a spout of fire just above their heads.

The square vanished in foul black smoke, the dragon roared like a furnace and shot by just above it, the tall green banner toppled, I heard shouts, screams, Inyx and Beryx roaring through the din. The dragon doubled up, leant in on a wing, and spouted again.

The uproar crescendoed. Easily now, the dragon lifted away.

The smoke convulsed and battered itself. Then, from its depths emerged, not scattered, broken fugitives, but a bank of haphazardly pointing spears.

Slowly the square coalesced beneath. The men staggered, some supporting others, coughed, choked, swiped at their eyes. Their bull-hide armor steamed like kettles and they beat their arms frantically to and fro. The sarissa ranks were ragged, the lines worse than doglegs: but they were intact. Even as I looked, a sooty green rag jerked upward in their midst.

Hawge's scream could have pulverized rocks. The square dressed ranks with frantic fumbling haste while the dragon whipped round and round overhead, re-stoking its fire. Beryx wrestled his maddened horse. Inyx was still roaring, hoarse with smoke. As the dragon turned over into its next dive, the sarissas opened and a flight of arrows met it high above fire-range.

Hawge swerved in mid-plummet, screamed with rage, and tore up into the higher air.

The square swayed as men propped themselves on others' shoulders. Some were running back into the smoke, retrieving sarissas, tearing home as the dragon dropped once more.

This time the arrows did not deter it. Three times it scourged them with flame, and three times the square sustained it, emerging disordered and distressed but unbroken beyond the smoke. But the sarissas were thinner, broken or burnt, and as the square moved, many wounded or disarmed men were helped along in its midst. I was hoarse with futile shouting, and my stomach had grown cold. How long before they faced the dragon, weaponless?

Once more Hawge dropped in that catapulting dive. This time the sarissas stayed upright, but a shining hail shot up from their midst full in the dragon's face.

In the midst of the volley Hawge twisted and shot out its wings. One got out of time. Beat wildly, un-coordinated. Seemed to crumple. Its own momentum slid Hawge side-long down the sky as it made a desperate recover, lost it. And hit with a thump that shook the earth, amid a barbaric yell of triumph from three hundred smoke-parched throats.

Very clearly, in the comparative lull as the dragon floundered, I heard Beryx's order. "Present—sarissas. Charge."

The front rank sarissas came to the horizontal. The square moved.

A phalanx charge is not the cavalry's delirious thunderbolt. It is delivered at a walk, measured, deliberate, and irresistible as death itself. I could picture my friends' faces: Iphas, Errith, Thrim, Asc, all cold with vengeance about to be assuaged.

Hawge had blundered to its feet. It waddled a few steps, clumsy as a grounded albatross, looking over its shoulder as it went. The square came on. Hawge's eyes revolved. Its head snaked along the ground. Then it turned and began lumbering forward too.

Fifty yards. Forty. I could hear Inyx calling them off, steady as if on parade. My fingernails had pierced my palms. Thirty. My throat ached with the expectation of fire. Hawge was breathing it, short pants, oily black smoke shooting above its head. Twenty yards. Inyx yelled, "Go!" And as the ranks broke into a trot to gain momentum the dragon swung its tail.

I think—I hope—most of the front rank died instantly. They were my friends. The tail mowed the entire rank down, smashing them into the ground, hurling them in the air like toys, crushing rib-cages and pelvises inside the bull-hides that could foil fire but not such giant blows. The second rank, trapped in the charge, fell over the bodies with sarissas going all ways as they tripped, the square sides spilt helplessly outward round the fallen, and with a tremendous brazen bellow Hawge lashed fire into the chaos and followed it in with sting and tooth and nail.

I cannot describe the rest: it is blotted by smoke and tears. I remember stray sarissas beating in the murk, the dragon's back that surfaced like a spiny whale, geysers of red-hearted black dust. A sweep of the tail flinging two bodies thirty feet into the air, the flash of steel as someone, in gallant despair, tackled it with a sword. A running archer caught by a fire-blast and turned to a falling meteor. A monstrous claw coming out of the smoke to dig in and twist as the dragon pivoted, and blood spouting from a body— dead, I pray—under the nails. The hideous, hideous noise.

And Beryx, with a sarissa for lance and his cloak over his horse's eyes, hurling them both at the dragon like some mortally wounded, pain-demented boar.

The sarissa pierced Hawge. I saw its head go in, somewhere at the root of a wing. The dragon let out a screech that muted all the others and whipped its head about on a gout of flame, the horse screamed as horribly as only horses can and tried to rear over backward with its front legs seared completely away, the dragon's tail caught it in mid-fall and hurled them both skyward like scarecrows, whiplashing to catch Beryx as he came down and hurl him away again like a catapulted stone. Then the smoke veiled it all.

III

Sunlight was beating on my head. The rain had passed, to leave a brisk, fair, brightening afternoon. Only my face was wet.

Gradually I realized I was seated, hands clenched between my knees, braced against cold uneven rock. I could smell only rain-washed air. Hear only an aching silence, punctured by faint, derisive yarks.

Painfully, I opened my eyes.

The fires had died. The smoke had blown away. Below me on the silent battlefield, Hawge was dining upon its spoils.

I have never purged that image. Some things should not be sung. I can still see it, though: the clear blue sky, the nude black earth, the pitiful debris of torn, broken, strewn bodies, red flesh and glaring new-bared bone amid the sheen and stare of broken weapons, the sepia blotches of sodden bull-hide, the thick red blots that marked pools and pools of drying blood. And the vast black bulk of the dragon couched full length among it, only the head moving as it scavenged. Idly, daintily, here and there.

No telling how long I sat there. Horror erases time. But presently I noticed the body of a horse, lying apart from the rest, and that reminded me of the Geat king whose horse died with him. And that connection shot me to my feet like a red-hot spur.

To do what I did then you would have to be beyond fear: this is not a boast, merely a note that beyond certain points fear ceases to exist. I walked down the hill, out over the blackened earth, up to the carnage, and within earshot I stopped and spoke.

"Hawge," I said.

The dragon's side loomed over me, monstrous as a ship, black, moving slightly as it breathed. Hawge did not bother to rise, or to turn its head. But one eye revolved, to take me in a green, crystalline, inhuman gaze.

I looked down. I knew the danger of a dragon's eyes. There were bodies at my feet. I remember wondering if Asc was one, lying here smashed and twisted with the impossible suppleness of the dead.

The dragon exhaled, a lazy, furnace draft.

<Man,> it replied.

The voice was curiously puny for so large a beast. Indeed it was more of a rasping whisper, hardly vocalized at all. It waited for me to go on. And what I must say next rose in my throat like bile.

"If my lord pleases," I said, "I should like to make a song, about this famous victory."

Hawge's head came round. It is quite true that dragons are very human: vain, with a sense of humor, delighting in riddles, power, gold and death. There was humor in that lidless eye which dwelt on me, but there was also an acuity to chill the blood.

<What,> asked Hawge, <do you want?>

After a moment to gather my wits I answered, "My lord has many . . . many . . ." I gestured around. "All that I ask is one."

Hawge pondered for what seemed an eternity. Then it sank its head, and blew a puff of rose-pink fire. And presently asked, <Which one?>

Ridiculous to say, I don't know yet. Perilous to reply,

The one who wounded you. Hawge waited. In desperation I said, "It will be a famous song."

Hawge rolled over. The crystalline eye roved from me to the corpses and back, and I felt it pierce through all the subterfuges to my very soul. Then the chin sank on the ground and the vast whisper said above me, <Leave his horse.>

As I turned in flight, a thin tongue of flame licked my calves and Hawge breathed after me, <Remember the song.>

With music or not, that search must remain unsung. There were men still breathing in that charnel house, and I could not, dared not succor them . . .

Beryx lay just inside the further edge. I saw the wink of steel amid the matted bull-hides, then a blood-red helmet plume. He was face down, legs doubled and twisted under him, arms flung wide as if he had tried to roll with the impact, face buried in the corpses beneath. The corselet was shattered like hammer-struck glass. All his right side was a ghastly mess of broken steel and bone splinters and raw flesh and crusting blood, with a frightful welling pit halfway down his ribs: the mark of the sting.

When I could see his face I did not recognize it, for all of it was black and half of it was burnt. I remember standing there, half-weeping as I sought a way to carry him, to carry him alone, to carry him with the honor he deserved.

Finally I got him over a shoulder, limbs dangling round me, and staggered drunkenly away. Hawge revolved a single eye to watch me go.

If the climb to the watershed was bad, the descent was worse. I kept slipping, and Beryx grew heavier and heavier. Nothing weighs like a lifeless man, and he was a tall one, and I am slight. Finally I had to rest. I set him by the track, thinking that now I could at least lay him out decently, trying not to think of the infinity between me and Astarien, left with no space to think of grief.

It was near sunset. The sky was full of wind-cloud, long plumes of fiery rose and lambent apricot tousled against halcyon blue. The air had chilled. My shadow was long. As I bent over Beryx, another shadow crossed it and I leapt to my feet.

He studied me across the body: a stocky, black-haired, gray-eyed Stiriann, with a farmer's coarse blue shirt and breeches and a most unfarmerly naked sword. Imagining looters, I was ready to fly at him like a faithful, futile dog. But he jerked his free hand downward and said, "Who's that?"

"Beryx," I said. "The king."

He frowned down at the body. I said, "Who are you?"

He answered without looking up, "Stavan. Coed Wrock." Almost belligerently I demanded, "What are you doing here?" And he responded in key.

"You're on my land," he said.

"Air and Water!" No doubt I was hardly a model of aplomb. "The quintessential pharr'az! 'You're on my land!' Well, there are three hundred other dead men and a dragon also on your land, and if I had a bier I'd be more than willing to get this one off!"

His eyes had not left Beryx. Now, not deigning to answer, he dropped on a knee, and I nearly leapt before noticing he had put down his sword. He went on staring. Just as I prepared to wring his neck, he sat back on his heels and began to pull off his shirt.

"In the Four's name!" I bawled. "He doesn't need a blanket, he needs a bier! And if you got off your behind and signaled Astarien you'd be more use than you've ever been in your—"

He lifted those passionless gray eyes and said as if I had not spoken, "Undo that flap-coat of yours while I cut some saplings. It's a litter he needs." And, as I went quite rabid, he pointed to the welling pit in Beryx's ribs and said, "Blood's wet. Heart's pumping: see how it makes? He's alive."

Whatever else befalls me, I shall number that week in Astarien as the worst in my entire life. It was not enough to be the sole survivor of a holocaust, nor to totter back with a king slung on a couple of shirts and saplings at the point of death, nor that I must bring him into that lunatic's stewpot of a town where the local government could not make itself heard, or try to nurse him in chaos worsened by scenes of insensate grief, all with the dragon still lying on my friends' bodies within wingbeat. I, a mere harper, had a kingdom landing round my ears. "Take it to the king." That week I learnt just how much they took.

Evacuees were still coming. Gerrar was beside himself: half the towns of Everran were asking where to put and how to feed them, every governor north of Saphar wanted to know what the dragon would do and what he should do next. The levy commanders in Saphar were ramping to sacrifice their green troops, the Guard wanted to give Inyx a military funeral. Quarred enquired if it were safe to summer their sheep in the Raskelf, the lords had illicitly raised the wine price, the Regent did not know what to tell Estar and Hazghend, and the farmer holding the phalanx's horses wanted to know for how long and who would pay for it. There were only three rays of sun: Kelflase, intact, in touch, sending the commander Sarras up next day to Astarien. Stavan. And the nurse.

It was Stavan who got us through Astarien, up to Gerrar's house, into a bedroom, and before I thought how to strip the king's armor had produced a thin, leathery, white-haired woman imperturbable enough to be his mother: which in fact she was. She took one look at the bed, the king, the household women in spasms around him, told me, "Clean sheets. Hot water. Lamp." Told Gerrar, "Get them out." And told Stavan himself, "Los Nuil. Wild honey. All you can rob."

Undoubtedly Thassal saved the king's life that night. She had his armor off with minimal disturbance, the surface splinters out, and the blood sponged off before Stavan reappeared with a bucketful of wild honeycomb, that we were instantly set to crush and sieve, before she bandaged it in a huge poultice over the entire wound.

Next she bade us find hethel oil: that night in Astarien, finding whiskers on a baby would have been a lesser enterprise. With that she soaked the burnt side of his face and bound it up in silk scarves annexed from the wardrobe of Gerrar's wife. And at midnight, when the spreading stain on the poultice made it clear the sting-pit had not closed, she undid the bandages, bent down, and sucked the wound.

As she spat in the nearest basin, I could not restrain a cry. She merely said, "If it don't clot, won't matter if I suck him dry."

Clot it did. When I said in wonder, "How did you know that?" she looked at me as if I were an idiot, and replied, "It's in all the songs. Dragon poison thins the blood."

For three days after that he lay at the river's brink. Considering the handling I gave him, it is a Sky-lords' gift that he lived so long. Thassal applied fresh poultices, and fed him honey thinned with water and mixed with yeldtar juice, which she made him swallow by stroking his throat.

"Yeldtar to keep him quiet. Water because he's bled. Honey's quick strength."

Unlike me, she never despaired. "He's a fighter," she said, watching his death-white face against the pillow. "He'll fight." And, as the cocks crew in Astarien's bleak dormitory-like streets four mornings later, he opened his eyes.

Thassal promptly pushed me behind the lamp. "You he knows." She fed him again, quietly but relentlessly making him finish the whole cup, then gently lowered his head. But when his eyes had closed, she stood there a long moment, and then she said a curious thing.

"So," she murmured. "They are green."

She probably saved his life times over as he mended, for a more fractious patient never filled a bed. He was hardly conscious when he tried to talk, and the smoke must have held poison, for it had seared his throat. Then nothing would do but wax tablets and stylus, and of course, being right-handed, he could not write. When he started to beat the bed-clothes Thassal hauled me upstairs, commanding, "Tell him the tale. Naught else to do."

So I told him. He turned his face to the wall and lay the rest of the day like a skinned pup, with Thassal seated silently by the bed. Coming up at lamp-time, I heard when she finally spoke.

"King," she said, "this won't do. Live folk need you. Those don't."

He did not move. But next morning he was propped up with the tablet against his knees and his lopsided turban making him look like a mad Quarred sheep lord, as he doggedly, grimly taught his left hand to write.

His first demand was a move to the lookout tower. Thassal shrugged. "He'll fret silly else." With that achieved, he summoned Sarras and Gerrar and me to a council, and then I had to contend not only with the rest of Everran but with a demonically active king.

First he summoned engineers, then ordered them to build a catapult. "We'll jam stones in the bastard's gullet." Informed that, unlike the dragon it would be immobile, he wrote in furious jagged capitals, "Then build one that's not!" While they digested that he sent for armorers to forge unbreakable sarissas, herb-doctors to compound a dragon-poison, hunters and more engineers to design a dragon pit, and Four knows what else. Between times he took over the evacuation, deployed the levies, dismissed the Regent, summoned the Council to Astarien, set a permanent dragon-watch, quelled the lords, expelled the royal physician who had been slung in a mule-litter and sent north so fast he was only fit to wring his hands, threw his tablets at me for suggesting he should rest, and requisitioned Gerrar's scribes so he could deal with the Confederacy.

After he regained his voice things speeded up. But when, not a month after the battle, he announced he was ready to get up, Thassal calmly demolished him.

"You have no clothes," she told him from the tower door. "And no one will bring you any. And if you try to get some I'll take that nightshirt off you as well."

Healthy, he would have laughed and admitted defeat. As it was, he lay back and said in that strained whisper, "You cursed woman. You should have been a general. Thank the Four you're not."

An hour later he had sent a mirror-signal for the Treasurer's inventory and was waving his tablets at me, saying, "Here, Harran, you're a wordsmith. Draft this."

I asked, "What is it, lord?" And he tossed me the stylus. "Proclamation. All the Confederacy. Champions. Anyone who can stick the dragon, I'll give them . . . give them . . ."

"It's usual to offer a daughter," I said flippantly, and then could have bitten off my tongue.

He did wince, but then it brought his first real laugh. "Better than that." He held his ribs. "Offer them—Maerdrigg's maerian."

I dropped the stylus. He said, "Heirloom, priceless, the luck of the house." Shrugged, and winced again. "Everran comes first."

He was still in great pain: the physician talked of extracting splinters when he was strong enough, but after three weeks not even Thassal could feed him yeldtar juice. "Saw it in Hazghend. A drug." So I would play for him, in the night watches where I had now been promoted as nurse.

I still see that little stone wedge of room, the pallet bed overhung by a goose-feather mattress Stavan commandeered the Four know where, the rough iron door, the archer's slit full of frostily starlit black, the tiny lamp flame on his strained, haggard face. I would play the little, simple airs of Everran's work and play: songs for all seasons from every Resh, the folk catches that outlast lore. When that failed, we would talk. One learns a great deal, talking at night. Sellithar must have been the only subject on which we never spoke.

After seven days Hawge had flown north-east amid a wave of frantic orders for the border garrisons to shelter the people and let the dragon be, and was now dormant after feeding heavily on a tardy cattle herd in the Coesterne hills. The field at Coed Wrock had been salved. The king had already commissioned a cairn, but that no one had found Inyx's body was his deepest grief.

"He was right," he said wistfully during another night conversation. "I shouldn't have tried it. I threw them—and him—away."

"I do not think so," was the best I could do. When he spoke in that quiet remorse so utterly unakin to self-pity was when I pitied him most. "It had to be attempted. They would say the same."

He shifted his head on the pillow. "All the same . . . I'd like to have begged his pardon. Told him he was right."

"He," I rejoined blandly, "would enjoy that."

We both chuckled. Then it was time for another of the bed-ridden's indignities: the sponging, the bed-pan, the food you cannot cut for yourself. Coming back, I beat up the pillows, which as usual were everywhere, and asked, as usual, "Is that better, lord?"

He smiled rather wearily as he lay back. Then he looked up. Whatever wreckage lay under the bandages, his eyes remained beautiful: long-lashed, vivid green almonds, full of impish light.

"Beryx," he said. "I can't expect to be 'lord' when I ask you to do things like that."

I murmured some demurral. He said, "That's an order," and then began laughing. "Oh, Four! I mean, that's an order—please." As he held his side, I thought, No wonder they died for you. If you command, you can also charm.

Like Thassal, Stavan had been invaluable: while I played Regent he wrought with Gerrar's household, materialized food and physic and sick-room furniture from thin air, excluded hysterical visitors, even managed to achieve quiet in the nearest streets. Later he provided for counselors, engineers, physicians, armorers, and all the king's other whimsies as well as me. When I asked why he stayed, he shrugged. "Nothing better to do."

That next night I was supping in Gerrar's former record room when he came in to announce, "Someone wanting you." With a mental groan I said, "Send him in," and looked up at a ghost.

He was propped on crutches in the doorway, wearing leg bandages, a soldier's under-tunic, and something like a leather corset over it: squat, black, gnarled as an old hethel tree, his calling in his face.

Quite deranged, I said when my breath returned, "We did look for you. I swear it. I am sorry. If you only tell me where you lie—"

At which he shot me a sharp black glance and growled, "For the Lords' sake uncross your eyes, harper. Pinch me if you like."

"Crawled away," he said, disposed in my chair. "After dark. Harper, spare us, don't cry in m'wine." Stiffly, he flexed a leg. "That's just burns." *Just.* "Tail hit me high. I've the father and mother of all belly-aches, and I spat blood for days, but I can get around in this." He touched the leather strapping. "Farmer made it. Hauled me into bed when I crawled there. I've just broken out. How's the king?"

I told him. He nodded. Then, with a quick glance under his brows, "Heard what you did."

"But not for you." It still kept me awake. "I told the dragon, just one. I didn't dare—"

"I didn't matter," he spoke brusquely, meaning it. "What matters is him."

"Lord," I said as I opened the tower door, striving not to grin from ear to ear and spoil the surprise, "lord, look what I picked up."

Inyx hopped past me. Beryx's head rocketed up. For one instant his face was all incredible, incredulous delight, he plunged up in bed, grabbed instinctively at his side, forgot it to throw out his arms—then in a flash radiance became the most desperate grief.

"Don't you start," Inyx growled. "Harper's already pinched me black and blue."

Beryx stuttered. Choked. Choked again. Tried to wrench his back to us. Inyx's very shape changed. With a violent effort, Beryx faced round and lifted his head. "No," it came almost on a sob. "You old fool—not that!"

He got control of himself. Very clearly, looking Inyx full in the face, making it an indictment, an explanation, his utmost recompense, he said, "You were right."

Inyx shoved away a cup-stand with a crutch and hopped over to the bed. "Lemme get off these things," he grunted. "Stand over."

Beryx moved his legs. Suddenly tears ran down his cheeks and as I closed the door I heard Inyx say in a voice I never believed could hold so much gentleness, "Si'sta . . . si'sta . . . That's a leader's price."

Inyx eased life greatly: a close friend, a fellow soldier, competent with things Beryx would delegate to no one else, which slowed him down and mended him faster. Inyx could also curb Beryx's worst fantasias. If Inyx went, "Mphh!" instead of, "Ah," the king would grin ruefully and drop the project, saving much wear and tear on messengers, Stavan, and assorted experts' self-esteem. Inyx also harmonized with Thassal, and to the physician's disgust thoroughly approved her doctoring, and he had tended enough campaign wounds to offer valid advice. But he was anxious to move the king.

"Too close," he told me. "And kingdom's like soldiers. What they can't see they don't believe." When Sarras, who gathered news as wool gathers burrs, told him that rumors of the king's death were already unsettling Tirs, he actually managed to tune Thassal and the physician on the need for an early splinter-probe.

Beryx wanted to go south first. Thassal told him sternly, "You can't act till you're moved. You can't move till they're out. If one worked down to an inner vein we could not stop you bleeding to death." At that he yielded, and the physician set to work.

Afterward he looked worse than on the battlefield: flat on his back, so thin he barely raised the bedclothes, so white I thought he had already bled to death. Helping change the bandages, I saw the pits they had left, and understood why. However, he recovered quickly, and mended faster for it, sleeping better, putting on flesh. Presently Thassal left his head unbandaged, merely rubbing hethel oil into the scar.

When I first saw that it took my breath. As I stood in the door, fighting to school my face, he glanced up and showed me I had failed.

"No," he said wryly, "I doubt they'll call me handsome again."

The scar began where the corselet-collar had met his jaw line, caught the corner of his mouth and swept up past his nostril, mercifully missing the eye, then reached right back to his ear: a rag-edged triangular purple welt fit to terrorize a child. I felt ridiculous tears prickle, and hurriedly burlesqued a triumphant-hero march on my harp. Thank the Sky-lords, he laughed.

But a couple of nights later I found him trying to lift his right arm, immobilized till then to help the wound in his side. As I came in he glanced up with a small worried frown, saying, "Come and rub this for me, Harran. I can't make the fool thing move."

The skin was icy, and the muscles had shrunk. Only natural, I told myself. But I told Thassal too, and next day came with her to look.

She freed the arm from the sling and laid it on the coverlet. Prodded. Poked. Felt his shoulder. Two lines rose between her brows, and she said to me, "Fetch the general."

Inyx hopped in. Listened. Looked. Felt in turn. Said, "Ah." Then he sat on the bed and spoke very softly to the king.

"Remember that lad Kirth? In Hazghend? Took a catapult graze just under the shoulder point?"

Beryx looked up at him. His face was stiff, and rather white about the mouth. Holding his eyes, steady as a phalanx charge, Inyx said, "Ah."

Beryx's eyes turned to the arm. The room was very quiet.

"It barely broke the skin." His voice was careful. "But he couldn't use the arm. We . . . sent him home."

Under his breath, Inyx said again, "Ah."

Beryx was still looking down. From the left his face was unmarred, springing nose and clean mouth, winged brow and long-lashed green eye, the strength and decision that go beyond handsomeness. But the steady grief in it tore my heart.

"Well, well," he said at last. Then he smiled at Inyx, a smile of cold steel courage, and said, "Here's one Berheage will be leading from behind."

Going out, Inyx spat in the stair-well and said to Thassal, "Four grant I never have to tell another thing like that."

She replied as she once had to me. "He's a fighter. He'll fight."

Only he did not. Like that inner vein cut by a splinter, it slowly bled his spirit away before our eyes. I do not know which was worse to watch: the decay, or his effort to conceal it. "Four send the dragon," prayed Inyx blasphemously. "Or a mutiny, or an invasion. Anything to wake him up."

I did not try myself: having gratefully abandoned all pretences of Regency, I had retired to my harp. I had a song to make, a battle-song, the most delicate jugglery a bard ever attempted, for I was determined to tell the truth, flatter the dragon, and yet leave honor with the losers at the end. It was in my mind that one day Hawge might recall that song. I was wrestling a tricky modulation in my parchment-lair when an explosion carried clear from the tower.

I flew upstairs. A dusty, spurry messenger was bobbing in the doorway, trying to fit in a wail. As a leonine roar fired him past me, I shot inside to find Beryx half out of bed, strewn with parchments and spitting fire like Hawge itself.

"My uncle!" he bellowed, hurling missives broadcast. "My beloved uncle! Doesn't think I'm fit to deal with this! Doesn't think at all! The ninny! The nincompoop! The— Inyx! Inyx! Rot it, where are you? Where's Stavan? Call Gerrar—get a horse-litter—take this thing off me! By the Sky-lords' faces, I'll *disembowel* him when I get back south!"

Thassal fairly bounced in with Inyx bursting after her, purple in the face. Beryx flung his sling at them left-handed, kicked back the quilts, shot to his feet, and promptly collapsed. Inyx shed crutches to arrive in time and pinned him down with a hand in the chest.

Beryx roared, "Get your paws off me!"

Inyx panted, "Can't."

The king thundered, "What!"

And Inyx gasped, "Can't. Over . . . balanced m'self."

There was a frightful hush. Then Beryx unwound, and began, albeit painfully, to laugh.

As Inyx levered himself upright, Thassal and I retrieved

parchments. I recognized the Quarred ram-horns on one huge red seal.

The king, eyes very bright and dangerous, said, "Do you know what they say? Quarred: 'Where the doughty warriors of Everran failed, our shepherds can hardly hope to succeed.' With a five thousand strong standing army and 'shepherds' who raid my Reshx every year! Holym: Most unusually concise. 'Branding cattle. Can't come.' Hazghend: 'Love and best wishes, Ragnor, I have pirates off Osgarien and Estar's hired my ships.' Estar: Oh, this is the pearl. 'We have a current fluidity problem. Our assembly has voted to censure the dragon at the next Confederate Council, and will apply trade sanctions on your behalf.' Trade sanctions! Shepherds! Branding! I fought for Hazghend, my grandfather saved Estar. Loyalty! Not to mention foresight! Let a dragon ruin your neighbor so you'll have to fight it yourself!"

Inyx was studying the Hazghend parchment. His brows knit. He said slowly, "This is a month old."

"My uncle the royal incubator!" Beryx erupted all over again. "He's sat on those for a month! The—the—incompetent!" It was the worst insult in his vocabulary. He hove himself up the bed. "Find me a horse-litter, Inyx. I can't rot here any longer, Four knows what else he's done. No, woman, blight your splinters. I'm going home!"

Over his head Inyx caught my eye, and very nearly achieved a wink.

Characteristically, the turmoil of departure did not make Beryx forget his debts. While I was packing my harp, Stavan came in, perched on the table, and presently remarked, "King sent for me."

I cocked an eye.

"Offered me a stewardship. Said, 'If you ran this mess, you'll run the palace in your sleep.' I said, I belong in Stiriand. He said, 'Then Gerrar shall rebuild the house at Coed Wrock.' " He shook his head. "Dictated the order there and then."

"You deserve it." I thought how I would miss him, how we had met. "Twice over."

He shrugged. Fingered my harp. Hesitated. Then, with a palpable jerk, he plunged.

"Harper . . . what do you know about aedryx?" he said.

"Aedryx?" I was puzzled. "I never heard of it."

"Them."

He was watching me oddly. "Who are they?" I asked, wondering what obscure branch of Stiriann folklore I had missed.

He looked down, growing still more reluctant. At last he said, "Wizards." A pause. "In the old days." Another pause. "There are songs."

"I've never heard them." I was professionally piqued.

He shot me another fleeting glance. Then he brought the words out as if loading a fireball catapult.

"They say . . . Lossian was one. And . . . he had green eyes."

Then he was off the table and gone before I could assemble a question to chase, let alone catch, the hint.

Thassal was yet more tantalizing. She saw Beryx to his horse-litter, and as she stood by it in the steep stony street I now knew so well, he held out his left hand. "Thank you," he said, "general. Now where?—ah." He hauled his right arm forward. "Here, pull this off."

She looked down at the great seal ring in her palm. It was a finghend, green and vivid as his eyes, worth a fortune. When Beryx gave, he did it with both hands.

"I doubt," she said, "Coed Wrock's enough."

"Coed Wrock's for Stavan. This is for you. Rot it, woman, how low should I value my life?"

His mock ferocity raised a faint flush on her cheek. Then, with Stavan's air of reaching a hard decision, she looked up.

"King," she said, "I'll give you a gift to match. If you need to know about aedryx—come to Coed Wrock."

Beryx started so violently he upset the horses. "Aedryx! How do you know?—what do you?—here, Thassal, listen— come back! Oh . . . let her go." He lay watching her gray skirt flick from sight. But all the way to Kelflase he was unnaturally silent. And what I found still odder was that he never, then or later, mentioned the incident to any of us.

After Kelflase a paven road replaced the half-finished horse-track, another sick-bed project, but it was still not fast enough for the king. Counselors might nurse their saddle-galls, the physician might bleat of convalescence, Inyx might cock an anxious eye. Beryx disembarked each night white and sweating worse than the horses, and climbed in next morning saying, "For the Four's sake, let's get on!"

With summer waxing, Saeverran's grass had hayed off, Saphar's vines were blowsy, heavy-laden, and the humid mornings beckoned to days of laziness. Earth-day had left every road thick with saplings which the refugees watered, as they harvested hay and weeded vines and filled every other occupation ingenuity could suggest. More and more often as we moved south Beryx was met by anxious local governors asking if the Treasury could finance a new well or renovated market for refugee work, by deme leaders swamped with Stiriand folk and fowls and stallions and worried it was permanent, by garrison commanders enquiring about strategy and wine-lords nervy about the market. Or simply by wives whose men had been levied and who asked, "When will he be back?" Small wonder he reached Saphar as thin and haggard and hectic as before Inyx arrived.

When we descended to Azilien it was afternoon, and the riverbanks were thick with small white and gold ahltaros flowers turned to the westering sun. The air had lost its springtime clarity. The city and the Helkent themselves looked vaguely smudged. As we clattered on to the bridge I saw Beryx thrust open the litter curtains with a hunger in his gaunt face. Then it changed.

Over the bridge breast appeared a floral archway, banners, a horde of bobbing heads, and the tall figure of the Regent, splendid in official robes.

Inyx's litter shot out a volley of soldier's oaths that closed on, "Unconquering heroes—eccch!" Four, I thought, as those determinedly gay smiles curdled my own stomach: you could have spared him this!

The advance-guard slowed. The cheering began. A citizens' band struck up the march I had burlesqued; the Regent advanced with outheld hand and a fulsome smile on his silly face. I heard Beryx snap at his horse-leader, "Halt!" As the Regent reached the litter, he thrust the curtains wide.

Nothing is so foolish as forced joy gone bad. The Regent's hands followed his jaw down. There was no mistaking the expression, and Beryx would have had it full face.

He made a valiant recovery. "My dear boy—my dear boy—whatever have you been doing—oh, dear oh dear—" To cap it, he tried to help Beryx out, a thing not even Inyx dared.

The king emerged between his arms, face white where it was not purple, jaw rigid with the double effort of standing alone and of concealing it. "No, uncle," he said with a glittering smile. "The question, surely, is: What have *you* been doing?"

I heard Inyx's demonically gleeful snort. Beryx cut through a cloud of excuse and explanation, extending his left arm for the ritual embrace.

The Regent would plainly have sooner cuddled a toad. The band was still thumping, grotesque in the widening hush, my sickened stomach had become a knot of rage. To be sure, they could not help it, any more than their well-meaning welcome: but let anyone say anything, I vowed, and harper or no harper, I'll put his teeth down his throat.

Beryx, as usual, was already in control. "You shouldn't have come down, uncle." A purr that barely hid the claws. "I'm not fit yet, I'll have to go straight home. But I shall expect you up there at the first advice." Right royal rage would precede a more than right royal rebuke. He climbed back in the litter, the Regent flapping behind him: jerked his head to the horse-leader, sat up straight, and yanked both curtains wide.

You may imagine his progress for yourself. All the way up the hill they were out to cheer him, and all the way they tried. He sat through it, back straight, jaw rigid, nodding to the odd acquaintance. I daresay he would sooner have been washed in boiling oil.

When he emerged at the gate-arch, Inyx and I dead-heated to his shoulder. "No, you old idiot," he said without venom. "You're no better than I am. Harran, give me a hand."

As we climbed his weight grew heavier, his breathing more painful, his face wetter, till I ached to cry, "For the

Lords' sake, let me carry you!" But I dared not suggest a half-minute's rest.

The armory guards saluted him when we passed: not a royal gesture, but a true salute, of soldiers to a defeated fellow, a gallantry they could understand. Seeing his face ease, I could have cheered them both.

We turned the corner. Reached the path to the royal rooms. And down from her outpaced maidens Sellithar came running, ethereal in a smoke-blue gown, glitter of golden hair and coronal, joy in those clear blue eyes.

"At last!" I never heard her sound more beautiful. "Where have you been?" And as she spoke, Beryx lifted his face.

She could not have helped it. It was a thing beyond anyone's help, too quick and instinctive and spontaneous to prevent. Her stride faltered, her eyes flared, her face shouted shock, horror, revulsion. And it was over, in that flash.

She caught her smile and her footing and ran forward, words tumbling as she forced joy and relief and welcome back into that lovely limpid voice. I felt Beryx go stiff, as if to meet a spear-thrust with his naked flesh.

His good arm was over my shoulder. As she reached him, he stood up straight and unmoving, and said in a voice that could have been everyday, "I'm glad to see you, Sellithar."

If protocol can be cruel, it may also be a mercy. In private, she might have broken down. Here, she turned white as he. Then blood and rank and discipline succored her, and she answered with the same formal falsity, "Welcome home, my lord."

She came with us to his apartments. As his body servants surged forward I felt his almost physical withdrawal, and understood. I too would have wanted to be alone. He smiled apologetically and said, "Kyvan, Ysk . . . I'm out of practice. Just tonight, will you let the general bed me down?"

Amid assurance and protestation they withdrew. I could not look at Sellithar. I knew if she tried to stay he would eject her, and I dared not imagine how. But she said at once, "Beryx, you must be exhausted. I'll see you to-morrow. Mind, you're not to get up until I do."

Ouch, I thought, recalling Thassal's iron decrees. He dredged up a smile, I hurried to escape before the door closed. He said, "Harran?" He was rocking on his feet. It was the merest whisper. "Will you . . . go to the queen?"

Her porter refused me entrance. When I overrode him with a king's command, I knew she would not be there. I stood in the arches of the little hall paneled in blonde imlann wood, tiled with a mosaic in palest limes, azures, and smoky lavenders, gweldryx flying among terrian blooms. The air bore her dry light scent, a blend of keerphars. Looking out to the paven paths and pools of the lily garden, I thought: alone. Not in her rooms, probably not in the royal apartments, not where her presence or un-escorted going would be remarked, certainly not where anyone could see. I went through the closing lilies, down the southern arbors, round to the little pleasance beneath my tower.

Sellithar was kneeling on the seat, elbows along the outer parapet, staring into the melted evening distance toward Tirs.

I went to her quickly. Then paused, and sat down. She did not move. I took my harp and played at random: an im-provisation, what Beryx called "thinking noise." A little wind rustled like dragon speech among the helliens.

"He would not let me come to Astarien." She spoke dully, without looking round. "I wanted to. To nurse him."

I made a soothing nothing on the harp.

"He never mentioned it." Her voice was duller, dead. "If he had, I could have . . ." She broke off. I played a hurried attempt at consolation, at erasure of that one small terrible word.

She straightened up. Her profile was still, and set, and curiously calm. "He will never forgive me," she said. "Not so long as I live."

Music failed me too. I knew it was the truth. Beryx was a devoted king, a humane general, a loyal friend, a generous master, probably a loving spouse. He would support you, lead you, defend you, rally you, comfort you: quite cheerfully die for you, over and above forgiving you wounds to his body, soul, and dignity. But never a wound to his pride.

I opened my mouth, but my silence had already replied. She cried, "Oh, Harran!" and flung herself round in a tempest of tears.

It was treachery, perfidy, base and unforgivable: but when the woman you love in is your arms, in distress, in your trust and in want of comforting, I defy anyone to be any nobler than me.

Her tears were over long before I stopped kissing her, embracing her, babbling all the usual inanities. Presently she lifted her eyes, tear-drenched, blue as terrian flowers, and studied me as if we had never met before. My heart had stopped when she gave a quick, shy smile, outlined my lips with a finger, and ducked her head.

"Harran," she said, when I let her speak again, "what shall we do?"

It was in my heart to say, Run away to Meldene and make you a harper's wife. But the heart is a very stupid organ at the best of times, whereas women are unfailingly full of wisdom, so I said nothing at all.

"I am," she said, "the queen."

I have remembered that, I said silently, these last three years.

"So . . ." she said.

"So," I tried not to sound bitter, "I had better leave."

She straightened in my arms, and I saw courage, maturity, accepted responsibility literally form before my eyes.

She kissed me. Then she said, "If you can bear it—I'd rather you were here. But . . ." her eyes filled with pain. "I have broken a real trust. I must not . . . break it in name." She looked into my face. "Can you bear that, my dear?"

No! I wanted to yell. I have already borne enough! Then I recalled what she would bear tomorrow, what Beryx had already borne in that one day, and was ashamed. "If you ask it," I said, "I can."

She kissed me again. Then she rose and said with no hint of bitterness, "You must go now. The king might have need of you."

The king did summon me next morning. He was in bed, conducting simultaneous breakfast, council, and correspondence, which latter he promptly delegated to me with an order to "light a fire under these Confederate ninnies, even if it's too late." The Regent made no appearance, unlike the army of servants forestalling his every need: but when scribes and council departed he waved them away, saying, "No, wait, Harran. Play for me a while. 'Calm me down.' "

A quotation from Thassal I had thought unheard. He was looking pulled and pale. I would have chosen something simple. But as he lay back, eyes closed, he asked, "How's your battle-song?"

79

I played what was done. He listened quietly, then bright-eyed, then openly laughing. At the end he cried, "You two-faced singing serpent!" and went to clap his hands.

As I sought desperately for words, he said, wistfully but without self-pity, "There are so many things you can't do one-handed. Ride a warhorse. Peel an apple. Play a harp, I suppose."

I did not add, use a sword and shield, wield a sarissa, draw a bow. He opened an eye and grinned. "Never mind, Harran. At least I've learnt to shave."

"Self-defense?" I inquired blandly, recalling certain horren-dous interludes at Astarien. He retorted with spirit, "The most horrible barber I ever suffered." And as we laughed together I gave thanks to the wisdom of women, which let me share laughter and memory with a whole heart.

A day or so later the first champion arrived.

He strode into the audience hall as if he owned it, wider than Asc and twice as tall as Inyx, his barrel chest cased in a gold-inlaid steel corselet, his fur trousers tucked into knee-high cross-laced boots, a double-headed axe over his shoulder, a silvered boar-crest helmet on the back of his blonde curls. His bright blue eyes and sweeping corn-gold moustache and general air of rambunctious confidence shouted Hazghend to the skies. Dropping the axe-head with a clang on the marble pavement, he boomed, "Where's this dragon of yours?"

"In Stiriand," replied Beryx, evidently used to Hazyk manners. He looked closer. "Gjarr—am I right?"

"Gjarr it is," nodded the giant. "How'd you know?"

"We met in Hazghend. Tyr . . . Kemmoth, I think. You'd gathered up a pair of corsairs. We took one off your hands."

"By Rienvur, that's right! Galley on my port side—somebody jumped aboard and chopped the captain, left us the starb'd one just before I sank. Nice piece of work." His eye said with perfect unconsciousness, perfect friendliness, Poor soul, you couldn't do it now. "Dragon tickle you up a bit, I see?"

"Just a little," Beryx replied gravely. "There'll be a mirror signal soon to report its position today. Do you want any help? Horses? Archers? Diversions?"

Gjarr laughed aloud, a splendid flash of white teeth in sea-bronzed face, and slapped the haft of his axe. "Oh, I think Skull-splitter here'll be all the help I need."

I saw Beryx and Inyx exchange one straight-faced sidelong glance. Then Beryx said demurely, "As you like. The maerian will always be here."

Hawge kept the axe: it was taken with the intricate swirl of fire-red hazians and scintillant blue-white thillians that made the hand-grip on the ivory haft.

The next was supreme archer of the Quarred army, born in the Hasselian marshes where they can shoot out a duck's eye before they talk, a lithe darting black snake of a man with the best reflexes I ever saw, a vanity that would have sat loose on Hawge, and a very canny wish to see the maerian before he risked his life. Beryx sent to the Treasury. As it was borne in, the sunlight turned it to a cataracted eye full of baleful, beautiful fire, and the archer licked his lips. He said, "I'll be back."

He took on Hawge from ambush. Unluckily, he chose a rock-heap, and when his first arrow went in an eye, Hawge demolished ambush and archer with one infuriated swipe, before using a hind claw to pluck the arrow out.

It had whole vision just in time for the next contender—contenders, I should say, for they were two big blonde

81

Hazyx as loud and cheerful as Gjarr, who liked to fight in tandem, one with spear, the other with axe. Hawge trod on the axeman when it turned to see what had pricked its other flank, and the spear-haft was wooden: an unhappy oversight.

After that they came thick and fast for a while, more Hazyx, hot to retrieve the national pride, a couple of Quarred phalanxmen, an Estarian mercenary wielding a mace, a Holmyx who, despite hearing my battle-song, went into action with horse and lance. Inyx watched them come and go with baleful amusement, Everran took a perverse pride in its unkillable bane, and Beryx grew grimmer with every disastrous trial.

He was walking now, though with difficulty, and still shy of strangers, but nothing would have kept him from the market when the first Confederate traders came. I went down too, for I love trade-days: new faces, new things, and if you are lucky, a new song.

This party was Estarian, sallow, meaty, dully-dressed but whistle-clean, the shrewdest bargainers in the Confederacy. They had come for hethel oil and, arriving the night before, had already unpacked and filled the town with drunken carriers. The bales of woven stuffs, tools, pottery, and Estar's myriad other manufactures were neatly disposed opposite the tall pointed Meldene oil jars, the scales were set up, half Saphar had begun its private chaffering, and traders and guildsmen were waiting for the king.

He took the high seat. Mint-tea was served, the overture began. It would last for hours: grave compliments, discreet news fishing, veiled probes for a weak bargain point, before anyone mentioned the goods, let be something so vulgar as a rate of exchange. Having seen them accept the new Beryx without blinking, I left on my own affairs.

A jewel merchant always came with the first Estarian traders, though he rented rooms all year in the north colonnade, and he did not barter but bought and sold for gold rhodellins all the precious stones of the Confederacy. Last year he had shown me a bracelet, a goldsmith's whimsy of fine-beaten gold, set with plaques of smoke-blue enamel to feather a chain of the tall graceful birds we call terrephaz, the blue dancers. Graingrowers say yazyx: thieves. No guildwife had thought it dear enough, and it had already been touted in Estar, so I doubted he had taken it back.

We sat in his outer room with a view up the steamy market bustle to the heights of Asterne above the palace roofs. A mirror signal was winking rapidly as the boy brought mint-tea. We had just opened a parcel of uncut maerians when a hullabaloo broke out and people began to run like startled goats.

The Estarian raised his brows: a suave, elegant person, his pose was never to be in haste. Then his tea-boy burst in, red-hot with news. "The dragon, harper, the dragon! Come to th'Raskelf 'n et all Quarred's flocks!"

I left without bothering to excuse myself. People were behaving as if Hawge were overhead. The Estarians looked affronted, the guildsmen panicky, a winded signaler was gasping at Beryx's side.

"Raslash . . . last night . . . Fire north. Shepherds . . . today . . . Lost whole flock!"

He had to breathe or burst. Over his crimson-faced heaving Beryx's eye shot round the market, and I jumped forward in response.

"Send Inyx here," he rapped. "Tell Asterne to confirm. Then get a scribe and rescind that proclamation and send the messengers immediately. No more champions." His mouth tightened. "Wasted lives and stirred it up!" And he turned with iron calm to the Estarians.

"Excuse this interruption, gentlemen. A slight problem in the north. Nothing to worry you."

It did more than worry them. Hurrying downhill behind the first messenger, I met him coming up on the chamberlain's arm. He had tried it alone and failed, and was plainly galled to the quick as well as infuriated by his helplessness. "Gone," I said before he could ask about the message. "Where are the—"

His eyes narrowed to blazing green chips. "Upped ensigns. Gone home. Risk your own gear, but you can't run oil over Bryve Elond with a dragon just up the road."

"Oh . . . Oh." The disaster was beyond words: the trade-route cut, our oil and wine unsold, Everran starved of cloth, tools, pottery, arms, the Estarians' news spreading the damage over the Confederacy. "The . . . The sheep?"

"Sent Inyx—here, Kyvan, that'll do. Harran can see to me." He held his side. "Rot it, I'll *have* to stop." We paused under the arch. "Told Inyx, take the levies. Mount archers, beat it off. Shift the flocks. Shepherds'll run in circles alone." I could feel his own urgency to be there, hot as iron in a forge. "Only one flock taken yet. We have to get them away. At any cost! Confederate stock. And I told them it was safe." His face twisted. "First the Guard, then the champions. Then the traders. Now the sheep. The thing's put a spell on me. Every choice I make is wrong."

IV

A week later Inyx came into the king's presence chamber, walking with a stick, his battered leather corselet black with soot, trousers nearly solid with horse-sweat, a helmet mark framing his sooty face under the flattened hair. "They're out," he growled, transferring his helmet from armpit to cup-stand. "Send me to shift fowls next time, not —ing sheep."

Kyvan rushed for a chair and wine, Beryx produced a brief tight smile. "How bad?" he asked.

Inyx took a long draught, wiped his moustache, and looked his king in the eye. "Three hundred and eighty," he said.

Beryx said nothing. I knew his thought was not of three hundred and eighty widows, their present grief or future livelihood, or of the three hundred and eighty themselves. He was thinking of the order that had sent them there.

"Good lads." Inyx's voice was slightly thickened. "Good as the Guard." His ultimate accolade. "Stood like rocks when I told 'em and shot like—like Hazyk skirmishers. Lost two more flocks, then Morran got 'em marshaled while I took the dragon on. Smart lad, that one. Bunched 'em up like a red Quarred dog and had 'em across Bryve Elond right after dark. Six turn-ups we had to cover him. And riding horses down between 'em to make ground for the next." He took another long swallow, and sighed. "But, Four, it's nasty work. The burns . . . Hospital camps all over the Raskelf. And a lot of 'em . . . went hard."

Beryx averted his face. The presence chamber is a winter room, small, intimate, with walls of folding rosewood panels and a thick crimson Quarred carpet to echo the rosewood roof. The fire was out, the panels folded back to admit dusty air and hot, glazed slaty summer blues and yellowed greens. But as Inyx spoke the room seemed to heat, to darken, to fill with men dying in anguish under the lurid glow of the dragon's breath.

Inyx shifted in his chair. "Not your fault." He sounded quite truculent. "We didn't ask for it, we've just got to deal with it as best we can. Same as any war." He grunted to his feet. "It's away to Saeverran now. Stand-easy for a bit."

At those first words something had moved in Beryx's face. Now it vanished and he looked up sharply. "Are you all right?"

Inyx stared. Then he produced one of his rare, acid grins. "*I* don't rush out with an iron basket round m' middle," he said rudely, "looking for a glorious death."

Beryx's face cleared in a laugh. "Go and find a bath, you old ly'ffanx. You stink."

Quarred was prompt with a sonorous official complaint. Beryx's reply, considerably pithier, said that help sent when asked would have prevented any damage. We had barely dispatched it when the skies over Saphar turned a sullen brown with smoke.

Hawge had left the Raskelf in something of a tantrum: baulked of its woolly feast, it had been harassed by a swarm of hard-riding, fast-shooting archers who did not wait to be smashed with a tail, scattered too quickly to be properly incinerated, and persistently fled in the wrong direction when chased. I have since pieced together the true story of that blend of desperate stands, foolhardy attacks, lightning retreats, and miraculous rallies by which Inyx, using raw troops over mountain country, not only held but rebuffed a dragon. He did less than justice to his part in it.

Hawge did not feed in Saeverran. It flew dead north for Kelflase and spewed fire all the way on the Slief beneath, then crossed the Kelf to dine on a big Gesarre vineyard's laborers. But it crossed Saeverran in a hot spell, during the summer's first westerly gale.

Sending Zarrar to the fires, I told him this would be his journeyman's work: from my very self I hid that I could not bear to go from Saphar, the king—and the queen.

Zarrar came back very quiet, though composed, and is only now making the songs. "Something like that," he said, "takes time."

The songs are terrible but magnificent: images of fire that rings the horizon like an endless incandescent worm, whose lakes lie amid flaming red-gold beaches with the stars of dying trees in their depths, fire that fills the zenith sky with scarlet to make midnight clear as noon, that comes down on the wind in squadron after squadron of reaching, racing, scarlet and vermilion flame, that roars louder than floodwater and at a mile distance sucks the breath from a man's lungs, that throws forward its skirmishers in swarm upon swarm of sparks that jump firebreaks and run across saturated roofs and reduce days of frantic labor to five minutes' jeering flare.

Against that spectacle he places the folk, the farmers, soldiers, refugees, beggars, hethel-lords, ditch-diggers, town governors. They rise in silhouette, blackened, singed, and desperate, often beaten, never conceding defeat, growing taller and taller until they dwarf the flames. The battle line that held the Saeverran road six hours with the cruel sun beating down undimmed from a whitened sky and the fire charging on a wind that never flagged along a front stretching from Kelflase valley nearly to Saeverran town. The breaking of that line when the wind veered, and whirlwinds bore live coals far over their heads so the fire, rekindling, overjumped the rear defenses and bore down on Saeverran itself. The townswomen who formed bucketchains from the wells to soak not only roofs but the surrounding land, before the exhausted fighters could outstrip the fire on the uplands, arriving to find the entire population of Astil marched up to reinforce them, the governor at its head. The three-day battle for Saeverran, islanded in a wave of flame, desiccated by the heat, lit by wind-borne sparks in fifty places at once, defended to the last wall, lost when the town-hall roof crumbles on both governors' heads.

After that come the leaderless survivors, striking northeast after the fire as it branches out over the Slief, the farms their owners lit without hesitation when they were in a counter-fire's path, the scores of little unsung stands on knoll or bare flat where it seemed the enemy might be stemmed. The Gebrians up from their arid plains, the hethel-lords ridden from Meldene with estate folk at their backs, the Saphar volunteers and homeless Stirianns, the Kelflase garrison who dammed the river and toiled like madmen to channel, pump, carry water south on their backs. The wind change that wheels the fire north to menace Astarien: and the last battle-front, spread across that upland valley behind a half-mile glacis of burnt, stamped, flattened earth. Women, children, grandmas, scribes and cripples and cooks, Gerrar at their head, swathed in wet cloaks, buckets and wet bags and green branches in their hands.

Zarrar has almost finished that song: how the rest of the

force made north through the night when the wind dropped to slow the fire, extending the defense till it ran from Kelflase to Deve Astar, with the Kelf borne in bucket-chains to their backs. How the fire came down the valley in one last tremendous charge so hot the tarsal trees did not burn but exploded in fountain upon fountain of red and white-hot sparks above the molten grass, while the heat vaporized the very air, and the defense hid in their cloaks as children raced each other to the falling sparks until sheer unbearable heat drove them back. So the last sparks to cross were beaten out by five brave souls who ran in to them and died there, asphyxiated by heat and smoke.

How the fire, baffled, choked to a halt: and the instant the heat eased the fighters surged in upon it with bucket and bag and branch, beating till they collapsed, till their boot soles burnt away, while the bucket chains stretched forward through the night like cables drawn to breaking point—and held. How, by unanimous election, it was Gerrar who sent the mirror signal next morning: Fire out on Saeverran Slief.

Once the fire crossed the road, manacles could not have kept Beryx home. Inyx did. He stumped in while Kyvan was prophesying doom, I was arguing, Sellithar weeping, and Beryx firing commands hither and yon and deaf to us all. He swung on Inyx, beginning, "Inyx, you—" and Inyx stopped him dead.

"I won't and neither will you. There'll be no time for nursemaiding there."

"Had to say it," he growled to me afterwards. "If he never speaks to me again."

Which seemed likely. Beryx had gone white as paper and then rounded on us, hissing, "Out! All of you! Out!" This last direct to Inyx, with a look to slaughter snakes.

We fell back on Inyx's quarters, the first time he invited me there. He had the gatehouse tower, with his own private lookout forever tramping up and down the stairs, which Inyx did not seem to mind. The rooms, kept scoured by a six-foot cavalry widow, were full of bizarre mementoes: a twisted iron joist from a corsair galley-ram, a seven-foot Quarred shepherd's crook with its steel spike and crozier, lopped in half. A dented company kettle, a two-handed Hazyk sword, a blood-stained battle order. A Hethox throwing spear thinner than your thumb, with a shovel-nose iron head that could halve a man, a set of worn-out horse-shoes behind a red leather bridle with silver bosses and su-perb ivory Holym forehead plate. An entire mirror-signal unit, the charred remnants of a Lyngthiran fire-cross, and letters in everything from wine to tar, all surmounted by a huge battle-painting where square-topped horses reared or kicked upside-down amid thousands of small stiff soldiers and a perfect hedgehog of spears.

"M'father's," Inyx said with pride. "Old man commis-sioned it for him after they kicked the corsairs out of Estar." By which I assumed "old man" meant Beryx's grandfather. "A long-serving family," I remarked.

"Um," said Inyx, and looked into his cup.

Beryx withdrew up Asterne to live with the mirror-signalers, sending down decrees with the feverishly awaited news bulletins and forbidding anyone to go up. When the fire was out, Sellithar asked me to play at her private thanks to Ilien. As we set out, I saw Inyx going slowly toward his tower, and said on impulse, "Lady . . . ask the general too?"

She shot me a look. Then she called him, and put the in-vitation with the exact warmth that was not pity in her harpsong voice.

We were all returning to the palace for a council of war—"our war," as Sellithar said, dimpling wickedly—when Beryx met us in the path.

He was strained and hollow-eyed and must have slept the week in that rag of crimson cloak, but he was walking fast, forgetting to hide his right arm, with an absorbed, impatient frown. "At last!" he burst out as he saw us. "Where the Four have you been?" Grabbing my arm, he put his right shoulder in Inyx's back, fielded Sellithar between us, and pushed us all toward the Treasury. "Come in here."

Striding over the stone flags nearly at his old pace, he said, "It's still near Gesarre." No need to ask, What? "But it won't stay there. It won't stay anywhere until it lairs. And if the lore's right, it will only lair when it has something to protect." We all stared like simpletons. "So we'll give it something. From this."

When no one spoke, he wheeled on Inyx in something less like defiance than abject plea. "For the Four's sake, this time I must be right!"

Inyx cleared his throat. A faint, awkward grin came. Then he said solemnly, "Ah."

Beryx's face lit up: reconciliation had been made.

He turned to me, balanced now. I said, "It's the lore. If we can try it, why not?"

Sellithar took a pace back, saying, "You'll be busy . . ." with that quiet dignity as new as the severe, refined lines of her cheek and throat, and Beryx swung quickly to her. "No, wait, Starflower. Help us to decide."

She flushed delicately, eyes brightened with pleasure if not hope, glanced along the scintillant racks. Then she said, "If I were you—I should send it Maerdrigg's maerian."

"Why not?" she went on. "It's beautiful enough. And you offered it to the champions." She paused. "And," she said candidly, "I never liked it very much."

Beryx stared a moment. Then he said abruptly, "No. Nor did I."

The maerian went north with some loose finghends, a packhorse load of gold, and Morran, Inyx's promising youngster, charged with delivery of the bait.

"All to plan, lord," he said, at stiff attention in the audience hall: a tall hazel-eyed bronzed boy hardly in his twenties, but already bearing the soldier's stamp. "We arrived three days after it fed." Nowadays, in Everran, such talk hardly caused a flinch. "Laid out the treasure, found a lookout. The dragon took off toward Feock, and the sun must have caught the gold. It made a big circle. Then it made a lot of little ones. Then it landed. When we left, it was sitting on the gold like," his cheek muscles twitched, "like a broody hen."

"Let us hope," Beryx said blandly, "that your simile is apt."

Three days later Hawge flew off with the treasure and Gjarr's axe in its mouth. For a week anxious mirror-signals followed it down the Helkent clean through Meldene: then Aslash on the Ven Elond road reported, "Entered the Kerymgjer Caves. Not seen since."

"Now," said Beryx with grim pleasure, "we'll shut the trap." He sent for local people, cave maps, engineers, wall builders, well-makers, and a score of other specialists, remarking, "If I can bury or wall it in there I'll willingly lose a score of Maerdrigg's maerians."

But even dragons cannot eat gold. Hawge emerged before our plans matured, and it was hungry. And the first edible thing it saw was a train of Holym traders, coming up the road with cattle to sell.

I found Beryx sitting alone at dusk in his presence room.

Without asking why he had sent for me, I sat down and began to play.

At last he sighed and opened his eyes. Then he rubbed his fingers up between his brows, the gesture of a tired man at the end of his wits.

"Harran," he said, "I want you to do something for me."

"Willingly, lord," I said.

"You won't be. The Kerymgjer caves—you know them? In the spurs just north of Bryve Elond." His teeth clenched. "Why, with all Everran to hide in, did it have to settle there? The engineers doubt we can bring the roof down. The mouth's too wide to wall. And you know the road. You know what will happen if our trade has to come past that."

"I know."

He looked up at me: no longer royal, even masterful. Just a weary man bearing a load of leadership with a line of disastrous decisions at his back.

"So the only thing left," he said, "is to parley. Make a," his teeth gritted, "treaty with it. So much gold—so many cattle—or whatever it wants to make it stay at home."

"You want me to draft the offer, lord?" I asked.

"No. I want you to carry it," he said.

Disbelief, shock, horror, indignation, I felt them all. Why me? I wanted to explode. Not me! I wanted to squeak. Some icy-nerved young warrior like Morran, some wily old hand like Inyx, take it yourself if you must, anything but give it to me! If I had been beyond fear at Coed Wrock, it did not last: I still woke sweating with that forge voice in my ears, that facetted eye reading my innermost thoughts. Then I thought how he had already fed her first lover to the dragon, and found myself shouting in silent mutiny, You shan't give it us both!

Some, I devoutly hope not all of this, had shown. Beryx

leant his brow in a palm and looked at the floor.

"It was not an order," he said at last, more tiredly. "It was a . . . request."

I strove to speak, and failed. I played something and it betrayed me, an angry, resentful chord.

"No," he said without looking up. "I know it's no job for you. Only I thought, you've spoken to it. And you made the song. It would have been a good . . . But Inyx can—no. I can't spare him. I'll go myself."

At that my tongue moved. "Beryx," it said, "don't be an idiot." He jumped. "I'll go."

He did not thank me for hazarding my life, offer me gold, jewels, half his dominions, or any other futile recompense. He merely smiled that rueful, disarming smile that could have melted Hawge, and said, "Well, you have used my name. At last."

"This time," I told my servant, "I will take the great robe." As he lifted it from the chest there was a knock. The outer door opened, and a hooded figure said in a voice like harpsong, "I have a message for the hearthbard. From the queen."

I had just wit to say, "That seam has opened. Will you mend it?" Then she was in my arms, eyes midnight black against a white wool cloak lined with swan's-down that looked muddy against her face.

"I can't bear it," she said, stifling sobs against me. "I can't—not you as well."

Ungallant as it may seem, I felt less bliss than embarrassment. What if she was missed? If someone came? "Love," I said rather stupidly, "I'm not going to fight with it. Only talk."

"No different . . ." Then she reared her head up. "How

dare he?" she demanded. "Why doesn't he send a soldier? The general? Why must it be you?"

Humanity being more perverse than dragons, I found myself saying, "I've spoken to it before. And I have an excuse: the song. What use would soldiers be in a word-fight? He can't go himself."

"Why not?"

"You know." Staring, I quoted her own words. "Without him, what would Everran do?"

"I don't care," she said flatly, "about Everran. Let it fry. We can go to Tirs. My father will secede."

"Love . . . Sellithar," I stammered. "I couldn't . . . I—it was you who talked about breaking trusts!"

"Before this!"

I looked around. Over her head I said, "I have given him very little. He has given me everything. Even you."

Slowly her face quieted, though not in conviction. Then she put a hand inside her cloak. "I thought you would say that. So I brought this. They'd laugh at it in Saphar, but in Tirs we know better." She held out her hand. "It's a talisman. We call them Lossian's Eyes."

I nearly dropped the thing on the spot. It was a flat, silver, single spiral gripping two stones, not beryl or finghend but some even paler green crystal, cut with high-shouldered faceting that made them twinkle like Hawge's own stare.

"No, take it," she thrust it urgently back at me. "It will keep you safe: even . . . there."

She fastened the clasp. I drew her near for a parting embrace. But she put her arms around me and whispered, "Don't go away from me. Not yet."

So I quitted Saphar unwillingly, but with joy in my heart: and also guilt.

★ ★ ★ ★ ★

In summer Ven Elond is usually crowded, but my four-man escort and I were almost alone as we climbed the gentle hills of Saphar Resh, while the Helkent drew ever closer to right and left, and the tall red crag of Lynghyrne, Fang of the Morning, rose ahead to mark the pass itself. Before Aslash, the country alters to the meager highlands where Tirianns learn to hunt, long stony slopes of rosewood and gastath and numberless sandstone scarps. The governor of Aslash received me with honor. I ordered my horse reshod, and retired to my harp.

Next morning was swelter hot, a true midsummer day, with a zenith hard and pale as turquoise, the hills dancing in a liquid haze of heat, dust curling from Aslash's unpaven square, and the sweat already thick under my shirt. The escort had found a local guide. The dragon watch reported Hawge had fed on a mob of mountain donkeys yesterday. Everything was auspicious. As I climbed on my horse in the shade of the thin-leaved, thick-twigged syvels, the governor, a taciturn retired soldier, glanced west across the baking white square and remarked, "Luck."

Recalling that Raskelf mirror-signal, I retorted with a tinge of sarcasm, "Thanks."

The Kerymgjer caves lie in the flank of the first spur north from Lynghyrne, a blue roan bulge under the Helkent's vermilion heights: as Beryx said, a perfect spy-post on the pass. We could see the cave mouth from well back. A trail of scorched and broken timber led up to its long, low black gash, a thread of black smoke spiraled idly above.

In the thin shade of a rosewood clump the guide halted. The escort exchanged looks that changed to blatant relief when I said, "Not you." Ants ran among the dusty stones, morvallin yarked over the crest. Climbing to earth, I said with spurious bravado, "Hold that till I come back." Gave them the horse, donned my robe, and took my harp.

The climb seemed endless. My boots turned on loose stones, my robe snagged on broken trees, the morvallin mocked me, I was hot and sweaty and enraged with fear as well as feeling utterly ridiculous. Harran the master harper, wearing his best feathers to be fried: what a song I'll make, I thought. And that fetched a bubble of silly laughter that recalled the phalanxmen marching to Coed Wrock. It also steadied me. I reached the cave lip in good order, if not good heart.

The Green Pool Caves are as famous as Deve Astar for the clear beryl of their great meandering subterranean lakes and the frosty ringed and knotted columns of their stalactites: they are also wet, dank, labyrinthine, and dark. I paused on the brink, reluctant to play hide and seek with a dragon in there, and as I paused, from the darkness came a drowsy flare of rose-pink flame.

It lit the whole outer cave, big as a banquet hall, roofed it in rose crystal and floored it in rose-flushed chrysoprase, so for a moment I could think of nothing else. Then I noticed Hawge itself.

It lay curved around the lake, tail vanishing into shadow, crested back casting a serrated isle of darkness on the glowing mere, head just below me on the cavern floor. The fireglow caught the huge, facetted, lidless eyes and made them twinkle like my talisman, threw out the bulging nostrils, the half-raised upper lip, the cavernous maw. On the ground between the nostrils, like a pearl before a swine, answering with its own fire to the dragon-light, lay Maerdrigg's maerian.

You may record among the Sky-lords' wonders that I did

not have to clear my throat. Nor did my voice stick. I said, "Hawge."

The upper lip twitched. The immense, rasping whisper responded.

<Man.>

I said, "You bade me make a song."

When it did not reply, I sat on the first rock bulge and began.

Every harper hopes that one song above all will outlast him, and that song is mine. There was much work and more struggle in its making, but it runs fluently as all good work should, sounding simple until you try to play it, exploiting all a harp's potential and the whole range of a voice. More notably, its sense is ambiguous. The dragon is so mighty that the men are dwarfed, foolish, puny things. From the dragon's viewpoint, splendidly true. Yet they persist in their insanity to the bitter end. From the dragon's view, justifiable homicide: stark courage, from the men's. Truth can be pitiable or valorous. It all depends which way you look.

The cave resounded to the final chord. Hawge breathed, a long, ocean draw. Water tinkled, far away. Accustomed to the twilight, I saw other things on the cave floor. The buttery glow of gold, a silver cup, probably some town's Ilien chalice. The fire-patterned haft of Gjarr's axe.

<What,> enquired Hawge, <do you want this time?>

Fear can be a fine inspiration. I sang my answer, painting Everran's waste. If I did not manage the fires so well as Zarrar, it was a harrowing picture that emerged, an uprooted population, many crippled, more ruined, the wreck of agriculture, the peril of trade. An entire country turned upside-down.

Hawge breathed peacefully in the darkness. <Go on,> it said.

You cannot bargain in song. "Hawge," I began, "if the country were whole there would be more food for you. And if it were brought here you would not have to go out— leaving your jewels alone."

That was a lucky shot. Hawge's eyes kindled. A tongue of fire shot past my nose and with a grind like crossed steel the dragon whispered, <This is my treasure. MY firestone.>

"Assuredly." I tried not to cough in the smoke. "And you should guard it. A bargain would be helpful to us both."

Hawge sank its chin into silence. At length I ventured, "How much—food—would you want?"

After another minute or so, Hawge named its terms.

<Thirty cattle each new moon. Ten sheep. Every second moon, a horse.> It considered. <Some of that white stuff the cattle lick. I like the taste. Almost as good as man.>

"Men are not included," I said in a hurry. "We do not grow them like the rest."

<Very well,> said Hawge. <Ten gold ingots. Every new moon.>

The eyes twirled slowly, leering up at me. It was openly laughing now. I wondered if it knew the exact contents of the Treasury. It would not have surprised me to hear it had read the Treasurer's mind.

"Very well," I said recklessly. Whatever it wants, Beryx had said, and I had already haggled once. "Thirty cattle, ten sheep, ten ingots. Salt, and a horse every second month."

Hawge blew a long smoke ring and added, <Alive.>

Trying not to be sick, I got to my feet, and answered, "They will be sent."

Turning its head a little, the dragon blew another idle jet

of flame. Its light shimmered on the lake, cut out the shadow in impenetrable black, glistened gold and silver on the immense mailed side whose every scale was big as a phalanxman's shield, glinted up the drooping spines, and turned the wing ridges to folds of thick black silk. The whole became a creature of magic that was resplendent, sumptuous. I had a crazy urge to go down and fondle it.

With an even crazier impulse I am quite definite was not mine, I said, "My lord is mightier than any army. What weapon could master such a lord?"

Then my heart leapt up between my eyes and I tried frantically to recall any cover within reach before the dragon leapt. Useless, I thought. It would sear or smash the hiding-place as well. I stood pathetically on the cave brink in my seven-colored robe, and Hawge gazed up at me, two globes of facetted green light with the maerian shining below them like a third, evilly mocking eye.

<Man,> said the vast empty whisper, and it held the gloating joy of one who jests in perfect safety with his own death, <Man, the weapon that could slay me has not been forged.>

"We cannot do it," said the Treasurer. "We can not do it!" He actually slammed a palm on his beloved ledger. "Not ten ingots a year comes in from Gebria and Stirianlase together! Not eight ingots a year comes in as fees and tribute! And with Stiriand burnt there'll be only half a vintage, and Saeverran and Findarre and Pensal have to be rebuilt, and there are the pensions and the refugees and we can't sell the oil! I tell you, my lord, your fool envoy has—"

A left hand with a plain gold seal ring cracked down on the parchment and stopped the rest in his throat.

"That treaty was made by a brave man," Beryx spoke so

softly it was pure menace, "in peril of his life. If you think you can drive a better bargain I recommend you try!"

Deciding to be ignorant of all but the Treasurer's words, trying not to let my chest swell, I stepped into the Treasury, asking, "What can't we do?"

"We can," the king retorted with fierce crispness before the Treasurer could speak. "We must. What's in hand here now?"

The old man blinked up at him, cowed but resentful. "Thirty ingots," he muttered. "That has to feed the refugees and rebuild towns and—"

"Sell the gems. Use that for Everran." As the Treasurer's lank white hair bristled in horror, he went on grimly, "That buys us three months. Harran, come and tell me about it. Everything you thought. Everything it said. Everything you thought it said. Anything at all."

He listened, coiled and tense. At Hawge's stipulation of, "alive," he gave a curt nod. "It's thought of poison. Rot it! Go on." But at the final exchange he leant right out of his chair and made me repeat it again and again.

"Not been forged." He sprang up and began to stride the audience hall as if he went on air. "Not been forged. By the Four, Harran, that would have been worth forty ingots a month!"

I shuddered. Hating to be a gloom-tongue, I said, "Lord, I think it's—no more than the truth."

"Bah!" He spun in a crimson swirl. "You forget your own lessons as well as your lore! Tell the truth two ways and now can't read it yourself. If the weapon's not yet forged it may be there isn't one, but it also means such a weapon's possible. It can be forged! And what does your lore say about dragons' vanity? It made you ask so it could boast, and it showed its weakness in the boast. Harran, I beg to return your compliment. It's you who is the fool!"

"But if there were such a weapon," I wailed, "how do we find it, when it hasn't been made?"

"Three months." He paused, vibrating with urgency. "In any case, Everran could never pay it alone for long . . . We'll go to the Confederacy. We want help to pay the dragon. And we'll search for the weapon as well." He looked at my face. "For the Four's love, Harran! At least it is a hope!"

V

When the king said, "Harran, I'm not a good word-smith: you'd better come along," it surprised me far less than finding he meant to begin in Holym, and northern Holym at that, which meant riding clean across Everran to the great border pass where Kemreswash heads. And like the rest of the palace, I most assuredly did not expect the king of Everran to set out with a harper and a pair of horse-handlers as his entire entourage. But he was adamant enough to out-shout Inyx, and I did not know all his purposes at the time.

The road north was painful. Beryx had not ridden before, and we began on the highway where the Guard had passed so merrily, thence entering the Raskelf, so mangled by Hawge. Empty sheep camps, burnt hillsides, hospital camps everywhere: and Beryx visited every one.

Across the Helken the road swung west into my own austere land, which as with all long-delayed homecomings was the same and not the same. The people I knew were changed, the places misremembered, and if the yeldtar still splashed crimson under the silver hethel leaves they now minded me of unsold oil. Beryx watched, and said nothing. To perception he added tact.

But in Stiriand we entered the oldest desolation of all. Nothing could have been more pathetic than Findtar and Pensal's blackened ruins crumbling in the summer glare amid acre upon acre of ruined vines. Pentyr's entire deme was the same. I was thankful to reach Dun Stiriand's sullen red fort, perched in its border-eyrie above the muddy stream of Kemreswash.

The Stirian governor had been summoned by mirror-signal from his keep, which is also a depot for the gold-washers who make a wild and risky living from the border streams, and Beryx told him flatly that their license fees would have to rise and their barter rate fall. "I have a dragon," he said, "asking ten ingots a month." When the governor flung up his hands, he added, "Tell them to visit Pentyr Resh."

A week more found us on the saddle between the Helkents' flaming red abutment and the delicate gray spines of the Histhira range, with Holym filling the eye to north, west, and south. Its long, rolling prospect of summer-browned and silvered plains was broken by stands of staring white helliens, tall black coastal elonds, and the short twisted trees named riendel for their lovely white and scarlet-filamented flowers, but there was not a town in sight.

While I wondered about directions, Beryx took a deep breath and squared his shoulders. "Let's begin," he said.

Holym is called cattle-land with reason: save a few mines near the Mellyngthir delta marshes, and some sheep running along the Quarred border, the cattle own it all. Nor do they keep a few head on each farm as in Everran. The Holym cattle are numbered by tens of thousands, they live wild on holdings big as a Resh, they are worked with horses by men who set small value on their necks, and they are not our short hairy red breed but huge smooth-skinned whites, blacks, yellows, and brindles, with horns long as bows and temperaments to match. The towns comprise a few houses along streets widened to handle such herds, and in place of markets there are stockyards tall as houses: moreover, the cattle jump out of them. This I have seen.

Instead of kings, Holym has an annual Council in the capital Holymlase, to which every Resh elects a delegate. It is supposed to voice the people's will to the biennially elected consul. The real ruler lives permanently in Holymlase, supposedly to fulfill the consul's commands, and is called the Scribe. But there is a schism in Holym politics, chiefly over border dealings with sheep lords from Quarred. One party supports free trade and an open border, the other insists Holym should be reserved to cattle alone. Those favoring trade are called Open, those against are the Closed. Add to this schism that all Holmyx prefer tending cattle to assemblies, that the council delegates are usually ignorant of all but their own Resh, and that Holym continually suffers violent floods or extravagant droughts, and you see why it is nicknamed the quiet Confederate.

A month or so before the Council gathered we reached the first town, Savel, an Open Resh. Its collection of wooden houses is built on stilts along streets the cattle had churned to deep red dust. Assembly day was also sale day, and since no Holmyx cares who buys his cattle, the town was bursting with sleek Estarians, haughty Quarreders, bellowing Hazyx, wild-eyed Holmyx, and wilder-eyed Holmyx cattle bellowing loudest of all.

With no time for a state visit's formalities, Beryx had sent a message to Holymlase, but Holmyx rarely heed government announcements, and nobody had the slightest idea who we were. Luckily a harper and two body servants are a good deal easier to bivouac with the drovers by the stockyard than a royal entourage.

The assembly meets at the back of the tavern, just beyond earshot of the beer: northern Holym does not drink wine. The Assembly Ruand was pleased to see us, but unfortunately, all but three cattle lords were busy with buyers, or even busier with a drought. After an hour or so the Ruand apologetically told Beryx, "We don't have an assembly quota. Would you want to begin now, and we could open assembly when they come along?"

Beryx looked at the audience. One was asleep, one looking over his shoulder at the beer, and the third haggling with a Quarred buyer. He looked at me. I sighed, and unwrapped my harp.

One must admit Holmyx are good listeners. When I finished the battle-song, the entire tavern was breathing on my neck, with some of the merrier fighting each other in lieu of Hawge. By the time I finished the plaint of Everran's ruin, half Savel was weeping in its beer and the assembly was ramping to assist us. Three lords each pledged a hundred cattle that summer, the delegate would support us at Council, we were offered a variety of beds and an undrinkable quantity of beer. I thought I saw why Beryx had begun in the north.

The next town, Caistax, was a Closed Resh. It had a big assembly, but when the herald tallied seventy I realized he had counted dogs and children too. Beryx's speech earned loud applause, and the Council delegate was entrusted with several motions urging Holym to do this or that, but nobody offered cattle, and nobody mentioned gold. When we asked about notable weapons, one kind soul did offer us his cattle-dog: "Takes 'em by the nose and they follow 'im anywhere."

This mute string merely made Beryx shrug. "We'll find it by chance," he said. "In the songs, they always do."

In a month we covered most of northern Holym, amassing promises of Council support, pledges of over a thousand cattle, no miraculous weapons, and no hope of gold. We reached Holymlase bronzed as drovers, accomplished beer-drinkers, with Beryx managing a horse as if he had ridden one-handed all his life. One thing I liked about Holym was that nobody seemed to notice either his arm or his scar.

Holymlase straddles the Mellyngthir and Histhira river junction, a big town full of splendid white town houses and less splendid mining depots, stockyards, and slaughter-houses which stink to the sky, pierced by a long line of wharves. It is busy, fast-moving, and violent, which comes of miners, drovers, and sailors mixed in taverns that sell wine as well as beer. The Council would meet that new moon. Looking back on our northern tour, I entered the chamber full of hope.

I never knew cattle were such problems to keep or to sell. For two days the Council droned over wild dogs, red fever, lung-rot, iniquitous Confederate and slaughterhouse buyers, drovers wanting higher wages, and shippers who charged exorbitant freights. The third day, when all the Council was hung over and two thirds of it asleep, the consul called, "the Everran delegate."

Gauging his audience's patience, Beryx offered a sum-mary of Hawge's deeds, a tally of its demands, and a bald request for help. "Everran cannot raise the cattle, let alone the gold. If we do not, the dragon will ruin us. Then it will move on the other Confederates."

Some delegates favored sending cattle. One thought they might spare "a gold ingot, at least." Several woke up. Then a Closed delegate jumped up with a passionate opposition to any government action, right down to accepting Everran immigrants. This roused the Open party. Southern dele-gates began to rumble about "leases" and "export-balance." In the midst of it, the Scribe rose to speak.

First he gave a recital of Holmyx finances at such low pitch and high speed that he lost most of the Council on the spot. I gathered there were fifty ingots in hand and three hundred due, but then we modulated into a tale of desperately needy government projects and more desperate government expenses, after which Holym was not merely living on credit but head over ears in debt. There followed an elucidation of the Confederacy pact which left me in the dark as well. Finally he moved to dragons, which were not covered by any clause of the pact, not being famine, pestilence, corsairs, or floods. It was unsure they could cross mountains. And, most clinching argument, there had never been one before.

At this Beryx rose and said clearly, "Their favorite food is cattle. Everran's are running out."

That caused a stir. One Open delegate moved that "help be sent." The Scribe claimed this was too vague. "What help?" Beryx caught the delegate's sleeve and whispered, "Three hundred cattle and five gold ingots a year." The Scribe re-sang Holmyx finances and concluded, "It can't be done." Then the Closed delegates rose in arms crying that stock sent must include sheep as well as cattle, the southern Opens grappled them over involving Quarred, the delegate altered his motion to "help on a voluntary basis," and the Council voted against.

Our Savel Ruand was also their delegate. He overtook us outside, saying awkwardly, "Our fellows will send the cattle; I'll throw in another hundred myself." Beryx gave him a smile I could see would probably double it. Then he grinned and said, "Better than I expected." The Holmyx looked startled. But then he grinned too, and they shook hands on the pact.

From Holymlase to Quarred's capital is further than round Everran. I wanted to ship downriver, then sail along the coast to the Hazghend isthmus, but Beryx said, "No time." We crossed south Holym's plains at the limit of horseflesh, riding long into the night, resting in the oven noons, while the trees thinned and the heat-waves jumped on the horizon and the grass turned to sheets of silvered beige that hurt the eyes.

In four days we reached the Quarred border, whence to Heshruan it is seven days' ride: first through the Hasselian marshes, cracked black soil, withered reeds, shepherds complaining bitterly of fever from a summer denied them in Everran, and then over Heshruan Slief, wider than Everran itself. We rode parched and wordless across tussocks of blonde taskgjer grass mixed with prickly shrubs, covered with flocks like huge gray earthbound clouds, and dotted with innumerable windmills about the steadings of Quarred lords.

There are no towns in northern Quarred, but these enormous steadings are towns in themselves, with palace, household, shepherds' barracks, and all a town's other trappings. Some even maintain a potter's shop. We reached the first at sunset, dusty, unshaven, filthy, and a'horseback. Quarred nobility rides in carriages. We followed the long avenue of matched black imported morhas trees to the palace, a low, green-roofed place, set in luscious gardens, with verandas wider than an audience hall, but the housekeeper, a sort of female chamberlain, met us at the outer gate and consigned us to "the men's quarters," without a second glance.

I raised my brows to Beryx. He grinned wickedly. We used the communal bath-house, shaved, and went to eat.

It was the apprentices' mess, also used for needy travelers. Shepherds, steading workers, and Ruands like treasurer and smith and carpenters have another mess, and shearers a special one of their own. When we finished the roast mutton, Beryx caught my eye.

The battle-song's applause brought in the shepherds' mess. My marching song produced a roar that drew the steading Ruands and the housekeeper's palace cohorts, and after Everran's plaint a flustered underling begged us, "Come up to the big house. There's been a mistake."

We were ushered off to the main audience hall where the sheep lord himself made amends like the prince he was, even producing a ten-years-matured Everran wine. He had Holym holdings and already knew our errand. Moreover, he had lost so much face over sending a king to eat with his apprentices that he passed us on with letters of urgent support to the Clan patriarch in Heshruan, and introductions to Clan steadings along the way. Luckier still, his patriarch was the current Ruand of the Tingrith as well.

In some way or other most Quarreders spring from eight enormous clans, but they are so intermarried and interbred it is impossible for an outlander to comment on any Quarreder without another taking umbrage for "the Family." Their government is called the Tingrith: the Eight. A person from each clan, usually an elder, often the patriarch, lives in Heshruan and holds the Tingrith seat until he dies, when a relative replaces him. It is more efficient than Holym, but it produces ferocious clan rivalries and an obsession with birth. In Quarred, if you are not "born" into the upper ranks of one of the Eight, you may as well emigrate at once.

Heshruan is most splendid, however: a brand-new capital—corsairs burnt the old one—full of elegant buildings, green parks, scented and flowering trees, and innumerable fountains fed from an artificial lake. You see the city for miles ahead, a vast green and white splash on the tawny uplands, appearing and vanishing with the movement of the earth.

The Clan Ruand first invited us to stay at the Ruler's palace, and then to the horse-races that afternoon. Beryx refused the first in favor of the Clan palace, and accepted the second. Quarreders love horses, which, unlike the Holmyx, they keep for sport and war. They are bred on the huge southern cape of Culphan Skos: I made a song of how we saw them as we sailed to Hazghend, great skeins of bronze and chestnut and mahogany running loose on the green southern uplands, above gray-blue cliffs and bright southern waves.

They looked quite as beautiful on the race-track. Beryx's eye brightened. I was more taken by the crowd: the men in dark clothes and huge white turbans—the higher the rank, the bigger the head—the women in filmy summer dresses with equally immense flowered hats. I thought it a pretty conceit, before I found the flowers were of cloth. Garlands should either be precious, or real. I saw Sellithar in her gold terrian coronal, and lost interest in the formalities, which were as numerous as the crowd.

Heshruan is extremely formal: greetings, clothes, precedence, all is significant and rigidly observed. There is also a massive load of ceremony. The Ruand drags a fifty-man entourage, the Lords' days are celebrated with processions, bands, strings of prancing cavalry, carriage loads of Clansmen, officials, and bedizened generals. When I asked where the soldiers were, Beryx grinned, "Ask Ragnor. Or wait till we head for Estar."

There are also daily banquets, horse-races, and afternoon entertainments, but never a harper plays. The populace are government scribes or Clan potentates, and soon I would have traded them all for one rowdy Holmyx in high-heeled boots and harpoon spurs, or a single shepherd cook with greenhide to uphold his trousers and salt under his tongue. In Heshruan everybody is climbing, up or down, and the ladder they use is words.

The Clans did receive us well, for if you cannot be "born" in Quarred the next best thing is to be visiting royalty. Especially Everran's, since the Eight drink our wine. But there were questions about Beryx's arm, a thing unheard of in Holym, and many open stares, especially from the unmarried girls. Being "unborn," I did not count, but Beryx collected a court wherever he went, one of whom confided to me that his scar was "so romantic," whatever she meant by that.

Recalling Astarien, I doubted our definitions would agree. But a few mornings later I woke from a dream of Sellithar, and going along the cavernous upstairs corridor in search of fresh air, met Beryx farewelling the nymph in question at his bedroom door.

She gave me a brazen smile, and blew a kiss back up the marble stairs. He looked positively sheepish. Then with a sudden, gleeful, small-boy's chuckle remarked, "You can do some things one-handed, after all."

I opened my mouth to invoke conjugal faith and a scale of other such pomposities. Recalled who I had last shared a bed with, and thought again. Essaying levity, I began, "If you end in a Clan paternity suit . . ."

His face shut like a door. He answered bleakly, "No chance of that."

But he had chosen the Clan palace for more than amorous intrigues. "If you want to plant in the Tingrith," he said, "you have to plough plenty of dirt." Three weeks we kicked our heels awaiting an audience, and in those three weeks he juggled the Clans more cunningly than ever I did the truth and Hawge. I could not follow half the scandal levers, the power and blood knots, and was reduced to seeking a notable weapon, which in Heshruan is as witty as hunting a sea in Hethria. The city is not even walled.

On audience morning, Beryx appeared in crimson cloak and coronal, saying, "Bring your robe." We walked silently to the Tingrith meeting house, past the resplendent guards and up the marble steps.

The Eight sat round a circular table in a rank of tremendous white turbans and shrewd leathery faces. None were below middle-age, and the Ruand's beard was white as the mushroom on his head, but all bore the mark of sheep lords, who work for their wealth with their own hands, and know it from the ground to the mighty pair of ram-horns behind them on the wall. Everyone bowed solemnly. We were ushered to chairs, and Beryx gave me a nod.

Quarreders understand fighting, especially with fire: dry storms scourge them every year. Their eyes flashed at the battle-song. I knew they felt for the warriors of Saeverran, and would honor Astarien's fellow conquerors. I could not resist an extempore coda for Inyx in the Raskelf, for it was their sheep he saved, and I felt they would favor a fighter more than one who merely begged.

Beryx told them the rest, this time including my interview, which won my first glances of respect, and adding Hawge's words, along with the weapon search. "We do not ask help forever," he concluded. "What we are buying is time. For the Confederacy as well as ourselves."

The Ruand's eye sharpened. He said formally, "Quarred hears you." Then the debate began.

Quarred's finances. Confederate claims and worths. Hawge's faith or probable lack of it. Within five speeches I knew there was a power-struggle in progress, for which we were just the rope in a tug-of-war. The northern Clans favored us, since they use the Raskelf, unlike the Southerners, who stretch down into the grain and fruit and horselands of Culphan Skos. But they were fighting for mastery of the Tingrith, not for our cause.

Beryx sat quiet, barely moving his eyes. The Ruand, also impassive, watched the battle sway to and fro.

Presently it resolved into a struggle for the two Heshruan lords, who have a foot in both camps. The Northerners quoted Hawge's taste for horses, Quarred's proximity to its lair, the Raskelf's importance, the threat to the wine trade, Hawge's invulnerability to all but this frail chance. All Beryx's arguments. The Southerners were against extortion, risk, and getting involved. The debate grew warm. Veiled thrusts about "biggest export," "biggest spenders," "unfair representation," "tax evaders," were exchanged, cryptic comments about the Army—northern soldiers, southern generals—and less cryptic comments about "favor from the Chair."

At last a Heshruan lord crumbled before the threat of Hawge near his march-line, and a long-faced Northerner with a beaky nose and bright blue eyes veiled in folds of leathery skin sat back and demanded, "Vote."

The Ruand straightened. "Those in favor," he asked slowly, "of sending Everran ten ingots a month?" Four hands went up. "Against?" Three. "As Vethyr clansman, I have one vote. I cast it against." The Northerner's blue eyes flashed. "As Ruand, I have the casting vote. I cast that . . . also against."

Into the silence he spoke in his slow, deliberate voice. "I will move that Quarred send three ingots a month for the present year. We have lost the Raskelf for this summer. It will be a future risk. A debit of a hundred and twenty gold ingots for an unknown number of years is too great a risk. Those in favor?"

I did not see the Northerner's look, but Beryx gave a tiny nod. Seven hands went up. "Carried," said the Ruand. "Three ingots a month."

"Three!" I burst out in the street. "When they sell their wool to Estar weight for weight in gold! And he's a Northerner! He uses the Raskelf! The old—old—"

"And he's a Quarreder," Beryx said composedly. "He remembers my Raskelf note. They like their dignity. And he knows quite well that if Everran's ruined, Quarred will lead the Confederacy. They've hankered after that for years."

"If Hawge crosses the range, he won't be leading anything!"

There was irony in his smile. "He knows I'll talk my tongue out now to move Estar. And I just might succeed. I do the work, Estar bears the cost. Quarred's no worse off with Hawge, and ahead in the Confederacy." He glanced down the clean, handsome street, and grimaced. "Let's saddle up and go."

The quickest way from Heshruan to Estar is straight east to the bridge where Khallien and Mellennor join. We approached it in ceremonial garb instead of our usual farmers' shirts and Holmyx boots, which I understood when we passed border guards on both sides, Quarred's with wearisome formality and Estar's with blunt demands for "identification" from the gray-clad soldiery. Beryx touched his coronal, gestured at my robe, and said with unbelievable hauteur, "Everran. And suite. Have your communications broken down?"

We sat an hour in the guard hut while it was proved they had not. Then with "cordial apologies" an unsmiling commander ushered us into Estar and a rabble fell on us waving wax tablets and shouting at the top of their lungs.

Estar is infatuated with "news." They use mirror-signals on clear days, smoke on dull ones, fires at night, town-crier is the land's most coveted post, and lords grow rich solely by maintaining news-takers in every Resh. These had left the nearest town after eavesdropping on the border signals, and meant to extract value for their sweat.

As the swarm landed, Beryx swept both hands before him in the scout's signal for "Halt. No road," and yelled, "Harran! This is yours!"

Later, when I read the signals and heard the criers, I could hardly credit it. Harpers have good memories, naturally. These could write as well, yet they put Saphar in Stiriand with Beryx challenging the dragon to single combat at its gates, had me leading the phalanx while Inyx ran away, gave Hawge four wings and horns, claimed it had incinerated the Saeverran fire-fighters, that it demanded maidens for food, and was now poised to descend on Estar. But when I exploded, Beryx said, "Don't disturb yourself. All that matters is 'poised to descend.' "

Not content with songs, they rushed us afterwards, all yelling at once. "What happened to your face, sir?" "Will your government fall because of the dragon?" "Is Everran bankrupt?" "What did you think of Quarred's help?" "How do you feel about the dragon in Everran, sir?"

Beryx had been forging steadily ahead, uttering inanities: at that last question, he spun on the fresh-faced youth, who recoiled. "How would you feel," he said harshly, "if it were in Estar?" And strode away.

We slept in Cushoth, a city bigger than Holymlase and still not the Resh-capital, lodging under siege from news-takers in the governor's house. I now saw fresh reason for Beryx's beginning in Holym. All Cushoth knew of us and wanted to see for themselves.

So we climbed on the dais in the town square, and I sang to immense crowds who stared, pointed, chattered, laughed, squabbled, and ate nuts throughout. Then the news-takers attacked again, this time catching me as well. "Why do you wear that robe?" "Who wrote the songs?" "Are you married?" "Is the royal marriage withstanding the dragon?" "Is that your own harp?" Beryx mouthed, "Steady," just before I burst, so since he judged them important, I strove to stay in earshot of courtesy.

This farce went on clear to Rustarra, amid town-criers competing for sensational catch-lines. "Confederacy crumbles." "Everran King appeals to Estar." "Everran bankrupt: Estar next?" "Harper says, Dragon is a hypnotist." "Death by sting and claw." "Nervous collapse of Everran queen." By the time we reached Rustarra, I would have paid Hawge to eat the lot.

Estar itself is stupefying: mostly dead-flat plains, every inch of them cultivated, mined, covered in towns or factories, which suck in the Confederacy's sheep, cattle, wool, meat, hides, fish, coal, iron, tin, copper, gold, oil, silk, linen, timber, and spew out artifacts. Grain it grows itself. Resh-size fields stretch from one to the other horizon, with tillers thick as ants. And everywhere else are innumerable people, all in a frenzy of activity for the Four know what.

Rustarra, the essence of Estar, spreads for miles round the Tarrilien estuary, which has been dredged, extended with moles, and lined with endless quays. Behind them lies the town center: grimy, ornately carved official buildings, then fortified tower-like lords' houses, then the city wall, in good repair and thick with military machinery. Outside are mile upon mile of dirty little houses, factory chimneys in place of trees, army barracks, City-Resh council houses, depots, stores, granaries, stables, slaughterhouses, reservoirs, and slums full of outcasts, all sunk in a dirty brown sludge that blots the sky, and making a noise to burden the earth.

At first I thought government was the two annually elected shophets who lead the Resh Assembly's six-monthly sessions: finding the shophets only execute its commands, I supposed rule was the assembly's. Then, seeing swarms of the loudest folk in Estar deafening assemblymen over causes from higher jugglers' wages to government-issued yeldtar juice for slaughterhouse fowls, I thought this to be the government, until I realized these wind-horns never mentioned anything like trade or wages. And then I found there are men who never stand for election, never enter the assembly, never become shophet, but quietly command all those who do.

The most obvious are the lords of trade, carriage, news, and manufacture, who live wealthily but vulgarly in mansions within Rustarra's walls and point Estar where their money wishes. Less obvious are the guilds. Estar's number millions, for every trade from doctor to horse-boy permits only dues-paying guildsmen to follow their work, and when they strike for higher wages or cold water on tap for street-sweepers, the lords, shophets, and assembly are obliged to bow. Yet it is not these millions who actually hold the power.

Guild leaders mostly live in the poorest house available, dress meanly, keep no horses, and strive to resemble their poorest subjects. But since I never saw one without white hands, frog's jowls, and a globular belly, I conclude that telling others to strike is a richer trade than doing it yourself.

All these people were agog to see us in the flesh. We housed with the shophets, banqueted with the lords, addressed the assembly, lectured the guilds, and were beset by news-takers, the whole of it only adding to Rustarra's noise.

"This is Estar," said Beryx. "Think later, talk first."

We soon attracted some wind-horns who deafened assemblymen on behalf of, "Everran's starving children," and were out-yelled by a group defending poor, innocent, mistreated Hawge: "An evolutionary treasure that must be preserved." We ourselves were objects of intense interest, for Estar thinks monarchy "so quaint," and royal retainers quainter still. I was asked how much the king paid me, if he beat me, if I could leave him or was a palace thrall, if my wages were "tied to inflation," if I had a guild to protect me, and if he censored my songs.

After that one flare at the border, Beryx had Estar's key, and would now, unblinking, tell the most stupendous lies. Asked if I really "bit the dragon to make it talk," I nearly choked with rage before catching a bland green eye.

So in self-defense I spread my own slanders, that Beryx used a whip on his chamberlain, dined off gold and threw the plates away, beheaded generals who disputed his orders—that one almost cracked Beryx's public face—and locked up his council for three days on bread and water before he consulted them. But next time a squat factory-lord's wife dripping fur and thillians asked if he "really had first choice of all Everran's virgins," he waved at me and answered demurely, "Ask my scribe: he knows court etiquette back to front."

Among the mountebanks a group of scholars, who are lorebards without music, invited me to a conference. These were called Draconists, their lore being dragons, so I went with alacrity, hoping to learn something of use.

First they asked if I were a master or a doctor, taking my robe for an Everran scholar's gown. Then they said songs were not "scientific data" and wanted to know if Hawge laid eggs or was marsupial, how many teeth it had, if it hibernated, and how much it weighed, before forgetting me in a furious combat over Hawge's classification as a "worm" or a "firedrake," and its descent from insects, on account of its eyes, or reptiles, on account of its legs. Later, some actually extracted money from the government and went off to study it, armed with theories of dragon-language and something called a "submission crouch." They lived three days round Kerymgjer before Hawge came out feeling peckish and ate the lot.

Away from these sideshows, Beryx was visiting lords and guild-leaders and making useful talk. A grain lord does not like to hear how Hawge ravaged a Resh in a night, nor a weaver lord how his wool-stores would burn: "all that grease." Nor does a weapon lord wish to consider how Estarian sarissas bent on Hawge like pins: "such a bad advertisement." Guild-leaders melted for Everran's jobless, while both lords and guild-leaders winced at the thought of drinking no more Everran wine. "We'll go to assembly," Beryx told me, "when we've won the assembly ground."

Meanwhile I searched for a weapon, not among the potentates, but in the slum taverns where Estar's surviving harpers play. I liked the slums. They are ridden with thieves and violence, hatred, envy, hardship, dirt, and beggars who would wheedle a gold ingot out of Hawge, but they are human as newsworthy Estarians are not. Moreover, they liked harpers: especially the harper of "Thorgan Fenglos" himself.

It means, The Moon-faced King. It refers to the scar, and at first I disliked it, for Feng is the moon's bad aspect, the lamp of robbers, demons, and ghosts. But in truth it was a sign of liking. They saw Beryx as a fellow loser, and would have wished to see him win.

But the harpers had less lore than I, and even in the

Confederacy's arsenal nobody knew of a notable weapon re-
cently made. After a week I gave up, and went home to find
Beryx's assembly assault prepared at last.

For three days shophets, delegates, and Beryx made
speeches which the news-takers regurgitated for the people,
while the wind-horns went hoarse and one news-taker
scaled the shophet's bath-house window to eavesdrop on
our talk and win "the inside news." On the third day, when
I was all but deaf and most orators voiceless, the assembly
was near a vote—but then some wind-horn made an oration
from the city wall on the moral outrage of a republic
backing a monarchy, corrupt by definition, against an innocent beast only wanting love and understanding to make it
sweet as mother's milk.

The news-takers were in ecstasy. The wind-horns went
hoarse. The guild-leaders suddenly recalled they were
against lords on principle, and Beryx was clearly a para-
mount lord. The lords, unnerved by the thought of Hawge
led on a string into Estar, leant on the assembly, which
voted Everran twelve ingots a month. At this the guild-
leaders announced to the news-takers, "Any aid to Everran,
and Estar will have a general strike."

This is apparently more fearful than the plague. The
lords bent, the shophets recalled the assembly, which obediently reversed its vote. Everran would get nothing at all.

Beryx came out of the assembly hall like a red-eyed
arrow, clove a phalanx of news-takers, grabbed my arm,
bellowed, "Get the gear!" bade our servants take the horses
to the Isthmus, and whipped me straight down to the docks.
Halfway along was a Hazghend whaler which had been dis-
charging oil. Beryx yelled up at her captain, "Are you
sailing? Yes? To Hazghend? Yes? No matter where! Will
you take two passengers? Yes? We're coming aboard!" And

we were out of Rustarra on that evening's ebb.

All through that I had not dared speak to him. His eyes were quite black, and the scar, which had been fading, stood out lividly. But when Rustarra was a mere yellow glow on the smirched horizon and an easterly was lifting the whaler with a horse's living roll and surge, so I was wondering if whale stink would make me sea-sick, he came swiftly across the after-deck to grip me by the arm.

"Four preserve me," he said, "from news-takers, puppet assemblies, Yea-saying shophets, and all other word bungle-ists." He broke into a laugh. "Except harpers, of course."

It was a surprise to find the sun shone and the world had color, after Estar's murk. We ran the coast westerly, across Belphan Fer and past the huge forehead of Culphan Skos, athwart the path of the late summer storms, which would blot the uplands in tumors of lightning-livid cloud and buffet us madly as they passed. But the whaler was two years out, her crew sick for home, and though the skipper was happy to land us at Hazghend's capital in Hazruan, rather than his home port of Tyr Saeveryr, he was not yielding way to storms. He laid his course further seaward, cutting across the vast bay of Belphan Wyre, straight for Culphan Saeveryr, "the cape where the wind turns," and shook out another reef as he went.

From the sea Hazghend is beautiful, a wild coast of cliff and cape with inlets so long their gores of tourmaline water dovetail straight into the mountains that draw snow in winter, are too rocky for anything but goats, and rise in their capricious splendor straight from the turbulent cobalt and emerald-shot sea. One moment it is eggshell blue, the next purple with thunder, then lost in white squalls of rain.

There are no factories. The air is clear as polished crystal, and as cold. You pass fisher-boats, or whalers, or freighters out for hire, or the long low galleys in which Hazyx go raiding. Ship-building is Hazghend's fourth-favorite occupation, after drinking, fighting, and going to sea.

Hazruan lies in the longest narrowest inlet of all, with Culphan Saeveryr's black-cliffed peninsula stretching south, and the gray morose bulk of Culphan Morglis squatted to its north. The inlet is walled in sheer after sheer of midnight green pines mirrored a darker green in green-tinged sea, with tiny fish-villages, shipyards, laid-up galleys, and careened schooners in the coves between. At the inlet's head, the massif lifts straight to Asterne Brenx's snow-tipped fang, and beneath it Hazruan's stockade and timbered roofs crown the red and gray cliff, over a crescent of beach crammed with everything from fishing dories to the galleys of Ragnor's lords. Hazyx fight corsairs when they are raided and hunt them when others pay, and are otherwise indistinguishable, except to themselves.

We clambered into a whaleboat amid cries of, "No trouble! Good fishing!" and were rowed into the uproar of taverns and fishing nets, impromptu auctions and barterings of spoil. Threading the crowd of blonde, bellowing Hazyx who brandished cups, axes, women, and oars, we reached the steps that Ragnor calls his front door.

They are bare holes in the cliff where you mount in single file, and all the way the two mighty catapults above Hazruan's stockade stare silently down on you. They can throw clear to the opposite cliff. Ragnor, as he puts it, "does not like to be surprised."

His hall tunes with Hazghend: ship timbers mostly, I suspect, high-treed and cavernous, hung with trophies more bizarre than Inyx's, above benches and trestle tables built to withstand Hazyk quarrels as well as their rumps. It is full of smoke from the huge rough-stone fireplace, with rushes on the floor and arm-thick tallow dips around the walls, a perfect corsairs' lair. But a hearthbard sat on the fire's right, and Ragnor himself, albeit on sealskins, occupied a king's chair. Already I felt at home.

As is the custom, we entered without ceremony. All friends are welcome, and if any enemy did get past the gate, the hall is full of Ragnor's blood-vowed warriors. When I let the hide door-curtain drop, Ragnor looked up sharply from his wine.

He is a golden bull of a man, red-faced, blue-eyed, burly as Gjarr, with a sword-cut across the nose to give him character. He pulled his head back as if struck. Then he almost shot out of his chair.

"By Rienvur's flaming steeds!" Hazyx do not follow the Sky-lords, but the Crimson Planet, master of war. "By the—it is!" That bellow shook the candle-flames. "Beryx! You skinny upland grape-squeezer, what have you done to your arm?"

I did not know whether to wince or curse. But to my utter amazement Beryx retorted, grinning, "You windy seaside octopus, a dragon dropped me on it."

"Dragon, uh?" rumbled Ragnor when we were seated at his high table, behind ornate silver goblets of Everran wine and huge portions of spit-roasted sheep. "Courtesy of Quarred," said Ragnor briefly, and at Beryx's look his blue eyes twinkled yet more brilliantly. "Well, let's hear."

"Courtesy of your hearthbard," answered Beryx, "and if mine isn't sick of it, he can tell the tale."

Hazyx are prodigal in appreciation as all else. Amid the thunder of beaten cups, two or three gold armrings came arching at my head, and Ragnor laughed and said, "Don't give those to Hawge." Then he looked at Beryx with a glinting grin.

"Well, you upland fox, you didn't come here for sheep— or cattle. Did you?" Ragnor may look a beer-swilling pirate, but you do not make yourself Ruand of Hazghend, and hold together a country unsecured by inheritance and rotten with blood-feuds, unless your sword arm is bettered by your head.

Beryx spat in the fire. He related our reception in Holym, Quarred, and Estar. Ragnor spat too.

"I owe you," he said, "for the corsairs. But then, you also owe me—yes?"

Beryx's grin was as glinting as his own. "Was it you who told me about the king and the yeldtars? Or did I tell you?"

The tale is hoary as harps: the tyrant asked by a green fellow tyrant for a ruler's recipe, who takes the messenger into his garden and silently uses his stick to lop the tallest yeldtar heads. Ragnor chuckled and slapped his thigh. "Ah, well, take that one. Gjarr's boots *were* getting a sight too big. We'll start even. What is it you want?"

"Seven gold ingots a month," Beryx said bluntly, "and a weapon that hasn't been forged."

In the next ten minutes he had every weapon in Hazruan at his feet or across his knees. Two-handed swords, curved lopping knives, double-headed axes, boot-top daggers, bows tall as a man or shorter than my arm, thrusting, throwing, fighting, hunting spears, maces and sling-throwers, jeweled, gold- and silver-chased, hafted or scabbarded in ivory, in blood-tinged wood or plain greasy iron. Beryx smiled at Ragnor across them, rather ruefully. "You know my Guard?" he said. "I took them to Coed Wrock."

Ragnor whistled. Then he laughed. "A poxy great

hedgehog that falls apart if one man gets out of step!"

"The dragon," Beryx replied, "was very taken with Gjarr's axe."

Ragnor frowned: then he sighed. Then he said, "So, Scarface." To my wonder, Beryx looked quite pleased. "I can't give you a weapon. As for gold . . . You know how I am. I don't have these measly account books and fat scribes to sit about playing treasuries. If it's here I give it away, and if it's not I go out and get some more. No sea-lord worth a dipper of pitch does otherwise. 'Open-handed'—you know how it goes."

Beryx nodded. I knew too. It is the first epithet Hazyk bards apply to a great king, the first thing warriors seek after a champion's prowess, the keel of Hazghend government.

Ragnor looked down the hall. "You could try to take it back, but—" A gleeful chuckle. "It'd be a long day's work."

Beryx nodded again. Ragnor shifted in his chair.

"Everran bad, uh?" he asked abruptly.

Beryx said, "Yes."

Ragnor pondered. "I've ten galleys beached. A day or so'd crew them. Which do you fancy—sheep or goats?"

Beryx shook his head. "You'd reach Heshruan no more than half strength. You'd never get back. And Rustarra's armed the mole with catapults."

"Flat-worms. No spirit of adventure," Ragnor complained. He looked sideways. His face softened. "Rienvur, gimme a catapult before word-throwers, any day."

Then, of a sudden, he began to strip off his gold arm-rings: flat, round, thick as thumbs, headed with boars and dragons, inlaid with enamel, running from wrist almost to shoulder on both arms. His golden torque followed, a couple of gold chains, his dagger with thillian-encrusted hilt. "Can't have the sword. I'll want that." Then he rose and bellowed down the hall. "Hoy! Hoy! You beer-guzzling gut-fillers! I want your gear!"

"Melt it down," he said across the heap. "I dunno what it'll make in ingots, but it ought to do one month. I'll send you more."

Beryx looked up at him. He was smiling, in a way that reminded me how he had looked at his thousand volunteers.

"Thanks," he said softly, "pirate." His mouth-corners lifted. "Now all I need is a . . . ship."

Ragnor flung both arms in the air and nearly snuffed the candle-flames. "You guzzling land-shark! Next time I'll take the dragon neat!"

He found us a ship, a low, lean schooner, "fastest thing with masts," but not even Ragnor the open-hearted and open-handed could find us a wind. We woke to a ferocious southerly, blasting up from the ice with all its chill and twice its power, and Ragnor shook his head. "No, Scarface," he said. "I'll give away gold, but not throw it. She'd never get round the cape."

Beryx bit his lip. "I'm over the three months," he said. "And new moon's in ten days."

Ragnor was at a loss. Then his face cleared. "Come on," he clapped Beryx's shoulder. "Best lore in the world: when you can't do anything else, get drunk."

He must have had a head like Hawge's hide, for he was drunk all of seven nights afterward. And every night the southerly pounded Hazghend, and every morning he and Beryx clambered to the spy-post to come down salt-rimed and teary and grimmer than before.

Beryx wanted to take a galley. Ragnor said, "Give you one and welcome, but she won't weather Morglis either. You'll swamp in the open bay." He stared out where Culphan Morglis humped gray and obdurate, with swathes of spray obscuring its crest as the fifteen-foot rollers came tearing in and blew up marbled and foaming and green as Hawge's eyes. "First of the season's busters. Thing must have the Eye on you, Scarface. Earliest one I've ever known."

Hazruan did its best to solace us. I learnt three fine sea-songs from the bard, and could have had other comfort if I chose. The Hazyk girls respect harpers, and find more subtle gallantries than, "Lie down, you pretty harlot," very much to their taste. The trouble was, Sellithar would not let me warm myself.

The eighth morning Ragnor slitted his eyes at the sea a long time, the look of a Holmyx measuring a well-known and wicked bull he means to yard. Then he said abruptly, "Give it a try."

He gave us his own war galley and chose the crew himself, weeding ruthlessly through brawny battalions. Then he swung up beneath the high, gaudily painted sternpost, laid a hand on the steering oar, and glanced along her seventy feet to the dragon head rearing with scarlet jaws and golden scales above her prow, the look of a man for a well-beloved sword. "Tie your ears on, Scarface," he said. "If anything can get you there, it's *Beraza*."

He had shipped five extra hands: "bailers." As he nodded one hulk to the steering oar, Beryx jumped up. Ragnor said rudely, "When I'm gutting sharks with m'war spear, I'll let you know." Beryx, with a grin, sat meekly down.

Ragnor took her out, the men rowing almost lazily, while she bucked crossways to the swell and the fine spray chased across her bows. Gradually the swells deepened. They put more power in their strokes. Two hours later the troughs were ten feet deep, Culphan Morglis lay over the sternpost, the ship was bounding like a maddened horse, and the bailers were working for their lives. Ragnor bellowed, "Give 'em a hand, harper! Good'n steady!" Shot a glance seaward and roared into the sea-roar, "Ready to tack!"

The rest is a blur of water and terror and unbroken singing that has permanently impaired my voice, from the green hill that sat on our bow as the stern whipped up to the incoming roller to the frenzy that succeeded it as the gale thrashed seas in on our quarter and the *Beraza* corkscrewed and leapt and dived and bucked like a lunatic netfloat with no two planks the same way at once, while the keel groaned and the bailers worked like madmen and Ragnor fought the steering oar with every tremendous muscle and roared pitilessly, "Port! Starb'd! Heave! Hold! Send her! C'mon, harper, sing!" While the oars bent like lathes as the rowers soused head-under and came up spluttering, then sobbing like winded horses, and Morglis slavered over its escaping prey, while the salt got up my nose, down my throat, into my lungs—until they set the sail with three men hauled back from overboard, before I sang for those whole thirty-six hours while *Beraza* plunged and rolled her heart out as she ran under sail and oar slantwise to the unrelenting wind, first north-east up the outer width of Belphan Wyre, then north-west up the narrow inner arm to Tistyr's blessed mole.

Ragnor called in the rags of a whisper to a staring Quarreder, "Catch t'warp!" The crew collapsed where they sat. The white-coated dripping ship finally fell still. And Beryx, who had been baling in the thick of it with his right arm anchored over a thwart, got out of the bilge in the scraps of his crimson cloak, looked over to Ragnor, and quietly shook his head.

Ragnor grinned back, slumped over the steering oar, a frosted snowman with wine-red eyes. "Wanna say anything," he whispered, "use that bard of yours. He's not too bad."

VI

Would you credit that, after Ragnor and his Hazyx rowed their hearts out to get us through the gale, we sat for six priceless hours while the Tistyr commander signaled Heshruan to be sure we were safe to admit? Quarred is permanently panicky about its border isthmus. Ridiculous, because, as Ragnor says, "If I did come, there's three hundred miles of coast to beach on. Why would I damn well walk?"

The clearance came at dusk. We hove the gold on a packhorse and ourselves on our beasts. Beryx lifted a hand to *Beraza*'s blur on the inky water, and said evenly, "Ride."

I am unlikely to forget that ride. Clear through the night, steering by the stars, up over Heshruan Slief till a huge ember-red dawn found me flogging the packhorse and Beryx flogging himself. I made him rest an hour by lying down and refusing to move. "And if you kick me, I'll make a song of it." The packhorse lay down in the absolute height of noon, the whole Slief aquake in the heat and our mouths too dry to hear ourselves curse. We split the gold, turned the horse loose, and rode in search of a steading, which took all afternoon.

They were lavishly kind: fresh packhorse, food and drink, demands that we sleep. Beryx looked at the western sky. In a lilac dusk the new moon hung, slim and cruel as a sliver of steel. He said, "Can't," in a whisper, and tottered out to his horse.

Only image-shards remain of that night. Flogging my innocent beast for slowing while I slept. A servant's arm around me when I woke. Beryx swaying drunkenly, chin on chest, reins knotted round wrist, against a sheaf of stars. Falling off in a wide red cloudless dawn, pulling Beryx after me, insisting, groggy but adamant, "New moon come. No use get there dead."

Woken with a vile headache, drenched in sweat by the implacable sun, I recall watering the horses in somebody's earth-tank. Riding on. The Helkents rising higher and higher, a red rampart in the east, and at last the road up to where Quarred and Everran meet. Staggering into the border-post to meet soldiers whose determination ran to drawn swords. Quarred border was closed for the night.

Perhaps it was fortunate, if only for the sake of this song. We slept on the border-post floor. Four, how I slept. As the first sun dyed the Lynghyrne, we were eating stale bread as we climbed to the saddle of the pass.

Thank the Four that Everran does not bother to ward its march. The saddle topped and Bryve Elond engulfed us, a long trough of silvery leaves over twisted stumpy black trunks, our own elonds at last, our own red mountains reared above. Everran, tenuous fawn, filled the V ahead. Beryx looked up, a stick man on a starven horse, and an immense golden-crowned indigo-shadowed thunderhead lit his dreamy smile.

Then he straightened with a jerk. A shape had plummeted from the cloud, so high it was toy-like, a mere blotted silhouette, but one you would never mistake. Four-legged, serpent-backed, winged with sails, trailing a sting of tail.

Next instant Beryx was by the packhorse, snatching the halter as he ripped out words. "Ride! You left, you right. Harran, back down the pass. If it chases you, jump off the horse." The servants fled. He tore madly at the pack bag and I forced my muscles to slide me down, drive me round to the other side.

He snarled, "Get out! Go!" My fingers shook as I whipped the pack off, tore at the buckles, he ran a few feet and tumbled the gold onto the ground, I copied without knowing why, he slapped his horse savagely on the rump and as it snorted away he snarled again, "You raving idiot— go!" I hit my own horse across the nose—and then it was too late.

Hawge's circles had grown faster and faster, lower, smaller, tremendous piston wingbeats expressing more than simple rage. Then fire shot from its nostrils and lashed along the ground. The grass ignited, the elonds went up in fiery fusillades. We and the horses and servants were yarded, walled in rails of flame.

Beryx took five paces back from the gold. I found myself at his shoulder. The dragon thundered round its trap, braked with a slam, spun and dropped, right in front of us.

This time it did not waddle. It came like a stalking cat, chin on the ground, spine sunk between the shoulders and then arching up, eyes like burning phosphorus. Only this back rose thirty feet high, the tail that lashed behind covered fifty feet in a sweep, and even the ripple of those huge shoulders was lost behind the lamps of eyes.

Straight over the fire they looked. Straight through the fire they came. They were brighter than the flames. They were bigger than the flames. They were opening, widening, there was nothing left around them, nothing existed but facetted, sentient, thought-obliterating crystal green . . .

A clear, hard, human voice said, "I have brought your gold."

My sight cleared with a pop. Hawge was right on top of us, crouched to spring, eyes on a level with mine. Beryx stood unflinching, head up, looking straight back—only later did I remember it—into that deadly gaze.

Hawge snorted. Red-hot derision does not cover it. Flames struck the ground, ricocheted and shot twenty feet in the air.

<Where,> its breath was fire ripping through helliens, <is my fire-stone—Man?>

Beryx spoke clearly, precisely. "I can get it back."

Hawge hissed: the cut of a giant whip.

"Give me," Beryx persisted, clearly, steadily, still not looking away, "five days."

Hawge spat. Then the upper lip lifted in gigantic parody of a human sneer, and the eyes altered from fury to a vicious malevolence.

<Go,> it whispered, <to your—Saphar. But I leave now—to HUNT!>

It leapt straight at and over us with a sixty-foot bound caught in the air by the first colossal wingbeat and driven upward on a roar like a wounded earthquake in its throes.

I stood quaking, knees unstrung, mind a quag of unpent fright. Beryx turned around.

"You fatuous oaf." His voice came out a note high, with the fine tremor of a fraying string. "You raving imbecile. You utter incompetent! You risked the pair of us! You should have . . ." he broke off. Walked unsteadily to the roadside, and was violently and comprehensively sick.

He had recovered by the time we caught the horses, whose panic made them nearly as dangerous as Hawge. I helped scoop up the gold. "Bring it along," he said huskily, struggling astride his beast.

I cried, "Where are you going?" and he looked down at me. His eyes were quite black, but this time it was not rage.

"Saphar," he said.

★ ★ ★ ★ ★

Down Ven Elond I just kept him in sight. I was seething with questions: Why had the maerian been unguarded, who could dare to rob a dragon's den, how was it done, how did he escape, how could Beryx hope to find him if the dragon could not? I had recalled a thick red-crusted slash under Hawge's right eye. I wanted to know how Beryx had looked in those eyes and not been paralyzed like a mouse, how their conversation had jumped so impossibly and what steps were missed and how Saphar came into it. Aslash, I thought in forlorn hope. Aslash will know.

In Aslash square Beryx slid down, ignored cries, greetings, questions, told the air, "Get me another horse," and walked straight, as by willpower, toward the governor's house. The governor met him halfway, his soldier's aplomb reduced to a frightened mask.

Beryx whispered, "How?"

"Last month the gold ran out. General's sent messages for you, sir—two, three times a day. The dragon flew two days ago. Came back yesterday. A terrible noise . . . like the Helkents had fallen down. It flew off. So high we lost touch—"

"Saphar?"

Beryx was just audible. The governor's voice shook.

"Sir, no one's been able to raise them since . . . the dragon flew."

Beryx turned away. In death itself he will not look like that. The governor caught his arm. "Sir, for the Four's sake, I'll send scouts, messengers, you can't go on like—"

Beryx freed himself as if unconscious of it. "Horse," he said to the ground. "Now."

Aslash signaled ahead. We had relays at Khatmel, Tirkeld, Asvelos, we rode in two-thirds of a day what I had managed in two. I covered the last miles neither asleep nor awake, a pair of legs attached to a horse. Whatever sustained Beryx, it was not flesh and blood.

The road dipped, rose, dipped, rose a last time and slid down to Azilien. Our horseshoes thumped on the verge, clattered on the paving. I did not want to think why they were so loud, any more than I wanted to look up.

Beryx rode onto the bridge. Drew rein: and slowly, so slowly, lifted his eyes.

Like the Perfumed Vale, Saphar had been slashed with fire. Smoke still wreathed feebly about its terraces, but it did not conceal the huge welts of ruin that crisscrossed the city, wider than houses, slashing in rubble and embers across streets, ripping contemptuously through walls, burning up chains of thatch, and reducing major buildings to heaps of fallen stone. People moved among the ruins, slowly, aimlessly, in the uncanny quiet. Some looked at me, and looked away: not in rejection but in blank disinterest.

I heard Beryx take a slow, deep breath. I knew where his eyes were. I had looked already, and the heart was ice in my breast.

The palace had taken the full brunt of Hawge's wrath. Most of it was roofless, much of it had burnt. Every tower was a truncated heap. A plume of smoke trailed from the Treasury. I knew how the gardens would look. Crazy fragments of wood, fabric, stone, had been strewn broadcast under the impact of the blows. Hawge must have used its tail, over and over, with the most deliberate malice, a child smashing another's dearest toy. What crowned Saphar was not a builder's gay extravaganza, but a trashy wreck.

I think we walked up through the town. I know we walked under Berrian's arch, for it was intact. Tugging and kicking and clambering over the rubble in the gatehouse, I could feel that eye, a mute, burning indictment on my back.

Beryx went straight to the queen's rooms. They were silent, a hideous tangle of crumpled wood. He searched quickly, efficiently, you would think rationally, unless you saw his eyes. I trailed like a shadow, with as much mind of my own.

He did not bother with his own rooms, any more than he had with Inyx's tower. After one cursory glance at the Treasury, he turned to the Asterne steps.

There are a hundred and fifty, ascending the pinnacle that makes a stempost at the plateau's eastern end. Some royal builder had planed and smoothed it into a tower, with guard rooms delved just below the circular summit where the mirror signalers watch. Some king, perhaps the tower-maker, crowned it with a little rotunda, six marble columns under a circle of peaked roof to shelter Asterne's silver wind-bells, designed to make music from the play of Air.

The rotunda had been smashed to smithereens. The mirror-signal unit was in ruins. A couple of morvallin fled yarking as our heads appeared: I know now why soldiers loathe them with such deadly hate. As I eyed a long smear of blood over the southern parapet I heard Beryx grunt.

Inyx lay under the western wall. He must have been struck by the tail, then clawed. What was left lay on its face, a bloody sword by the limp right hand, the wide desert-fighter's shoulders still clad in a rag of mail. This time he would not trouble me with ghosts.

I grew aware that Beryx was speaking, in a remote, numbed voice.

"He was waiting for the message. From Aslash. He would have been sure I'd come—"

His voice broke. He looked down. Then he went on, in the same tone, but now on a note of valediction.

"At least he used the sword."

We walked back to the stairs. The guard-room door was ajar. In passing he gave it a shove, glanced in, and spun in his stride.

Sellithar was under the table, against the rear wall: huddled like an embryo. The folds of blue silk had caught his eye. She yielded to our touch, as a wooden doll's limbs assume a position, and hold.

Beryx looked at her with those black eyes empty of all but perception. But then he touched her cheek and said gently, "Sellithar."

She blinked. Slowly, her eyes came into focus. She saw me. The woodenness broke and with a great sob she hurled herself into my arms.

She cried dry-eyed, enormous racking sobs. I do not know what I did. I loved her, had thought her dead, and against all reason had her restored. What Beryx saw, or felt at her choice of comforter, hardly mattered at all.

Presently, between the sobs, came words.

"We saw it coming . . . He brought me up here. On the steps. He said, 'When it sees us, we'll run. You run in there.' "

I could look at Beryx then. He was listening with that same intent detachment. Sounding quite calm, he said, "He knew it would follow him. He must have meant to get in one good cut . . . I wonder why he missed?"

"He didn't." I recalled that red-crusted slash under the insect eye. When I told him, he nodded slowly, equably. "Good." Then the pupils contracted and his eyes filled with a laughter green and cold and cruel as Hawge's own.

"I'm glad," he said, "he managed that."

He turned away. "Bring her down, Harran. We've a lot to do."

"Search for the maerian?" The mere thought appalled me.

"I never meant to search for it," he answered calmly. "I wanted five days for evacuation. Four should be enough."

Just before he left the door I regained my wits. "Wh-where are we going?" I managed. And he glanced back in surprise.

"Maer Selloth," he said. "There's nowhere else."

Saphar was less prostrate than it seemed. Kyvan emerged from the palace rubble with prayers on his lips and a fresh crimson cloak over his arm, there were five or six rational counselors. Inyx had sent the entire mirror-signal watch down from Asterne, and using his souvenir unit they restored the city's tongue that day. Best of all, Morran met us at the gate-arch, announcing composedly, "Five hundred of the Guard fit and reported for duty, sir. We've been fighting fires."

A lord's wife with a whole house took charge of Sellithar. "I know what she needs, poor lamb." Beryx set up his quarters on the market's intact side, and with a harper for aide plunged into the task of uprooting a court, relocating a government, and moving lock, stock, and barrel out of a ruined city with zombies for half its inhabitants.

The details were endless: the Holym cattle, the Quarred gold, the remnant of the oil, the coming vintage, refugees, the dragon, the treasury, the court, the Army, communications, word to Maer Selloth . . . He cut through it like a knife, cold and tireless. On the fourth morning we rode out behind Sellithar's horse litter, leaving a post of signalers and a gallant handful of council, lords, guildsmen, and soldiers behind. Ahead of us the rest of Saphar streamed on foot, horse, and carriage down the southern road.

Tirs had taken few Stiriand refugees and less damage from Hawge. Its long foothills are poor toward Bryve

Elond, but eastward are fertile grain valleys, and Everran's orchards. Countless songs praise the Tirien apple-buds that blow in white and blush-pink clouds against the red Helkent rock and the blue spring sky. It was less pretty in autumn, with the poor land dull yellow and fawn and the rocks showing through while the storms swept north to soak us in steady succession, but the Azilien valley is charming, a tiny clear river that chuckles below green norgal and finlythe and the odd rivannon, while iron crags of rust and vermilion thrust steadily higher above.

Maer Selloth is a stronghold, set atop a mountain knee above Azilien's source, a red wall girdled about the hill summit with the keep lowering atop. At its back is Everran's only border post: Bryve Tirien, giving on the gorge where the Mellennor heads. Both Quarred and Estar have an interest in that pass, and have not been above using it. It was in my mind that Beryx might mean to use it too.

I knew he would feel Saphar's ruin as a failed trust, as piercing to the king as the manner of Inyx's death had been to the comrade and friend. He never spoke of that. Only, as we rode up to Maer Selloth, I saw him lift his eyes to the citadel, intact, undefeated, with a yearning that held pain and shame and grief. Then he said quietly, "Harran, when you have time . . . Inyx. Could you make—a song?"

I was grateful that there were several songs to make in Maer Selloth. The town is small and primitive, grossly over-crowded, there was friction with the people who feared, if they did not say it, that we would bring the dragon on them. Another hearthbard served there, and no Resh lord is happy when his king descends on him, even if that king is his son-in-law. Especially a lord like Tenevel, when he is less subject than ally, and the king is in exile, or what might be seen as outright flight.

Tenevel was courteous enough. He took in Saphar's folk readily if not warmly, he met Beryx on his threshold with a grave, reserved smile: a dark man—Sellithar favors her mother—with a Tiriann's whippy build and ruler's decision in an alert hunter's eye. But ruling had taught him ruthlessness as well.

Hawge returned to complete Saphar's ruin, expelling the garrison to Asleax on the Maer Selloth road, leveling the very walls, before it went to gorge on Holym cattle and gloat over Ragnor's gold. Nobody thought that would last. I consoled myself with Sellithar's regained color, thawed numbness, and a gaiety I rarely saw in Saphar, and if I was not making songs, escaped to the streets.

I had sought more than weapons in the Confederacy. Whenever I met the rare bard with more lore than I, I would toss Stavan's question into the talk. "What do you know of aedryx?" I would ask.

Estarians had never heard of them. A Holymlase bard said they were wizards, but all long dead. A Quarred steading harper told me flatly that "aedryx is an old word for towers—towers of guard—" and cited eight: Stiriand, Histhira, Tirien, Hazghend, Tyrwash, Berfylghja, Havos, and Heagian.

An Everran fort, a range, a direction, a country, and four phantoms were only riddles, cryptic, maddening. Another Quarred bard claimed Havos had been in Bryve Elond. "Its ruins are that hump just at the saddle-top." The others he did not know. Ragnor's hearthbard said aedryx were "connected with Lossian," but having only two couplets of the song, he had discarded it. He did know they were wizards, and he added an odd phrase. "Wizards," he said, "of the mind."

I had greater hopes of Tirs, if only from Sellithar's talisman. Many new riddles were itching in my own mind. Beyond Stavan's connection of aedryx and Lossian and "green eyes" and Beryx's own reaction to Thassal's gift, there was the way he had looked in the dragon's eyes unharmed. The way they seemed to read each other's thoughts. Moreover, if I understood aright, he had not only met Hawge's eyes but told it an outright lie. And been believed. Recalling how Hawge had seen through me on the battlefield, I grew itchier still.

Tenevel's bard laughed at the talisman, "an old upland tale." He had heard of aedryx, but never bothered with the lore. "Dead wizards, surely, are hardly memorable?" He preferred sugary compliments on my battle-song and eager interest in what I was making next. I returned an Estarian no-reply, and went back to the streets.

Then, walking up a squalid hillside alley jammed with rickety shops and refugees, I heard a song.

> *When the bitter water*
> *Catches ahltar's daughter*
> *Who will save her eyes?*

The voice was thin, unaccompanied, but true. The tune was strange to me. It had a fey, elusive quality alien to the songs of men.

> *When the Flametree's tower*
> *Falls to apple-flower*
> *Who can swear it lies?*

I tracked it through the trash and piled goods and people's beds and howling urchins to an even smaller alley that was torch-lit before mid-afternoon.

When fengsoth and fenghend
Run with Ilien's finghend
Women will be wise—

In the gutter a man was sitting, face uplifted to the patchy yellow flare as he sang. The white eyes in the gaunt, nobly-boned old head told me he was blind, as so many great harpers are. He was also hairless, thin as a wraith, wrapped in the rags of what had been a hearthbard's robe. He sat in the gutter with an empty, dirty cap beside him and sang without so much as hope of an audience, because singing was all he had.

As wise as havos' brother
Who has the Air for mother—
Sees the light and dies.

Feeling as if I had seen my own death, I waited till the end. Then I sat on my heels and asked, "Father, where did you learn that?"

He turned his vacant stare. I said, "I am Everran's hearthbard. And I never heard it before."

His features showed a flash of eroded contempt, but he lacked the spirit even to scorn ignorant youth. He said in that husk of a superb voice, "I had it from my father. It is very old."

"Who made it?" I asked. "And for whom?"

He was seeking some context to make it intelligible. My heart bled for a lifetime spent besieging apathy and ignorance. But he was a harper: if we have lore, we will try to pass it on.

"It was made by Delostar," he said. "A wizard. He made it for his sister. She was kin to Lossian."

He was too old to move to the keep: the honor he deserved would only have wearied or filled him with emptiness. I took him into his great-niece's shop behind us, got him a place by the kitchen fire, a bowl of bacon and beans—they were ready enough to serve the royal bard. When he had eaten, and might believe I was in earnest, I said, "What do you know about aedryx?" Already knowing that this time there would be a reply.

When I left it was far on in the autumn evening, and it astonished me to find Maer Selloth festooned in leaping yellow fire. Then I remembered it was Iahn's day, which Tirianns celebrate at home. Doubtless a risky proceeding, among the wooden houses of Maer Selloth, but one which has bestowed its name: with its constellation of yellow cockades perched there in the black of the hidden mountains, it did indeed resemble the Shadow of the Stars.

Bracing myself, I climbed toward the keep, trying to hurry lest Beryx should want to honor the day, with my new lore leaden on my feet. But just beyond the gatehouse I was startled to meet Morran, and Morran in a hurry. Startled, because he had the knack of making speed without haste, and more startled because he snatched my arm and whisked me straight out onto the battlements.

"Have you seen the king?" He was breathing hard. "I thought not. I looked for you everywhere, I was coming to find you—" A spurting bonfire caught his face: the cheekbones were bosses, the jaw clenched in a rigor of rage. "You don't know what's happened? Hawge has moved, crossed the road south of Veth Tirien, hit the Tirilien Vale. No, listen. It's worse than that. Tenevel came to the king. You know how they—Yes. And it's been getting worse. Beryx said, 'Evacuate.' Tenevel looked at him. Then he said, 'To

143

Estar?' No, I didn't hit him. I'm a guard. The king—"

He swallowed. "Tenevel stuck his chin out and looked hard as rocks. Then he said, 'Everran has fed the dragon. I will not gorge it in Tirs.' Beryx said, 'How will you stop it?' Tenevel stuck. Then he said, 'If there is no other way, I will remove the curse.'

"No, don't. Stand still. There's more. Beryx said nothing. That made Tenevel push it. He said, 'I have never shamed my hearth. But now I must think of my Resh.' No! Be quiet. Beryx was . . . how he's been. That woke him up. 'Explain yourself,' he said. 'Tirs must have addled my wits.' That stirred Tenevel up too. 'Very well,' he said. 'Go out of my city, before you are its bane.' Beryx said, 'This is still Everran.' Tenevel said, 'Not any more. I am going to se-cede—' No, wait! Beryx said, 'You will find Hawge harder to dethrone.' Tenevel said, 'I think not. I know the lore. King-summoned, if not king-slain. Leave Tirs, and it will follow you.' "

Morran took a deep breath. I could see his jaw muscles trembling.

"He—Beryx—the king said, 'Will you cast out Everran, or only me?' Tenevel said, 'Go or stay, the people may choose. But whoever leaves, there is one you will not take. You left my daughter to go junketing abroad: it did not save Saphar and you nearly murdered her. You have made her unhappy, in that northern tomb. And in five years you have not given her a child.' "

The fires roared below us, glinting on his tears, the rage and grief of a man whose loyalty, his life's deepest piety, has been outraged. I was beyond tears. As I made for the gate he hurried behind me, talking faster still. "I said, 'Let me take the Guard and see to this.' He said, 'Shall I murder a host and vassal? Get out!' I don't know what to do. Harper—"

"Do nothing," I said. "He would not want it. To him, Tenevel has the right. He could not save his own kingdom. He cannot kill someone trying to defend theirs."

Morran said furiously, "Tenevel has *no* right—"

I said, "You are a soldier, take orders. You can do no more."

Sellithar had her maiden rooms. Beryx, refusing to evict Tenevel's family, had lodged in the turret above. Hurrying upstairs, I sought something to play. Music speaks, if not so plainly as words. Sympathy he would deny, counsel he would not tolerate, pity he would spurn like burning brands. He had maimed himself, humbled himself to the Confederacy, lost his friend and his capital. Now his kingdom was crumbling and his queen would go as well.

I dared not think of Sellithar. If ever I had hoped to win her, it was not like this. But then I remembered Tenevel, turning his king out like a mendicant weaver, casting Sellithar's barrenness in his face, talking of "my" Resh to the man who gave it him, and I did not tiptoe in as I had intended, I almost kicked down the door.

Beryx had drawn a chair to the window-slit. He was leaning forward, chin on palm, elbow on the sill. The fires lit his profile: incisive, unyielding, unreadable. But his pride would see to that. I jerked up a stool and began to play.

If music can speak scorn, that should have scalded Tenevel's ears. When I finished, the last thing I expected was for Beryx to remark in quiet amusement, "Harran, I can still fight my own wars."

Not wishing to be as pitiless as Tenevel, as Morran, I did not respond, *How?*

"I've been thinking," he mused, "about that . . . What do you know of aedryx, Harran?"

My breath stopped. I think my neck bristled. After the

afternoon it was too pat, too apposite, too like Hawge—with a sinking in my stomach, I answered, "Nothing good."

"Tell me," he said.

"They were wizards," I began. "A long time ago: even before Berrian. They ruled this country—all of it, the whole Confederacy. They had magic powers." Wizards of the mind. "Not like the children's tales, staffs and spells and potions. They could . . . see through walls. Talk to each other fifty miles apart." Read men's thoughts. "Something like . . . mesmerize anyone who looked at them." Like Hawge. "They could blind, stun, kill—with nothing but their eyes. And . . . the worst was, they were evil. Cruel. Selfish. They tore the country apart. In the end, they destroyed each other. For a whim. For," I could hear Asc's deep voice saying it, "sheer wantonness."

He was still looking beyond Maer Selloth's luminance, into the empty north. He sounded curiously distant.

"Were they born—or made?"

"Eh?" I said.

"Were they born with magic—or was it taught to them?"

"I don't know." I felt stupid. "Asvith only told me what they did."

Slowly, Beryx straightened up.

"We have tried soldiers," he said. His voice was very soft, quite impersonal. With shock I saw my restoration had been superfluous: under that shell was not surrender but a fire that burnt steadily, unquenched. "We have tried champions. Bribes. Treaties. We can't find a hero. But we might find a wizard—if we tried."

Suddenly I was filled with unreasoning, instinctive fear. "Lord," I said. "Lord . . . the old harper who told me, said, 'I am singing songs of the aedryx to remind me that there are—worse things than Hawge.' "

His voice was very low. "There is nothing else."

"Surely there must be something?" The fear was still on me, the inexplicable, irrational warning that the remedy would be worse than the bane. "Or someone? Must you . . ."

"I must," he said it softly, cold as steel. "I will."

Something else was in the room with us: an awareness, a willful, incalculable power, answerable to nothing, wayward, mocking, capable of destroying the world for a jest. I had a terrifying sense that with those few words the king I knew had already transformed himself.

"Lord," I said desperately, "they're dead!"

He looked round at me. The fires' glow masked the scar. All I saw was the puck of a mouth-corner and the glint of a half-veiled eye.

"I think," he said, almost casually, "that I have aedric blood."

"Berrian," he went on in that light, unstressed voice. "A long time ago. But I heard my nurse once, talking. She said, 'Oh, he's Berheage sure enough. He's got the aedric eyes.' My father wouldn't explain. The one time I saw him afraid. But you say aedryx magic was in their eyes. And I could look at the dragon. You shouldn't be able to. But did you ever think about Berrian's crest? An eye. Berrian. Lossian. Lossian had . . . green eyes."

I must have choked. He nodded. "You've heard that one?"

"It's impossible!" I burst out. "The aedryx are gone! You don't have the magic! All you have is the blood!"

He smiled at me: a fey, gentle, blood-chilling smile. "A weapon," he repeated, softly, "that has not been forged."

I dropped my harp. His arm, his pride, his friend, his capital, I had seen what prices he would pay to save Everran. Never, in my wildest nightmares, had I imagined such a price as this.

He was still smiling, with that perverse gaiety that chilled my spine. "So if we don't have a wizard," he murmured, "and a wizard is the weapon—one will have to be made."

My voice came out a croak. "It . . . you . . . How?"

He stood up, lightly, but with a smooth, leisured movement quite unlike his usual swift decisiveness. "I think," he said, "that since I am no longer welcome in Tirs . . . I shall go to Coed Wrock."

The Four know what drove me to it: shame, loyalty, insanity, the thing in harpers' blood that cannot be gainsaid. "Then I am coming with you," I announced.

He laughed. "Yes," he said, still chuckling, "if ever there was a time to 'appraise the men of valor,' it will be now."

VII

We rode up to Coed Wrock at the heels of a storm on a windy autumn afternoon. The black and ochre valley was sodden, the sky full of turbulent gray thunder-wrack, with a yellow window flaring in the west. The house had a smoking chimney, gables, half a roof. Workmen had emerged from the scaffolding to look up with Stavan at the rest of the naked king-beam, and Thassal had been to the well. When she saw us she paused, bucket in hand: but not from surprise.

"So?" said Beryx across the makeshift kitchen table.

Thassal rested her hands on the planks either side the pot of fresh mint-tea. Again I felt a struggle, the breaking of ancient secrets, deeply sealed.

She took a long breath. Then she lifted her head and plunged.

"This family," she said, "has aedric blood."

"So," retorted Beryx promptly, "has mine."

Thassal's mouth curved in a tiny smile. "You know that, ah? Then you know why we keep it quiet." He waited. "There were—aedryx—in Everran in Berheage times. The last of them. Did you never hear of the Sorcerers?" His eyes narrowed. "Ah. Your forefather . . . hunted them down. Had them killed. Burnt. Drowned. Harpers made a demon of . . . Lossian. Ah. He was bad, but he was flesh and blood. There were other lines . . ."

"Stiriand," I murmured, "Histhira, Tirien." And she looked round sharply: then nodded, accepting that the rest

149

must be revealed. "Ah. My family springs from—a branch of the Stiriands."

That, I thought, explained their aloofness, their unconscious air of being more than farmers. The blood, and the need to hide. I too had heard of the Sorcerer hunts, the whole country crazy with fear, sisters accusing brothers, sons their fathers, innocents massacred by a lunatic mob driven by a fanatic king. I understood his fanaticism now.

"My husband never knew," Thassal was saying. "Stirianns have long memories. Even now, stories would start. Broomsticks at midnight. Wildfire round the house." A tiny smile. "Resurrecting the king." He laughed. "So this must still be—be—"

"Under the seal?"

"Ah." She paused. I could feel his impatience. At last he prompted, "You know the magic?" Thassal flatly shook her head. "You know someone who does?" Another shake. "Could you teach it, then?"

She looked thoroughly disconcerted for the first time since I had known her. Her gray eyes widened. "You?"

"I do have the blood."

Her eyes held disbelief, wonder, consternation. She shook her head violently. "No. Not you. It would be—would be—"

"It might be," his tone was quiet iron, "the only thing I can do."

"No," she said again. "No." And the iron became steel.

"Hawge has wasted Everran. Destroyed Saphar. There's no help in the Confederacy." Still she shook her head. "Tirs is going to secede."

That broke her. "Si'sta," she said in a rush. "I don't know the magic. Or anyone who does. But—" again the breaking of generations-old seals. "When they were failing, the aedryx, they made a—a fellowship. Families with aedric blood. Not the magic, just the blood. They helped each other. Hid each other. The children remembered. We . . . still do." She looked at him again. "There may be someone to—who knows the magic." A forlorn hope, staving off the worst. "I do know the password. And another family . . ."

Beryx stood up and smiled at her. "Accepted, general. Just give me the word and tell me the direction. Whatever I do with it, your hands are clean."

The password was quite simple: Tingrith. Eight. I wondered what the link was with Quarred and what other cupboards might hold aedric skeletons, as it led us from family to family, through disbelief, wild denial, timid concession. Then consternation at his purpose, then the reluctant yielding of another name, another family. But always the road was the same.

When we came down from the uplands east of Saeverran and Gebria's arid dusty red stretched before us, Beryx slitted his eyes as if to see over the horizon and said slowly, "I wonder where this will end."

It ended in one of the tiny Gebros garrisons, a collection of shanties and disused barracks about a brackish well that tunneled eighty feet to the waterline. The Gebros dwarfed it all, thirty feet of cut stone facing a rubble core, dusty, abraded by countless sandstorms, and cut sword-straight across the wilderness as far as we could see, an outmoded defense that remained an awesome monument. Beryx pondered it with admiration. "A determined old tyrant," he said. "One day I'll dam the Kemreswash, and build him a garden to match his wall."

Round the cracked table, beating off flies, feeling sand grate under our boots, our elbows, in our very tea, we renewed the search. The house Ruand was a desiccated black-burnt bull-necked Gebrian, who sent his family to bed at the start, and at the end scratched his ear.

"Lord," he said, "the only family I know is the one who sent you here."

Beryx said nothing. Watching the line of his jaw, I thought, If you did not build the Gebros, you kept the builder's will.

The Gebrian must have agreed, for he scratched his ear again. Then he said slowly, "All I can give you is a tale, and even harpers don't heed it, even out here. But they say there's a . . . big red rock. In the desert. With a spring. And green grass all year round. It's femaere work. That's what they call devils out here. If you try to drink at the spring, the femaere sends you mad, you run out in the desert and die." He shrugged. "Hardly worth the breath, but—it's the best I can do."

Inwardly I sighed. What Beryx would say I already knew.

"Is there anything about the direction? How far back it might be?"

The Gebrian looked under his brows. "Lord," he said, dropping word on word, "it's not back west. It's out in Hethria."

The sand grated on the earth floor, whispered in the cracked wall slabs, gritted in my hair, while I tried not to cringe as before me rose those endless, pathless, nameless red miles whose heat and thirst can kill you without waiting help from its savages. The Gebrian watched Beryx, and Beryx studied him. I knew he was not weighing the tale's truth or worth, or his own course, or the risks of it: he was gauging how far the Gebrian would go.

That Gebrian must have had aedric blood, or at least soothsayer's, for he read Beryx truly as I. He sighed, let a hand fall on the table, and said, "I'll try to guide you, lord.

If I don't, you'll go on anyway."

In truth, it is easier than you might think to travel in Hethria. Direction is easy, you go from where you are to where the next water is. We had one thing in our favor, that it was autumn, and the storms might have raised some herbage and left some transient pools. We took a pack-horse with a little food and two enormous cow-hide waterskins, bows, our swords, and Gebrian desert robes, voluminous blue things falling from neck to toe, which the true desert-marcher tops with a black turban of fine wool cloth swathed over nose and mouth and neck and head: the sun's worst peril is the way it sucks moisture from any naked skin. In fact, it is easier to cross than to enter Hethria, for the Gebros nowadays is gateless, and we first had to ask the garrison commander for men to open the walled-up arch.

Phengis had no fixed plan. "Just follow the waters, and hope to meet some Hethox. They should be hunting this country now. And if the spring's real, they're the only ones who'll know."

I knew Beryx had grinned at him from the dance of his eyes, so vivid above the dull black wool. "Lead on," he said. "It should be an interesting ride."

Interesting it was: at our crossing point the Gebros marches with a twenty-mile width of sand-hills, and autumn had brought them alive with quick-shooting grass, runners of sappy green weed, grasshoppers and locusts and birds and exotic, unknown flowers. Nor is all Hethria sand. There were ranges beyond the first of it, long and low, rarely making peaks, slanted chines of rock that run in slabs like a stone dragon's mail, muted indigo, rusty red, reddish purple, purplish blue, crouched above the land like the last eroded capes of a vanished sea. Which they were: we found shells at some of our camps, and once Phengis nodded up at a gorge side and said, "A Hethox told me his 'father-long-time-gone' used to sit fishing up there." The ranges fascinated me far more than the spectacular mirages, for they have a savor of antiquity, of half-forgotten lore, and a self-awareness as well.

Through the ranges run dry river-beds that must have carried mighty streams, for their gorges make a jest of Bryve Kemreswash. They are like Air's own axe-clefts, rents in the stuff of earth, like dropped lava settled into crazy shapes, and their colors eclipse any maerian: lambent copper, molten gold, flaming orange, red as the inside of a fire, all set off by the staring white desert helliens. Femaerel, Gebrians call them: ghost-trees. The key is eminently true.

In these gorges were rock pools from the rain, or so large they rarely go dry, or fed by some secret, inexhaustible spring, and to them comes all the life of Hethria. I spent many enchanted evenings watching the tiny thorn-head lizards, the spotted log-lizards, the big dragonish yellow wyresparyx, the hopping lydyrs of a dozen kinds, and the birds coming to drink. I never saw such birds: gray birds with pink bellies like flying apple-flower, white birds with sulphur yellow crests above their snowy heads, small birds like rainbow bits, black birds with breath-taking crimson under their satin breasts. Phengis laughed at my wonder. "Oh," he said, "there's plenty of life in Hethria."

Its human life took us by surprise. Riding along a gorge we rounded a bend upon a waterhole in a little bay of grass, and from the grass rose copper-black naked men with stick-like legs, pot-bellies, strings about their loins and foreheads, and hair that rose like a bramble-bush. They confronted us, silent, with empty hands.

Phengis reined up hard. "Don't move," he whispered tautly. "They're not happy. They've got the spears between their toes in the grass."

Dropping the reins, he lifted both hands, then called something in a harsh gibberish. When there was no reply, he muttered over his shoulder, "Hold out your hands."

Dutifully, we held them out. There was an endless pause. Then, one by one, the Hethox lifted a foot and the spear came with it, ten feet long, wicked shovel-nose blade gleaming in the sun. They took off the spear-throwers and leant on the hafts with a foot tucked on the other knee, while a gray-haired patriarch as naked as the rest but considerably fatter waddled up to Phengis's horse.

When they had talked awhile in the guttural tongue, Phengis swung down, grinning now. "He remembers me," he said. "Three pieces of iron and some salt, and we can join their camp."

The iron was arrowheads, since we were not sacrificing our swords. The salt was much appreciated. Dinner in return was not what I appreciated. Faced with a wooden dish of cold, cooked, white three-inch grubs, charred locusts, some pounded grass seed, and a lizard's leg, I nearly had no dinner at all. However, the Hethox had quite as much trouble being polite about our dried cheese and flour cakes.

They were very hospitable: they told us interminable tales and then thumped our backs and roared with laughter, showing perfect white teeth, they offered us a bag of grass-seed flour, and tried to teach me music blown on a six-foot hollow log. They were delighted by my harp, and made me play it over and over, in the midst of which I looked round to see two or three young gallants doing a perfect mime.

I imitated a Hethox trying to eat dried cheese. They rolled on the ground. One of them mimicked me stalking a lizard, crawling on hands and knees, treading on my gown, trying to rewind my turban, throwing my hands up and saying, "Four take you, you little pest!" They had the intonation pat. Beryx glanced at Phengis, who merely nodded. "They always watch you," he said, "a good while first."

Finally, when we were all replete with food and fellowship, Phengis turned to the Ruand and said something that ended in, "femaere—chxgos?"

Every smile went out, phut! The Ruand's reply was short and definite, with a chop of the hand. Waving at Beryx, Phengis embarked on a long and complicated speech which broke down as he tried to describe Hawge. At last he said to the blank stares, "Wyresparyx, ah?" Nods. "Wyresparyx . . . wyre." He turned to Beryx. "How long is Hawge?" He paced it out across the camp. Eyes popped. He pointed to the fire, opened his mouth and roared, *Hawge!*

The children stampeded. The Ruand looked perturbed. Phengis pointed west and harangued him again. The Ruand retorted with vehemence, "Femaere," and chops of the hand. Phengis sat down and said slowly, "They know about it. It's a very bad spirit place. They like us. They don't want us to go."

I saw Beryx's hand clench. "Can you persuade them?"

Phengis looked awkward. "They want . . . rather a high price. Magic. To protect them if we wake the femaere. They want," he nodded to my harp, "that."

Beryx sighed. At last he said, "We might find others."

I sat staring into the sand. He had given me a great deal. He had given me everything. But everything has its price.

I turned my harp over. My father had given it to me when I left Vethmel: his own harp, his heart's core, laid casually in my hands. Its syrel-wood sounding board was rubbed bare of varnish but still sweet and true, keys and strings renewed more often than I have years. They could not play it. They would ruin it. Its voice would die forever. It would never be heard again.

I heard myself say, sounding miles away, "I can always get another harp. We may never get another chance."

The Ruand drew us a map, building tiny sandhills, making U-shaped hollows which mean "sit-downs": a day's march. There were five. At the end, he gestured south-east and made an emphatic sign that needed no interpretation. He clapped both hands over his eyes.

As our morning mint-tea boiled Beryx said, "Phengis, this should be simple enough. A big red rock, three waters on, bearing south-east?" The Gebrian nodded. "Then I want you to go back. No, listen. This will be a dangerous meeting, if there is a meeting at all. I don't want to leave Everran wondering if it has a king. I don't want to risk more lives than I must. You have a family. Harran and I don't."

"And," said Phengis flatly, "I don't like leaving things half done."

In the end they compromised. At sight of the rock, Phengis would return to this camp until news came, or until new moon. They fixed a code of smoke-signals, and we saddled up.

A Hethox march is little shorter than a rider's day, but before we found the second water the rock was in sight.

It was actually a cluster of rocks. First they looked like giant red mushrooms, then misshapen domes, then they climbed above the desert like some Hethrian fantasy of Earth itself. There is no range. They rise sheer from level sands, big as hills but solid stone, a cluster of piled, smoothed, rounded monoliths that change color with distance and the day's passing marks. Sunlit bubbles of delicate lavender, misty blue tinged with pink, deepening to red, steeped in gold at dawn, paling at noon to a cross between blood and rust, darkening to vermilion, lambent blood-red at sunset, dying in wonderful old golds and rose-black shadows as they take the dark. For three days we watched them play this silent diapason of light. Once Beryx said quietly, "If we never come back, it was worth it. Just for this."

Without Phengis, the silence of Hethria seemed to rise up over us, a vast unbroken listening where bird and beast and our intrusive passage were no more than the scurry of ants. We talked little. Nor did we scout. As Beryx said, "If there is an aedr here, he's seen us coming. If he doesn't want us, he'll make us stop."

It was an unpleasant thought. I rode in to the rock towers' feet with a tingle down my back.

On the north-west side a series of huge red headlands embayed desert herbage and spindly trees, and nothing else. Beryx said, "Sun-wise is lucky." We rode right-handed round the towers' base.

Noon came and went and still we crawled under those majestic fronts, marveling at their height, the colors' subtlety, the sculpturing of Earth. The water-skins were low; the horses were looking for their daily drink. A small frown had gathered between Beryx's brows. Then we doubled another great bulging red flank, and reined sharply up.

Before us a new bay sloped gently down from the towers' lap, half a mile wide, a quarter long, but this was not a patchwork of sand and herbage. This was unbroken green, the green of desert grass in full season, thick and tall and showing a silken sheen as the wind moved upon acres of seeds, rippling, swaying like a harvest in that arid place. Close beside us a bare sheet of rock was filmed with seepage, the watery blue of reflected sky with a great red spire trembling and shivering across its width.

We stared in wonder. Then Beryx released a long, slow breath.

I glanced round. He had been quartering the valley like a soldier, but now he shook his head. Then he gave me a small dry grin and remarked, "Let's hope trespassers can argue first."

We rode into the valley, our horses snatching greedily at the fresh new feed. Nothing woke, nothing moved but wind and light. But then came a dull thunder, and up over a hidden rise poured a cloud of shining shimmering dappled gray and floating white.

As our horses whinnied, Beryx let out a grunt. "Not phantoms, at least."

In a moment they were all around, nickering, sniffing and play-nipping at our beasts: all grays, tall, beautifully made, sleek and superb as moonlight, a score of mares, foals, and yearlings, with a big stallion circling warily at the rear. Wondering if aedryx could change shape like were-wolves, I looked warily back. Beryx grinned and clicked to his horse.

The grays circled us, then angled off to vanish in another fold of grass. The valley remained empty. A hundred yards from the cliff we looked at each other, not daring to speak. Then we heard the noise.

Somewhere ahead of us someone was whistling lustily and hammering rock on rock.

It was a strange tune, a jaunty teasing wagtail of a thing that would have suited a harp. I was already storing it in my head. *Chirrup, chirr, chirr!* went the whistler. *What! What!* went the stones. *What! What!*

Beryx jerked his chin and said, "There."

Just ahead and above us a narrow gut ran into the cliffs at such an angle that we had not previously noticed it. At its mouth a figure in a gray robe and black desert turban sat on its heels in a bare place, striking a long narrow flint over a block. The chips flew with echoing cracks. The striker whistled on, oblivious, *chirrup, chirr, what, what!*

Beryx's eyes became green chips of mirth. He rode up in shouting distance and called, "Hello! I am looking for the master of the house!"

The figure broke off its hammering and looked sidelong down at us. As from Hawge's stare, I had an instinctive urge to duck.

But down the line of arm looked a pair of almost rectangular gray eyes as clear as rainwater and no more threatening, with dark rims of lash and fine deep crowsfeet sunk in dark-bronzed skin. A clear, resonant, unmistakably feminine voice said with equally unmistakable acerbity, "Well, Everran. Hast ta'en tha time over that."

Beryx recovered first. Perhaps he had expected such things, perhaps not. His eyes danced. He swung down from his horse and answered politely, "Well, ma'am, your directions were hardly . . . direct."

She struck the stone again. It was rusty-yellow, steel blue where freshly chipped, not a local piece. It was bedded on a patch of old hide while she struck it with some kind of chisel, perhaps bone, and a rock hammer. Her precise, expert blows at opposite angles were making a thing like a saw, with several teeth.

Beryx watched a moment. Then he said with the tiniest hint of reproof, "If you knew I was coming, ma'am, you also know why I came."

"The dragon," she said. *What! What!* She cocked her head and turned the blade this way and that. Then she glanced up, and the gray eyes held a chilling hilarity. "And tha wonders if I'm aedric, and if I'll rid thee of it. Yes, I am. And no, I won't."

Beryx's levity vanished. He said levelly, "I don't know why."

"Had sooner . . . make a scythe . . . in Eskan Helken," she was talking as she unraveled a thin leather lace between her teeth, "than meddle in such affairs."

His brows straightened. "But . . . you could kill it?"

"Ah. I could."

He paused. Then he said, "Not for anything Everran can give?"

She replied with the Gebrian negative: an upward jerk of the chin, a tongue's short, decided click.

When he said nothing, she reached behind her for a curved wooden handle, smooth and sheeny with use, split at the head. Working the flint in, she began to lace it on, hands flying unerringly to and fro.

Beryx said, "Will you teach me how to kill it, then?"

"Tha?" It was scorn unparalleled.

"If you won't kill it," he answered steadily, "I must have someone who will."

Her hands stopped. She looked round at him, the gray eyes chill, but no longer with mirth. "Tha couldst not learn."

"I am," he said without boast, "descended from Berrian."

"Ah." She resumed work. "With who knows what sort of mongrel blood crossed in? Berheage!" A snort. "Dost not know tha line's true name."

Beryx's eyes began to glow. Very evenly he said, "Do you?"

She chuckled. "What would it mean if I told thee? Dost not even know what tha used for the dragon's toy. Ah, I warrant that one walks o' late at nights!"

Beryx stiffened. "That stone," he said, "came with Berrian."

161

She was whipping the lace-end, quick and expert as the rest. "Berrian! A slip that fell off the tree upon treasure waylost. And built it a cage where his betters hoved before him. Dost not know what tha little dung-heap stands upon? That was Ker Thillian'eage. Home of forekin to Maerdrigg himself."

"And to you?"

She snorted acridly. "I am Fengthira of Havos. Dost not know that either. Not like tha man." I tried to crawl under the saddle. "Art ignorant as all tha . . . line."

"If I am ignorant," Beryx said quietly, "I am willing to learn."

She slid the tools into the hide and stood up. "Hast had a long ride, Everran." That freezing merriment was back in her eyes. "Wilt have a longer one home."

Beryx was becoming roused: let be the churlishness of her talk, he had been born a king. I doubt he was "thee'd" in the nursery.

"Ma'am," he said silkily, "if you came to Everran, which I know is unlikely, and if I had a palace, which I have not, you would not find such a welcome at its door."

Her eyes lit with a genuine laugh. "Hast a sting to tha tongue, at least." She slid the bundle to the ground, and folded her hands on the scythe haft. Fine-boned hands, but roughened from hard labor, with raised veins that belied her ageless voice. "Well? Use it then."

"We have tried every weapon against Hawge," he said, "except wizardry. You are the only wizard we can find. You said you can kill it, but you won't. You say I can't learn. But the dragon told us, the weapon that would slay it has not been forged."

"So tha'lt be the weapon? And make me the smith?"

"Yes."

"Dost not know what tha askst." Now the ice was in her voice.

"But I do ask."

"Forged! Art more likely to break. Break like a rotten flint!"

"Surely, ma'am," it was open irony, "not with a skilful smith?"

"Wilt dare me, ah? A wise smith don't try to temper flints."

"Then," he said, "I had rather be a broken flint than one that was never tried at all."

Her eye held danger, open threat. "So tha'lt be broken, ah?"

Deliberately, he answered, "Yes."

She paused. He held her eyes. Suddenly they twinkled with another of those disconcerting shifts to mirth. "I've broken a good many colts in my life. I've never broken a king."

He looked half-affronted, half-amused. She cocked her head, studying him. Then she said abruptly, "Take off tha clothes."

That did shake him. He balked and stared.

"Take off tha clothes. Dost buy a horse in a blanket, or first take a look?"

For a moment I thought he would refuse. Then he began to pull his turban off.

She watched unblinking every detail of his one-handed struggle with the robe, the buttons of his shirt. I doubt she could have found a quicker, simpler way of humiliating him. As the shirt came off she said, "Whoa," and began to walk round him, running her eyes up and down as if he were indeed a colt.

"Hot-headed." She poked the huge livid scars on his side. "Headstrong. Tck. Tha own fault." I saw his jaw stiffen, his chin come up. If he refused counsel, he relished criticism less. But he held his tongue. She felt the arm, and nodded. "Smashed the great nerve." She pushed it aside to touch the sting-pit. "Troubles thee still?"

He said flatly, "No." And she flicked her eyes up. "Th'art ignorant. Try not to be a fool."

He flushed and clenched his teeth.

"Dost think," she said, "aedryx need strength in naught below the neck? Th'are better stayers than a Quarred mare."

She came round and studied the scarred side of his face. He looked straight ahead like a soldier on parade.

"Thorgan Fenglos," she said musingly. "Does Everran suffer blemish in its kings?"

His muscles tightened as if at a punch. "I am king," he answered, almost under his breath, "by inheritance."

"Ah. And what does queen think of it?"

Had I been Beryx, it would have ended there. He turned white, making the scar stand out worse than ever, but he did not speak.

She went on with that deliberate, probing cruelty, "Not like it much?"

Looking somewhere over her head he answered, just audibly, "No."

Her lashes flicked up. "And barren as well?"

He shut his eyes. This time it was a mere whisper. "Yes."

"Ah." Then, idly, "Poor child." She walked away, not troubling to look back. "Put on tha clothes."

Silently, he obeyed.

When he looked up, she said dispassionately, "Head-strong. Crippled. Green. Crossbred as well. I doubt I'd take the horse. Why should I trouble with the man?"

That was too much. "Because," he said through his teeth, "I may be maimed, I may be mongrel, but I am Everran's only hope. I don't want to learn for pride, or for power; I am not willful, and I have no time for wantonness. But I have a kingdom, ma'am, and whatever must be done to save it, by the Sky-lords' faces, I will do!"

He glared full in her face, his eyes blazing green. She shook her head. Then, to my utter amazement, her own lashes sparkled with tears.

"Ah," she said. "Th'art Heagian, sure enough. Straight back to that glorious old clown. Never mind wryve-lan'x, take wryve-lethar. And care naught that t'will bring the roof on tha own head."

She swiped a hand over her eyes and half swung away. Beryx stood, utterly bewildered, until she blinked away the tears.

"Tha man shall take the beasts back," she said crisply. "And we'll do without that." I gasped as his sword slid from the scabbard, turned a somersault, and landed on a rock ledge twenty feet above. "Tha might take to me when tha temper's up. And get it up tha will."

She turned toward the rock mouth, and paused. Beryx had not moved.

"Well? What art waiting for?"

"This is not a 'man.' " Beryx's look was icy as her own. "This is my comrade and hearthbard, who brought me away from Coed Wrock. But for him I should not be here."

Fengthira gave me one razor look. "More fool he," she said, and I knew it was no cliché. My secret had been read.

Beryx still waited. She scowled. "Wilt try my patience already? What else?"

"We are two days," he said, "from water. Our horses have had none today."

That made her soften. "Bring them up. Take off bridles. They'll follow. And leave tha ironmongery here." Her eyes flicked to self-mockery this time. "I can't abide cold iron. I'm a 'sorcerer.' "

We unsaddled; she said, "Come then. No, not tha. The beasts."

And to my wonder they filed after her like dogs. As the last rump vanished, Beryx, recovering some of his poise, murmured ruefully, "I'll pay high for that."

The cleft climbed steeply, narrow, gloomy, twisting, slippery with wet. Fengthira directed the horses. "Ware that slab. And t'drop." We groped after as best we could, until the light returned in a fierce blue glare.

We were on a V-shaped pocket of soil rising to the next monolith, hidden from all but the sky, its checquer of greenery framed in fiery red and distant blue. A glance showed me vegetables, a grain patch, a pair of elegant finlythes, a long slope of natural grass to more trees above. The horses were drinking at the cleft-top: a spring, no doubt, deepened and rimmed with rock slabs to make a pool before it seeped downhill, framed by fishbone ferns and overhung by giant tree-ferns, an enchanted and enchanting well.

When the horses finished, Fengthira said, "Down. Come back with the rest." As they retreated obediently, she turned with a flick of her eye.

"Too full of How and Why to settle First. I'll tell then, and spare all our tongues. This is Eskan Helken." Red Castle, I translated, wondering who had named it. "The spring rises there," she nodded uphill, "and t'was here before me. I only make it last. With Ruanbr'arx, yes: the Arts. Wryvurx, the weatherwords. But I steer, not brew, the storms. And that was wryve-lan'x with the horses, mastery of beasts. Not 'prentice work. The grays are mine: they go with my name." Fengthira: moonlight. "I like horses better than men, so I use Ruanbr'arx to keep men away. And this is my garden, since I'm not Hethox and don't like aedric hunts. Take nine lydyr with wryve-lan'x, but you'll sicken when the tenth hops up. Not that plants," she added thoughtfully, "don't squeak when you pull them out."

We crossed the garden, seamed with tiny irrigation channels. "This lives by honest sweat. No Ruanbr'arx'll master weeds." Beyond a handkerchief lawn under the finlythes we climbed to the valley head. "And this is my house."

It was backed against the rock beside an even tinier spring thickly bedded in mint. A dirt-floored veranda was roofed by norgal bark that rested on a beam between two trees, overgrown with some climbing vine's black and scarlet flowers. A single stone step, a natural boulder, led inside. The walls were latticed branch and vine, then native rock, which held a fireplace and an irregular door. The furniture, table, chairs, a hanging cupboard, was unsquared wood, tools were propped in a corner, utensils by the hearth. A lydel hung by its curled tail from a roof-beam, chattering with pointed furry face and huge irate black eyes.

"Ah," said Fengthira, propping up her scythe. "Strangers. Must put up with them." She surveyed us. "And now th'art here, I suppose tha must be fed."

Beryx's lip twitched. He said meekly, "Ma'am, I do know how to cook."

"Ah. Like tha harper shaves. Garden. Lettuces and some corn." She tossed off her turban to reveal an arrogantly boned face under a crop of iron-gray hair, I walked outside and stood spellbound as all Hethria spread below me, an eagle's vision on the wing.

"Lettuces," commanded Fengthira. "Wilt have long enough to gawp at that."

We gawped at it after we ate, silently watching Hethria's solemn evening hymnal to the light. When the last red glow had left the horizon, Fengthira stirred and announced, "Harper shall do the garden. I'll cook."

Beryx asked demurely, "Am I the horse-boy?"

And she gave him a darkling glance. "Th'art the 'prentice," she said grimly. "Tha'lt have work enough."

We laid our bedding in the outer room, though I doubt either of us truly slept. Fengthira rose with the dawn. After breakfast, grain porridge and honey from the safe, she said, "Now." Going to her tool-heap she unearthed a long plaited hide rope.

"Four!" said Beryx in laughing alarm. "Are you going to throw and tie me like a Holmyx steer?" And she gave him a straight look. "Ah. Stand up. Put tha hands behind tha back."

He was not laughing now. "Wilt be taught?" she demanded. "Or not?"

Tight-lipped, he did as he was told. She tied his wrists with a horse-breaker's hitch, ordered, "Outside," ran the rope over a tree-fork, said, "put tha feet together," and tied his ankles too. Then she told me curtly, "Down the garden." As I went, I heard her go on in that curt, intent voice, "The first lesson for aedryx is to know thaself."

While I pottered among the irrigation channels the sun climbed, the meager dew dried away. I went to the spring and drank. A black and white saeveryr twirled on a fern limb, mocking me. Eskan Helken was quiet as a tomb. I climbed to the finlythes and sat in the shade, back against a trunk: but all Hethria's prospect could not fill my thoughts.

Fengthira was in the shade before I saw her, a dappled

gray ghost with a pot of mint-tea and a pair of mugs. Her turban was off. There was sweat on her temples and her finely fleshed face was sharp with strain, or weariness. Over her arm hung four pieces of severed hide rope.

"Sit!" she said sternly. "Pour that out."

As I poured the tea, she began, with her customary deftness, to splice the rope. "No," she said without looking up. "Don't take him any. Don't go near him. If he sees thee now he'll never speak to thee again."

I sat winded by that clairvoyance, wondering wildly what she had done to him.

"Teach me to kill a dragon," she growled under her breath. "And ruined my good rope. Had to cut it off him in the end." My mouth flew open and she gave me a rapier glance. "For his good, not mine. The stronger they are, the harder they fight. And I've not used Phare these twenty years. He might have broken my hold."

"What—what is Phare?" I got out at last. I was very afraid of her, not least for myself.

"Sight." A dour smile. "Into minds." Once again she anticipated me. "Reading thought, that's Scarthe, but thought's not all of a mind. That's where tha thinks tha thinkst. Really just where tha thinks in words. Under that tha thinkst without them. That's where tha thinks more than tha thinkst."

"I—see." I was remembering how, before words can be spoken, they must first be formed in thought.

She nodded, reaching for another end. "Ah. Tha doesna like tha thought-words read. Tha likes it less when someone shares them first."

"Er—" I said timidly.

"With Scarthe," she said dryly, "needst not know. With Phare, tha dost."

I thought suddenly of how we think, assured of utter privacy, and frantically tried not to think at all. She smiled sardonically and I knew she had read that too.

"Phare goes further. Hast a memory, ah? Some canst open when tha likes, some not. But t'is all there. All that ever happened to thee. Phare shows it all."

"Four," I whispered, feeling sick. "It would be like reliving—"

"Tha whole life," she nodded. "With someone inside, sharing it."

I shuddered, thinking I understood why she had had to cut the rope at the last. She smiled again, more grimly still. "Ah. But tha thinks with tha body too. Muscles. Lungs. Heart. Tha never 'thinks' of it while tha lives. Wait till someone takes control of them."

She glanced sidelong. "A ride on a bolter, ah. And no jumping off. Hast senses too. Phare steals them. Sight, touch, taste, smell. All lost. And speech. No, listen to the rest. Art only hearing it. Under that comes the part that tha thinks never thinks at all. The fire under the kettles. The things tha durst not, cannot think. The things tha wilt not let thaself think." I stared at her, open-mouthed. "Phare makes tha think them. Through someone else. Some fight when they lose their muscles. They all fight when it comes to that. But by then t'is too late. Art under control. Canst only feel. Not act."

Her nostrils flared. "Now tha knowst why I tied him. I don't like Phare. But without Phare, canst not learn. Dost not know thaself." She finished the last splice and reached for her tea. "He knows now. Leave him be till he gets over it."

We worked in the garden till noon, then climbed back to the finlythes and went to sleep. At last, when the sun was almost down, she took me up to the house, made more mint-tea, and gave me one of the mugs, thickly laced with honey, steaming and sweet. "Take that out to him," she ordered. "Up t'hill. And bring him back." As I looked at her in consternation she added, "Better if t'is thee, the first."

Beryx was lying flat and straight on his face in the grass at the coign of the northern cliff, both arms over his head as if for a shield. He could not have moved all day. Grass seeds had fallen on his clothes, great patches of sweat had dried white on the back of his shirt. When my approach became audible, I saw his back muscles crawl and tighten as he clenched his whole body in defense.

I sat by his shoulder and put the mug between us: at such times, music had always been my speech. The light commenced its evening descant, the silence of Hethria enveloped us, while I sought in vain for an opening chord.

But then, stiffly, painfully, he untangled his arms. Keeping his face averted, he rolled over, sat up, and took the tea, cupping it against his right hand as if to warm them both. His movements were slow, forced, cramped, as if he had been beaten all over and the bruises were stiffened: but these bruises were not on the bone.

With a little sigh, he set down the cup. "Thank you, Harran," he said, sounding spent and shaky, and forced himself to glance up. Instantly his eyes jerked away as if the contact had hurt, and I pulled mine away in shock, for his had the stricken, shattered look of one who has taken a mortal wound: and known it.

Desperately, wanting to help, remembering my orders, I said, "Lord . . . you will be too cold up here."

He went stiff all over. Then he managed to get up. His hands were trembling. Under his breath he said, "Yes."

We walked across the hill, me aching for a helpful word, he with the kind of desperate courage that goes forward because otherwise it will run away. But at the firelit door that too failed him. He ducked his head as he entered, as I had done to avoid meeting Hawge's eyes.

Busy over the fire, Fengthira merely said, this time in a neutral tone, "Sit." And not till we had eaten did she so much as look at him.

By then he had swung round, left arm on the table, in profile to her. She did not speak, but whatever she did, the mere touch of her eyes made him flinch as if hit on a burn.

"Ah," she said under her breath. With that same desperate courage he turned and looked her full in the face.

"Whoa," she said, after a moment, and a small, not unkind smile moved the muscle of her cheek. "Needst not slaughter Hawge tonight."

His eyes dropped. He let out a long, shaky breath.

She said, "Pass me the cup." As he reached out, she nodded. "If tha canst hear, then canst learn to speak."

Beryx looked up in perplexity. Fengthira said, <Not with the tongue.> And I too stared astounded, for her lips had not moved.

Her eyes turned to me. <So canst hear?> It came with probing interest. <Wilt be an aedr too?>

Before I could start a panicky disclaimer, her eyes had moved away again. She watched Beryx for a long, silent moment, and in that moment her pupils contracted as if the light had changed and her clear gray irises assumed the shimmer of molten lead.

Then she said, <Tell me tha name.>

He swung on her with something like irritation to shield him, opened his mouth, and choked.

Fengthira watched impassively. He tried again. Coughed. Retched, gasped, fighting for speech as drowning men fight for air.

172

<No,> she said. <Must use lathare. Speak with the mind.>

Perhaps it was reaction. More likely it was inevitable. He was a king, and proud, he had suffered as much as both would bear, and now he could not so much as proclaim a mutiny. His face contorted as he fought to yell at her, he struggled as if manacled, clawed the air. Then came up with a bound that overthrew the chair, and charged.

Looking full in his face, Fengthira made a single smooth hand sweep and ordered, <Stop.>

He brought up as if he had hit a wall. She held him with those eyes whose hot shimmer had brightened to a midday summer horizon, while he fought to come at her, completely beside himself. Then she said, <Stand still.>

He stood. If you can call it standing, when he was fighting to move with every atom of his physical strength. His eyes were quite black. Sweat poured off him. I think he actually foamed at the mouth.

Fengthira gave him a moment to see it was futile, and said aloud, "Rope."

When I did not move, she repeated, "Rope. Hast lost tha feet?"

She did not raise her voice but I scuttled like a mouse. As I came back, she ordered, <Put tha hands behind tha back.>

Beryx's eyes turned greener and blazed with active resistance. Fengthira's widened a little, shimmering brighter still. I heard her breathe. Slowly, irresistibly, his hands were drawn behind his back.

"Tie . . . them. Tie . . . t'other . . . end . . . to kingpost."

The words were spaced, as in phases of a mighty effort. My hands shook as I obeyed.

She waited a moment longer. Then she let go her breath and relaxed in the chair.

Beryx flew at her like a chained mastiff and brought up

with a jerk that should have torn his shoulders off. He was beyond reason, beyond capitulation, let be any attempt at obedience. He did his best to break the rope or break his arms or uproot the kingpost, while Fengthira leant back, regained her breath, and wiped her brow.

"As well he brought thee," she said without looking round. "If I'd that to hold without a rope, he'd not have needed swords."

She watched a little longer, a breaker waiting for the colt to tire himself out. When Beryx was standing, winded and tottery, she said, <Art fighting me. Shouldst be fighting thaself.>

He gave her a look of pure demonic hate. She sighed. "Make up the fire, harper. And take tha bed outside. T'will be a long old night."

When I woke in the morning watches it was quiet inside. I peeped round the jamb. The ember glow showed me Fengthira hunched chin on fist like a roosting owl, the gleam of a half-lidded eye. And Beryx, sitting on his heels against the kingpost, glaring implacably back. Before I could withdraw, Fengthira said without look or movement, "Make up the fire before tha goes."

When I woke again pale golden light was creeping down the tower sides, turning them to sheets of maerian fire. Neither of them had moved. Fengthira said, "Tha'lt be cook today as well as garden-boy." She went on, to my unborn question, "Make me some tea, and take something thaself. But not to him."

Beryx was red-eyed and mad-looking as a half-manned hawk. He had begun to pace to and fro. As he turned I saw the blood on the rope, the raw welts on his wrists.

"Ah," said Fengthira with irony, watching me. "If tha'dst write *Aedr*, must spill more than ink." She turned her attention back to Beryx and kept it there while she drank her tea. Even as she said, "Now see tha to my plants."

Nothing had altered at noon. At sunset Fengthira was red-eyed too, and her face had aged ten years. Beryx was past movement. He was hunched against the kingpost, head on his chest, eyes shut, every muscle of his body shouting unbroken, unyielding rebelliousness. I thought a little desperately that he would kill himself before he consented to try what she demanded, let be master it.

"Ah," Fengthira agreed wryly. "If he fought himself like he's fighting me, t'would have been over last night." She rubbed the small of her back and shook her head at me. "Naught tha canst do. My work. And my own fault."

Lying in my blankets, I heard her say, with tongue or mind-speech, <Wake up.>

Beryx answered with a baited snarl. Fengthira spoke with relentless patience. <Tell me tha name.> There was no reply.

When the stars counted midnight I thought of the fire. Fengthira did not raise an eyelid, but Beryx, still jammed against the kingpost, lifted his head to watch me with the dregs of exhausted belligerence. Fengthira repeated, quietly as ever, <Tell me tha name.>

He glared round at her. Then he said in a clear furious voice indistinguishable from his spoken one except it gave no hint of his condition. <You know my name! Four blast you, say something else!>

I spun round, open-mouthed. Fengthira's face broke into a slow, tired smile.

"Everran," she said, her mouth corners curling, "tha'rt enough to make me take up hawks. What wilt answer then?"

Beryx looked as stunned as I. He swallowed. There was a pause. Then, in that rather uninflected but uncannily normal voice, he said, <I—can I—shall I—have something to drink?>

Fengthira rose, stretching with the effort of age. <Shalt have whatever tha likes.> Her eyes twinkled. <Wilt slay me, if th'art ta'en off the leash?>

As Beryx looked up at her I saw his eyes lose their frost of hostility, waking to a shame-faced acknowledgement, a tentative, rueful response. His mouth corners puckered, caked with dry saliva from foam and thirst.

<No,> he answered. <I'm too stiff.>

"Use the knife," Fengthira bade me resignedly. "T'will be the end of my rope." Taking the bucket she went out with that old woman's gait.

Beryx drank water, we all drank mint-tea, then I bathed his wrists in the hot water before Fengthira dressed them with a honey poultice and bandages thick enough for a horse. Beryx grinned, a little stiffly, and opened his mouth.

"No," she said calmly into that rekindled green glare. "Not till tha canst use Lathare sooner than tha talks." She stood up. "And not," she added, "till the falconer has had some sleep."

They both slept the length of the next day, and the night as well. Beryx seemed better the following morning, his eyes rid of that haunted, wounded look I had seen on the hill. At breakfast he said abruptly, <Will it all be—like that?>

Fengthira's eyes crinkled as they lifted from yet another splice. "Th'art manned now," she answered gravely. "All tha needst is work."

Work him she did, first with her in the house, then outside, then making him help me in the garden as they talked, driving him with quiet relentlessness. He neither complained nor rebelled, but by the time we sat down under the finlythes his shirt was drenched and his muscles trembled when he relaxed.

After we woke, she sent him to the lower valley. <Hast salt with thee? Give the horses a handful then, and tell me how they look. They'll come when they see thee. And tha, harper, bring me up some . . . >

I forget what I brought. I was straining honeycomb for a new poultice while she scolded the lydel for trying to rob the safe, when we both heard Beryx call, shout, with urgency, with near panic in his voice.

<Fengthira! There's something coming! Not a man—! A—a—>

Fengthira's eyes went blank for one short flash. Her answer's force and vehemence nearly drove me on my face.

<Lie down! Cover tha head! Shut tha eyes! Don't look at him!>

On the words she was out of the house. I ran with emergency's instinctive response. She crossed the garden like an adolescent hurdler, beds and channels taken in her stride. Tumbling from the cleft, I reached the lower valley in time to see her racing, swift as one of her own horses, toward the mob.

They were jammed in a clump, ears back, on the point of flight. When she called something they broke, thundering away as horses do in panic, flat out, scattering like quail. She tore past. I ran up behind.

Beryx was doubled on his face in the grass, arms over his head, flattened in more than obedience. Something was circling him, at a slow walking speed, waving and bending like a sheet of paper in the wind.

It was flat: tall as a man, and shaped like a man, but

when it turned sidelong it was flat as a portrait out of its frame. It did not walk as a man does, but slid along all of a piece over the grass. As it revolved I saw a long black robe stained with ash and blood, its folds immobile, a pair of hands folded on the breast. In the throat was a huge wound, wet and open. Its long black hair was dabbled with blood and its face was whiter than marble and as expressionless, but the eyes were awake. Milky white, shot with flecks of golden fire, like a pair of conscious, blind yet living maerians.

As it came swaying and dipping toward us my blood curdled, my limbs froze, my tongue dried in my mouth. Still breathing hard, Fengthira stepped over Beryx and spoke in a clear, adamant voice.

"Helve!" she said. "Arskan vist, Maerdrigg. Imsar math!"

It halted, swaying, as if uncertain. She stared at it, her eyes cold and hard.

It faded. Slowly, it disintegrated. It was gone. The sun was shining through open, empty air.

I found my legs had let me down with a thump. Fengthira stared a moment longer, before she stepped back, exhaling a long sigh, and bent to touch Beryx. He flinched. She said, "No, me. Canst get up."

He unwound himself, and sat up. He was shaking. He looked mutely up at Fengthira, who nodded, but without a smile.

"Ah," she said. "Hast ta'en his stone. He wants it back."

We had climbed halfway up the cleft before Beryx broke out, <Why me? And why now? When I don't even have it any more?>

Fengthira's reply carried back to me, the reluctant last.

"Has probably followed all tha line. Probably followed

the one who has it now. But tha hast power. So canst see him. And power draws them. They have none of their own. They come to it."

"Ah, t'will make work troublesome," she apparently answered his thought. "If I had not come? He would have sucked thee dry. Then he would have gone to take his maerian."

As I shuddered, she answered my own question. "Aye. He'll come back."

Instead of letting us sleep in the veranda, she herded us into her own rock chamber and lit a lamp, which she had never done before. "Hethel's too scarce to waste." She arranged us on the floor, Beryx in the middle, and as we lay down gave me a quick, dry smile. "Quiet thaself, harper. The Dead are with thee always. Even if hast never seen them before."

I neither expected nor intended to sleep, but I must have dozed, for I woke with a start. The lamplight showed me Beryx, eyes tight shut, flat and rigid on his back, and Fengthira, up on an elbow. And in the doorway the white glow of those phantom maerians.

As if to a living man, Fengthira jerked her chin up and gave her tongue a sharp clear click. Then she spoke, more in sadness than anything, saying, "Helve, Maerdrigg. T'is not the time."

The maerians faded. Fengthira lay down. I heard her say, <Go to sleep, then.> I was adrift myself when the lydel on the roof broke into a wild yatter and we heard it tear up a tree in a rain of leaves and bark.

This time Fengthira spoke with outright exasperation. "Tha wast vexatious alive, and art more vexatious dead. Dost expect him to find it now, green as grass, and with thee addling my work? Hast need to drink Velandryxe thaself. Helve, tha stupid creature! Go away!" And after that nothing troubled us again.

Eskan Helken next morning had grown less idyllic, but daylight nerved me to ask what it had been. Fengthira, feeding breakfast crumbs to the lydel on her shoulder, looked up as I opened my mouth.

"Maerdrigg," she said. "The last Maerheage. The stone came to them with his father Thilliansar, for the marriage of Maersoth, Darrhan's daughter: his only trueborn child. Maerdrigg killed five uncles to keep the maerian when his grandfather died, and he had six sons out of wedlock himself. The last was Vorn: the Tooth. They changed it to Vyrne: the Last. He slew his brothers to get the succession, and Maerdrigg saw nothing. He still had his maerian. Then Vorn slew Maerdrigg as well. Hast seen him as he died: the Dead that walk must do it in their dying shape. And he walks because, dead or alive, he is bound to his maerian."

She glanced at Beryx. "After the Vyrnes fell, Berrian found the stone. When tha hast the skill, had best give it back. Yes, tha'lt have the art. And we had best begin on it. More than Everran is waiting on thee now."

She came round the table to stand behind him. The lydel tweaked her hair. She said, "Quiet, brat," and put her right hand lightly on the nape of Beryx's neck. "Look at that wall," she said.

He had stiffened at her touch. Now he turned his eyes obediently to the latticed frame.

They widened. He caught his breath and held it until Fengthira lifted her hand. Then he let it out without noticing and turned to stare at her with a bright wonder, close to joy.

"Pharaone," she nodded, smiling a small, stern smile.

"Farsight. Pretty, ah? And simple—for thee." Something that might have been envy tinged her voice. "Do it again, then. By thaself."

Beryx turned without hesitation, his eyes widening. They did not turn black this time. The irises brightened, no longer cool, but vivid as a finghend held against the sun, sparked with stars of living light.

Fengthira watched, alert and still. The glow intensified, beginning to weave as sunlight does in water, to twist in ever more swiftly dancing strands—she put a hand on his neck and said, "Whoa. Come back."

He came up blinking as if he had been submerged: shook his head. Turned to me with a quick eager glance as if to share whatever he had seen: checked, and gave Fengthira an enquiring look.

"Hearing, yes," she said. "Lathare, if he were taught. But not the Sights. Must go through Phare for those." His look sharpened. "Si'sta. Hast his ear for music, but canst tha build his songs? Ah. That's in the blood. As Ruanbr'arx is in thine."

Gathering up mugs, I felt a moment's envy. Then I recalled the apprenticeship for such a gift, and gave thanks mine was for the harp.

As I washed up I heard the quick, absorbed, technical exchanges of craftsmen at their work. Then a break. Then Fengthira said sharply, "Whoa!" and Beryx's chair went over with a crash.

<I must!> The explosion was not rage but anguish. <It can't go on, I must go back!>

"And do what?" she cut in icily.

<You know, you saw,> he cried.

She snapped back, "And I let thee see for learning, not so tha shouldst rush back to run tha people about the

181

country one jump ahead of its teeth. What more canst tha do? Hast learnt nothing else."

I heard him charge to and fro, a rush of rebellious, anguished, despairing steps. Fengthira said coldly, "Canst do as much for them as Maerdrigg for his maerian."

His feet stopped. Then they returned to the chair. His mind's speech held torment twisted to a rage of purpose. <What comes next?>

"Work," she replied. "All of us. W'ave burnt more wood these three days than I do in a week."

We went to the lower valley, where she called the horses. We saddled ours. She said, "We'll take tha packhorse," and tossed the much-abused hide rope over its back. Then she fixed her eye on a dry gray mare, and after a moment the mare came up, bending her head as if for a bridle, standing while Fengthira hopped from a rock to her back, moving off as if given the office with rein and heel.

Even Beryx's distraction broke at that. "Wryve-lan'x," Fengthira told him. "Shalt do it in time. Like all the rest."

Outside the valley the mare halted. "Find a dead tree," Fengthira commanded. "Use Pharaone. As tha wouldst with eyes."

Beryx checked his horse, frowning, troubled more by the past vision than the present task. This time his eyes merely blanked as Fengthira's had the day before, then he swung his horse to the right.

The frail, spindly, desert tree, barely six feet high, was already rotting. They have a short life. I thought of an axe, but Fengthira shook her head, her eyes shot one gray flash, and the tree snapped at the butt as if at a lightning strike. "Axynbr'arve," she told Beryx. "Another high art. Tha'lt learn that too. This time, canst pick up the bits."

By noon we were heaving and hauling the packhorse up the cleft to unload the wood, while Fengthira made mint-tea and took it down to the finlythes. I was more than happy to rest, but Beryx was still on the rack.

When we finished, Fengthira sighed and said, "That guide of thine. Had aedric blood, ah? Speak to him, then. Send him back to Everran. Say th'art making a weapon. Canst give them hope, if hast nothing else."

Beryx's face lit: then it grew dubious, which made her snort. "Couldst boil a kettle twice that size. But I'd best ward harper first. Look here." My eyes rose involuntarily, and hers took them, drawing me into a silent gray moonlit world of unknown, unnamable shapes . . .

I was back amid sunlit green and finlythe shade, with Fengthira watching me closely and Beryx breathing hard, sweat on his face, looking shakenly delighted and partially consoled.

"Wilt be a song indeed," she told me with one of her dour smiles, "if canst make a song of that." I knew she meant what I had seen. "Letharthir," she added to Beryx. "If I'd not shut his mind, tha'dst have deafened him." She shifted the teapot. "Shouldst practice Pharaone, but . . . Th'art strong. And time's short. Phathire, then. This 'prenticeship should be hasty enough even for thee."

By the time I finished the garden, Beryx's fretful restlessness had become absorption, almost awe. He shot me a yearning look, and Fengthira chuckled.

"Show him, then. Canst do it. No, harper, no call to pull back like a touchy colt. Just look in his eyes. Tha'lt see, if hast not the Sight."

Beryx's eagerness steeled me. I met his eyes.

They were green, scintillant, dancing with energy in place of mirth, but now the pupils widened to swallow green in black, and then black cleared to light. And in it, as in a tiny crystal, figures moved.

I was looking up at some half-built edifice where men swarmed like zealous ants, driving sledge-teams that hauled up dressed-stone slabs, winching, heaving, levering them into place, shoveling containers of rubble to pace the rising stone. Close by a tall man in a crimson cloak with a gold coronal on his dark hair exhorted a group, stabbing his finger on a piece of parchment, waving here and there, and all around us stretched the arid lands of Hethria, bisected to the north by the courses of a mighty wall.

<The Gebros.> Beryx sounded literally inside my ear. His eyes sparkled at me through the finlythe shade. <That's Phathire. Not records, not lore, not hearsay. You're there, Harran! Can you—but you don't have to imagine. You saw.> He laughed in open delight.

"Hark'ee, Everran," Fengthira broke in sternly. "No Sight is a toy, least of all Phathire. Mayst use Pharaone as tha likes—except on Everran. Except on Everran," she repeated inflexibly. "But Phathire tha'll not use without me by. Th'are more things in Pharaon Lethar than tha knowst. If tha fetches one like Vorn or Lossian or thy or my plaguey ancestors, t'may be more than I can persuade back."

<Oh,> said Beryx, crestfallen. Then his eyes narrowed. In some amusement, she answered his thought.

"Ah. There's a sight for the future. Yxphare. But tha'll not play with that. It's no art, it's a gift, and a double-edged gift. And yes, I can do it. T'is bred in my line. But it comes to me, I don't seek for it. And yes, it told me tha wast coming. And no, it did not say I should teach thee, which is why I tried thee first. All I saw was a picture in the well there: Eskan Helken, and the two of you riding up." She climbed to her feet. "Now shalt stretch tha muscles. I need flour to feed you two great gowks."

So we took turns grinding her small desert grain on a saddle quern until supper. When we finished, Beryx was still on the dance, so Fengthira made him wash up.

As he strode back on to the verandah her eyes twinkled and she said, "We need to 'calm thee down.'" It was Thassal's very intonation. "And harper's lost his harp. Well—" she went inside, and brought out a long bundle of what had been ornate brocade, gray shot with smoke-like patterns and wonderful watery lights. "See what canst do with that."

It had a globular sounding drum and two necks long as my arm, seven strings above and seven beneath. The wood was rosewood, dark as polished blood: the frets were plum-red, blue-shot hazians.

"Aivrifel," she said, when I finally dared to touch, and a whisper of wind-music breathed under my hand, like Asterne's silver bells transposed for strings. "Seven honeys. Aedric music. That was—" she broke off. "Drat it! I forgot. That was Darrhan's own. We'd have Maerdrigg plaguing us all night."

Then her frown cleared. "Sing," she said, with an impish girl's grin. "I'll be tha harp."

One would hardly ask Fengthira if she could keep in tune. Nor could I bring to mind a song that would not prove delicate, to say the least. In the end I birthed a new one, hardly formed yet, a catch for the saeveryr over Eskan Helken's spring.

When I finished the verse she whistled a reprise for interlude, sweet and true and what was in my very mind for a harp. "Go on," she ordered grinning, as my mouth fell open, and accompanied me for the rest. At the end she said,

"Ah." And I felt all Hazghend's armrings poor against that one small word.

Later she sang with me, playing with her voice as she had with her whistling, round and over and through the melody, harmonizing, improvising, plaiting it all into a master's whole. When we finished she smiled to herself, and understanding that joy in skill and gift I smiled back, feeling a kinship with her at last.

Though Maerdrigg did not trouble us, at breakfast Fengthira wore an abstracted frown. She eyed Beryx, on edge to begin. Then she said, "Everran, tha canst wash up. Come, harper. I've a thing to show."

We walked down hill into Eskan Helken's crisp new sunlight, that turned a spider's web to glittering silver lace. "Havos," she said absently. "Spider. My line." Her mouth was wry. "Si'sta. Sights tha canst learn alone, but what comes next is Commands. And for that he needs—a mind."

"I can't do it," she went on, rather roughly. "Canst not be teacher and lesson both. Hast given a harp to this. Canst give something more?"

My breath dried. To live with a wizard was bad enough, to watch Beryx become one was growing worse. But I had not thought to make his prentice work.

Fengthira pressed me no more than Beryx himself had when the Hethox wanted my harp. All that pressed me was Everran—and myself.

"Good," she said, before I spoke. Then, cryptically, ironically, "Hast won more than tha knowst. And now, si'sta. The first command is Scarthe. Reading thoughts."

"Ah," she said as I backed away. "I know very well there's that in tha mind he should never know. And that tha'd hide it to spare him as well as thaself. Needst not blush. T'is one reason I like horses better than men. Their morals are simpler. Hast a mare, tha holds her. Canst not, someone takes her away. No blame either side. No need to hackle either. I know tha canst help it no more than the stallion that wants the mare." She chuckled. "Hurt tha dignity, have I? Well, I can give thee a command, bid thee forget her for—seven days. Should be enough. He'll not learn Phare from me."

I was still seething, but what was there to say? I looked up, and that silent gray world enveloped me.

"No, tha'll not feel it." She moved me up the hill. "And nor will he." Under her breath she added, "I hope."

Inside the house Beryx was pacing to and fro. "Sit." she said. "Art worse than a corn-fed colt. And tha." I sat, feeling as if it were to face the surgeon's knife. "Scarthe," she told Beryx. "Look in his eyes."

Beryx looked at her instead, and came to his feet with a bound, breaking out fiercely, <No!>

"Spare me," she said wearily. "I know tha knowst the way of Scarthe and tha scruples of eavesdropping and what it will do to him—and thee. Harper has done tha squirming for thee. And agreed to it."

Beryx began half a dozen protests and fell back on a violent, <No!>

"Then go back to Everran," Fengthira snapped, "and watch tha people's ruin. T'will save thee plaguing me."

Beryx went fire-red and struggled for words. Fengthira's eyes were bleak and pitiless. She said, "Take tha choice."

Their eyes clashed. Then he spun round, biting his lip, his eyes full of rage and shame, and I looked up into his gaze.

How does it feel? I remember thinking. There should be some sensation, surely? Then the first intuition of another's presence, that wild beast instinct that warns when we are approached by stealth. Then a sudden recollection of Fengthira describing Phare, and then panic, because the one thing you cannot do outside sleep or skill is to stop your speaking thoughts. Then it began to hurt.

<Rot you!> Beryx was yelling at the top of his voice. <Blast and blight you before the Four and every other Face!>

He became incoherent in the mental equivalent of choking rage. Fengthira's voice sliced into it. "If tha'dst be an aedr, must pay the price. I told thee, tha didst not know what tha asked."

He whipped round for the door. She said, no louder but cutting as a razor, "Shalt not throw tha tantrums with me." He spun as if jerked round by the shoulder, raging now on his own behalf. She said, "Wilt go back on the rope?"

He very nearly flew at her. He was on tiptoe, teetering for the charge. Fengthira assumed that deadly stillness of an aedr poised to strike.

"Art a king," she said, "and wast never gainsaid in tha life. More's the pity. Hot-headed. A forked stick for a mouth. Run over them that council thee for tha own good, and if tha must heed it, fly off like a brat in the sulks." It was deliberate provocation now, a flogging rather than a single lash. "Kick the pricker out of the yard and not just kick against the pricks. But if I come to break thee, by the sands of Deve Saldryx Korven," her eyes were alight now too, cold and perilous, "tha'lt answer to the bridle, whether tha wilt or not."

Beryx had his eyes shut, jammed tight. He was white as he had been red, shaking from head to foot, and I knew it was neither fear nor rage nor pain. It was a battle for control.

Fengthira paused a moment, still coiled. Then she said

in a neutral tone, "Come back here."

He opened his eyes and walked unsteadily to his chair. With startling kindness she said, "Good lad."

Beryx suddenly began to laugh. I doubt he too was thinking of his phalanxmen, whom he had called good lads.

When he broke off, hiccupping, Fengthira nodded. "I said tha'dst get tha temper up. Well, hast it down now. And hast made an almighty bungle of tha first Command. Do it again."

Beryx looked at her in wordless despair. I wanted to protest too, but you might as well try to bend a mountain of adamant.

Either Beryx improved or I grew inured, for it was easier after that, even if we took all morning to satisfy Fengthira. After a time she made me bring wood, boil tea, occupy my mind while he worked, which in some ways was worse than before. Finally she sat back and shook her head.

"Hast a touch," she said, "like a brick-maker stitching silk. But there's no helping that. Art too strong, and needst more practice. Other minds." Beryx had been sitting with his hand over his eyes. At that he gave her a mute look of appeal, and she shook her head. "We'll let it be."

They banished me to the verandah with the aivrifel and spent the afternoon practicing the Sights. When Fengthira's quietly commanding, <Harper?> recalled me, Beryx's eyes were black-smudged and he looked fine-drawn and taut.

"I'll teach thee Letharthir too," said Fengthira, "for the skill, though I doubt there'll be need of it." She gave a small chuckle. "Not with Hawge. Sit down, harper. Over there." She stood behind Beryx, a hand on his neck, face assuming that intent workman's look.

"Now," she said brusquely, "don't fight me. Dost hear?"

We were both rigid already. At that Beryx shut his eyes. She gave him a shake. "Open thine eyes. And tha, harper, look at him."

His eyes were normal, green and cool. Then they dilated. The pupils flared. Something violent was going on behind them, a struggle, or a struggle suppressed. A form of Phare, I think. Whatever it was, it passed. His pupils contracted to pinpoints, and then the irises seemed to expand instead, but they were no longer cool and dark. They were luminous with a hot, living light, shot with white facet-stars, crystalline, enormous, all-engulfing, the mesmeric stare of a hunting feline, of a dragon itself—

My own yell reverberated in my ears. Beryx was kneeling over me, holding me on the floor one-handed with a face of frantic concern and bitter remorse, crying, <Harran, Harran, it's all right. Do you hear me? Oh, Four, what have I done to him! Listen, do you hear? It's all right!>

His face was human, his eyes were dark green almonds rimmed in long black lash, not lidless, facetted, crystalline . . . I felt myself relax. Fengthira's face appeared above me, past crisis ousted by professional interest.

"Didst not tell me," she remarked, "Hawge had looked at thee. Else I would not have put thee to that."

Beryx glanced up blankly. "Ah," she said. "Dragons use a kind of Letharthir. And," her voice lost all expression, "their eyes are green." She shrugged. "No Letharthir. And enough for tonight."

But as we watched the sunset she clapped a hand to her head, exclaimed, "Thor'stang! Clot!" And darted inside. "Everran," she called, "find me sixteen small stones. About the same size."

Not daring to laugh, we scratched about like small boys in the dirt. Inside she had lit the lamp and drawn with a knife on the table, a big square divided into sixty-four smaller ones.

"Sit, Everran," she commanded, rapidly ranking stones on the outermost squares. "This is Thor'stang. Kings'-war. Canst move on any untaken square in any direction as far as tha likes. Takest an enemy's piece by jumping over it. First to lose all loses the war."

A flicker of interest lightened Beryx's fatigue. He sat down, his face assuming a soldier's cast: I knew he was a devotee of chess. With a glance under her lashes, Fengthira added softly, "The rest tha'lt learn . . . as tha goest."

Five minutes later she was chuckling, while Beryx leant back with a look of patent unbelief. "This one," she said, "tha plays in the mind. Canst use Scarthe. And Letharthir. And Fengthir. If tha canst."

Beryx was wide awake now. He gave her a calculating glance. She looked limpidly back. His eyes narrowed. Hers opened, gray and depthless; he made a wild movement like a man overbalancing off a cliff and she chuckled again. "No, if tha tries Scarthe outright I'll take thee with Letharthir and tha'lt give me the rest of the game."

Beryx looked down at the board. <What is Fengthir?> he asked.

"Scarthe," she replied, "with commands mixed into what tha reads. Then withdraw, without any of it known."

His eyes gleamed. Such subterfuges appealed to his soldier's mind. Fengthira gave him another limpid look and said, "With masters, they tossed up a pebble and whoever caught it with axynbr'arve took first move. But I'll give thee first hold."

There was a long pause. Then, still holding her eyes, Beryx reached out for a stone.

<Rot it!> he yelled. <You never thought about moving there!>

"Ah," she retorted, laughing. "And thy Scarthe was clear as a flag in a bramble-bush, so tha readst a lie. Try again."

When I went to bed the game had gone three-quarters of an hour without a piece being moved. When I woke later they were still at it. I caught Beryx's profile: alert, a pucker in the mouth-corner, a glint in the eye. As Fengthira glanced up, the same imp laughed back. At sunrise they were asleep, but a heap of pebbles was piled on the table, and atop it, a triumph banner, lay a scrap of faded gray rag.

"Shalt have tha revenge tonight," said Fengthira at breakfast, and as my stomach sank she gave me a smile. "Comfort thee, harper. Wilt not have to stand like an ox this time."

"Calke," she told Beryx. "The hammer, not the needle. Should suit thee, th'art ever Through, not Round. Give harper a Command."

Beryx said to me, <Stand up.> I obeyed.

He looked at Fengthira. "Next time," she told me, "refuse."

I sat tight. Beryx's eyes opened, the green growing hot and starred. Something niggled in my mind. I shut it out. His eyes kindled, began to weave in sheets of translucent green light . . .

"No," said Fengthira flatly. "Canst not use Letharthir. Or Fengthir. This is outright command. Again."

This time it came with a drillman's crack, <Stand up!> And sheer surprise shot me out of my chair. But Fengthira shook her head. "Wilt fright a lydyr off a corn-patch. Not stop a charging bull. Again."

Ready now, I knotted my muscles, and though the command was a firm push I defeated it. Beryx's eyes grew hotter, not faltering before Fengthira said, "Again." And this time I was hauled bodily, irresistibly to my feet.

192

Beryx wiped his face, drawing deep breaths, his forearms trembling. I sat down. Fengthira said, "Again. Wilt have to get tha temper up, I see." He turned, and as I braced myself she leant over and gave him a smart clip on the ear.

I should think my boots rose a good foot off the ground. As I landed with a bump Beryx let out a furious, <Ow!> and jerked his head away, and Fengthira laughed outright. "I have thy measure now, Everran," she said, grinning. "T'is hit or miss, with thee. Again."

He gave her a choleric look, and this time I shot straight to my feet.

"Better," she conceded. "Walk away, harper. Stop him, Everran." I managed five steps and was dragged to a halt. "Bring him back."

If Beryx had his temper up, mine was rising too. On the way back I resisted in earnest. As I stood panting by the table Fengthira said, "Let him go, Everran." She nodded to me. "Now hit him. With tha fist."

My fist doubled fiercely, and relaxed. Beryx's eyes changed. As we stared at each other in dismay, Fengthira snapped, "Art such a mouse as that?"

That did it. I rushed him. I have not come to fisticuffs since childhood, and Beryx had a soldier's reflexes of defense, but there was more bile in me than I knew. I swung a haymaker and kicked him in the shins as he ducked and next moment we were at it in earnest, clinched together, butting, kicking, rolling over and over like a pair of farm-yard dogs.

It was shameful as well as stupid: my king, my friend, with one arm to my two and no savor for the fight. But all sorts of buried grudges surface in such a fracas. Not only two days' humiliation rankled in me but three years' envy and frustration, and I daresay my two arms had cost him bitter jealousy, if he never admitted it even to himself. They also gave me the advantage. I was sitting on his chest before he remembered what he was.

My hands flew in the air, something kicked me head over heels and he was on his feet before I could get up. His eyes shot a sharp green flare. I was pinned in my tracks. And as I fought to escape, those twisting sheets of emerald fire altered: for the first time I saw malice, a cruel, gloating exultation, look out of Beryx's eyes.

Next moment the constraint broke. I sat down plump against the wall while Beryx stood panting, the malice gone, eyeing me in something like bewilderment. But I was aware that in his mind a residue of that moment remained.

"Now tha understandst Calke," said Fengthira. She sounded remote, impersonal, and quite terrifying. "Look here."

Beryx looked round. Then he cried out and tried to jerk a hand to his eyes. Failed. His head went back, his spine arched, he turned a somersault and rolled thrashing and kicking, "Still!" hissed Fengthira and my leap was pinned to the floor. But her eyes, white-hot and frightful, stayed on him.

Then I was released. Beryx collapsed, face down, twitching. In her normal voice Fengthira said, "Get up."

He rolled over, and tried. He was shaking too badly. He looked up at her, and to my horrified amazement, he was in naked fear.

"Ah," said Fengthira quietly. "T'was unjust. And unkind. And not what tha expected. Hark'ee, Everran. That Command has undone better men than thee. T'is what shows aedryx their true nature. And teaches them that nature's vice. Not the power, or the use of it. The pleasure in its abuse. Didst taste it? Ah." For he had bent his head.

"None of us are proof. T'is why I live in Eskan Helken, out of temptation's way. But tha canst not play hermit, and I'll not have it happen to thee. So I gave thee a lesson to last. 'Mind the fire,' twenty times over can't match one good singe."

He sat silent, head bowed. She glanced at me, and I too ducked my eyes in shame, but there was amusement in her voice.

"And now y'ave both blown off the steam, maybe ye'll be fit for making tea."

She was right. When she had made mint-tea, and Beryx revived, and she said, "Try a bout, then," we began timidly, but grew warm without enmity. Beryx's power became a challenge to me, a compensation to him. Once he grunted in amusement as he stopped my fist an inch from his nose, once I laughed aloud as I passed his guard and heel-tapped him on his back. Even when I realized those hot green eyes full of fighter's merriment were reading not only my eyes but my thoughts, it seemed just one more tactic, to be foiled if I could. When Fengthira said, "Whoa," we grinned at each other as we broke apart.

Fengthira sighed, leant back in her chair, and closed her eyes. "Art out of the smelter, Everran." She looked weary for the first time. "Now must forge the steel. The higher arts."

Beryx looked daunted. She opened her eyes.

"Wryve-lan'x first. Comes easiest. And t'will be most important to thee." She clicked her tongue, and the lydel, which had been most affectionate since Maerdrigg's visit, dropped chittering on her shoulder. She dipped a finger in the honey jar, and as it clutched with its paws like a child she shot him a warning glance. "Take care with this. Th'art heavy-handed enough with a man, and I'm fond of it. Use Scarthe first."

Beryx's mouth opened: and shut. He eyed the lydel, with more trepidation, I should imagine, than he had his first boy's spear.

It seemed a long time he studied it. His eyes did not take fire, but stilled, and deepened, and presently I realized with shock that it was a good five minutes since he had blinked. Then at last he relaxed with a long sigh, while the lydel, ignoring him, composedly cleaned its paws.

"The best tha hast done," said Fengthira, and cocked her head.

<It was . . .> He looked at the lydel in wonder. <They see differently. No color at all. And blurry. And right round to your ears. They don't think in words. But their senses are— It knows us apart, it knows how we feel, just by the smell.> He glanced at me and chuckled. <You and I are sweat-dirt-stranger-ecch-temper-got-over. She's homeground-honey-yum-yum-yum.>

As I broke into a laugh, Fengthira, smiling too, said, "Good. Now bring it to thee."

<Owf!> Then his eyes began to dance. <Er . . . how? I don't want another dose of the—ah—cells.>

Fengthira snorted, but with a quirk in her lips. "Th'art true Heagian. Unquenchable. And askst, How, with the whole battery of Ruanbr'arx in tha armory? Find out."

Beryx pondered a very long moment. His eyes darkened, then, very slowly, showed a soft fire, and died. The lydel paid no heed at all.

<Oh,> he said ruefully, and began again.

This time the fire was hotter. The lydel chittered and wrinkled its nose: then it scurried across the table, to bounce from his knee onto the chairback and up into the roof, and he glanced at Fengthira with laughter that was a shade unsure.

"No cells," she said. "It did not like thy smell, and tha letst it go. Well enough. We'll try the horses now."

A horse's perception so fascinated Beryx that it was some time before he could be brought to use a command at all. Next they tried the saeveryr over the well. Then Fengthira said, "Now stretch thaself. Find a wild lydyr out there and bring it to me."

It took so long I had lost track of Beryx's slow, wide-spaced breaths and begun to watch the clouds pattern, trying to find a rhythm that would take their dreamy changes without sending an audience to sleep. But then came a scutter in the cleft.

The lydyr hopped out, leisurely as if on its own affairs, a little furry melon with paws and tail and pink blurry eyes which were oddly fixed. It stopped, sat up; rubbed a paw up its face, then suddenly jerked its head up and was off down the cleft as fast as jumps would carry it, while Beryx and Fengthira laughed.

"Men first," she said, "to learn the Commands, and give thee practice and—later—the strength. Because a mind without words is harder than one like tha own. And easier than something with no mind at all." Beryx looked uneasy. "Tomorrow," she said. "Wilt need tha sleep."

After breakfast she came with me to the garden, while Beryx washed up. When we finished she glanced round at me and said, "Yes, mayst watch if tha wants."

We went back inside. She sat Beryx down at the table, put a hand on his neck, and said, "Move that honey-jar."

After a moment it slid along the wood. Fengthira removed her hand and said, "Alone."

Beryx eyed the jar apprehensively, and set his teeth.

His eyes kindled, wove into sheets of light, wove brighter, faster, until they dissolved in a blur of white-hot green like a wheel spun against the sun, his breaths became huge heaving gasps, the sweat trickled down his face. And the jar did not move.

Without comment Fengthira said, "Again."

After the fourth attempt she said, "Let be." And he dropped back, utterly spent.

"Axynbr'arve is hard," she said. "Must use another level of power. Mostly, the only way there is to jump." She went over to the tool-heap and unearthed her rope.

Beryx looked at her beseechingly. She merely clicked her tongue. He stood up and put his hands behind his back. She tied them, backed him to the kingpost, and ran the rope round and round him all the way to his feet. Then she went to the table and took up a stone.

He had gone white, and was gritting his teeth. She grinned. "Dost not like to play the fairground shy, ah? Then get tha temper up." And she under-armed the pebble straight at his face.

Beryx ducked with a soldier's quick economic grace. Fengthira nodded and aimed the next one at his chest. That did not miss.

He winced. His eyes began to glow. As her arm went back for the next throw, they shot one brief green flash and her hand stopped in mid-air.

"Tck, tck," she said. "Axynbr'arve is with things, not minds." She frowned. "Must be a Command, then. Look here."

I first realized when it seemed to take far too long. Then I heard Fengthira begin to breathe. I looked at her hands, and they were clenched, saw her back was arched, snatched a glance at her eyes and hastily averted mine before that molten white focus burnt them clean away.

Beryx was panting too, eyes white-hot as hers. The air strained like fabric being pulled in two, there was a ringing in my ears. I covered them, so I only saw Beryx's convulsive gasp before he went limp in the ropes, while Fengthira, breath whooping, leant hard on the back of her chair.

"Art growing," she said between lungfuls, "difficult—Everran." His look was not defiance but apology. "I know—couldst not help thaself. We all face up sometime. Good practice, too. But tha'll stand now." She turned for another pebble, swung, and threw.

It took him right between the eyes and it came far harder than the others, flung by mind rather than muscle, I suspect. He had tried to dodge it, and failed. He stood lowering, while a point of blood slowly welled, broke and trickled down his nose, and I wished I dared protest, and Fengthira weighed the next stone.

"Temper," she said, "is like Yxphare. Double-edged. Canst use it for . . . or against." The pebble took him fairly on the center of his right collarbone and he yelled with the rage of pain. <You cursed bitch!>

Fengthira merely took another stone. As she cupped it in her hand, he struggled with mind and muscle, eyes boiling now. She flicked it at his face. His eyes sparked savagely: the pebble shot up and over and took her with still greater impetus right in the middle of the chest.

"All . . . right," she croaked, hunched on the floor while I fluttered in panic, not least that she would leave me with a royal wizard helpless in bonds I could not loose. Beryx was shouting, just as panicky if from a somewhat nobler cause. <Fengthira, are you all right? Are you—did I—Four, I didn't mean to—I never meant it to hit you, I'm sorry—>

<Calm thaself,> she responded, rubbing gingerly at her chest. It had struck just below the hollow of the collar-bones, on the breastbone itself. <Ow,> she commented, deliberately mimicking him. <Hast a heavy eye, Everran. Harper, help me up.>

She got up heavily, while he seethed with anxiety and remorse and his own impotence. Her lip twitched. "Art not an aedr-slayer yet. Or a master's-butcher: though t'has been known. Or even a woman killer. W'are tougher than tha thinks." Tenderly, she moved to the table, leant on the chair, and took another stone.

Beryx deliberately shut his eyes. Fengthira broke into a chuckle and caught her breath. "Rest easy. Wilt not hit me again."

Distrustfully, he opened his eyes. She flicked the pebble without moving her hand, in a green flash he hurled it back, but this time it rebounded even more fiercely and too swiftly for him to stop. "Ha," said Fengthira as it thudded into his ribs. "Mayst save tha lamentations for thaself."

<Owf,> he said when he opened his eyes. <And I can't even rub.>

Fengthira smiled briefly. "Untie him, harper. Everran, look here."

As I slipped the last knot he stepped away from the post, rubbing at his right wrist, then at each successive bruise. "Hast learnt axynbr'arve," said Fengthira. "Pick up tha mess."

He eyed her a moment, before he turned. His eyes flashed. One by one each missile flew back to the table, and he looked round to Fengthira with a small triumphant smile.

"That," she said, "was worth a bruise or two." She scanned him. "If my lydel thought tha stank, had best alter

200

it. The pair of you. Hot water. And shave. Lookst like a hedgehog with green eyes. Then sit out there and let harper play with the aivrifel. No, canst not go on now. Wilt be little use to Everran if I kill thee in the breaking yard."

She vanished, leaving us to boil the kettle and shave in the spring's mirror and then strip down. As we scrubbed, Beryx said apologetically, <Harran, could you do my back? I can't reach that side.>

I was shocked at his loss of flesh: every rib showed, even the big spinal muscles had wasted to reveal the vertebrae, and his shoulders were pure bone. With the beard off his face looked worse, gaunt and drawn, a mere frame for the intensely, abnormally vivid green eyes. They were no longer just striking. They were compelling, fascinating, the very irises seemed awake, they had that constant weave and dance of light in a green flowing stream . . .

<Harran! Stop it!>

Somebody jerked my arm. Beryx's face snapped from the green, looking almost appalled. "Stop what?" I asked, rubbing my eyes. <You were going under,> he answered curtly, and turned away.

I watched his averted profile: clean mouth, springing nose, jaw made more emphatic by the loss of flesh, the long-lashed eye. Only, I thought with a sense of loss, it was no longer safe to look at that. It was a wizard's now.

Before I had felt out two chords on the aivrifel he was asleep, and he slept like the dead the whole afternoon. Fengthira came once, looked, nodded, and went away. Overhead the clouds passed, heavy woolpacks that dappled Eskan Helken with shadows slow and dream-like as the shapes in Fengthira's inner world.

I began to make a song for it: all minors, which the aivrifel favored, dwindling cadenzas, single mysterious chords, till the very structure grew tenuous and I had to pull it together with one of those gifts that come when you are seeking something else. A gem in its own way, an elfin, haunting motif like the shadow of remembered joy. I looked up to see Fengthira with its echo in her eyes.

"Ah," she said. "Hast understood what it will mean." And cut off my questions by prodding Beryx. "Wake up, Everran. Sleepst like a hedgehog, too."

The next two days were largely a reprise. They played Thor'stang, wrestled mentally, robbed Fengthira's hive with Beryx keeping off the bees, threw pebbles and failed to hit each other, all to my boredom and their great delight. The third morning we came in to find the fire out cold and Fengthira sitting with folded hands by the hearth.

"Wryviane," she told Beryx. "Must light it if tha'd eat. Go on. T'will be easy enough."

I brought twigs and shredded grass and bigger sticks. Beryx stood before the hearth as a fighter does, four-square, balanced lightly on the balls of his feet. He drew a breath that seemed to go forever. Then without any warning his eyes lashed and a jet of flame went roaring up the wall. "Whoa!" shouted Fengthira. "I said light the fire, not burn down the house!"

They did not work that day. It was humid, enervating, the clouds had thickened, and by noon there was a darkening boil in the north that presaged a storm. We watched it from the verandah. Or at least, I watched it, for Beryx was looking at Fengthira instead.

She turned to answer his thought as she had so often answered mine. "Yxphare," she said, "comes from my line. Scarthe's my own gift. But tha'rt Heagian. Flame-tree. So fire-work comes easy to thee. Tha springst from Th'Iahn, who was one of the greatest aedryx ever made. Not born: he came late to it, like thee. One day, mayst use Phathire for the tale. Berrian was eighth generation, across the blanket to a Slief Manuighend concubine. Slief Manuighend is what tha callst Heshruan Slief. T'was all Heagian country once. Berfylghja and Tirien were their offshoots, as Tyrwash was from Hazghend. No, not the Hazghend tha knowst. Thine are corsairs, no more. Hazghend was the line of Vorn. In tha Tirs was its tower. Stiriand and Histhira were in Holym. And Havos was in Bryve Elond."

She glanced away to the storm. "The first Fengthira brought them Maerheage blood. She was got by Maerdrigg's eldest son, that was killed by his brother Vorn. There's Maerheage in tha line too, but that's another tale. They were all cross-bred, the old Tingrith, just like Quarreders. And yes, I am the last of my line. I came here after the Sorcerer hunts."

"Ah," she smiled with irony as we both sat up with a jerk. "Six of tha generations past. Pure aedryx are like dragons: they live long, unless th'are killed."

No wonder, I thought, that she had "thee'd" us both like boys. But she was measuring the storm as Ragnor had the sea, a known, conquerable element.

"I'll teach thee Wryvurx," she said. "May come in useful. That will miss us, but t'is coming this way."

They climbed Eskan Helken's north wall, and for a long time I watched them, two tiny tense figures in wildly blown robes against the crescendoing storm. It seemed impossible they could master such a tumult of the skies. But slowly, slower than the cloud-shadows' motion, I saw a change in the heavy bruise-black of the storm wall, that makes Gebrians spit because the rain is going past: an arch appeared in it. Then it became a black mountain piled above a white-mouthed cave, as the rain front pivoted head-on to us, and that white slowly climbed to fill the sky, while the horizon shortened under its feet. When thunder and lightning were simultaneous and the first drops blew through that gusty, eerie light, they came down, Beryx wet enough to have stayed there, Fengthira quietly satisfied.

It was a splendid storm. The towers poured such cascades it doused the fire, the thunder drove the lydel under Fengthira's arm, and we all had to hide in the rock chamber till it passed. "T'will feed the spring," said Fengthira, "a full three moons." She eyed the sopping house. "Find some kindling, Everran, and light the fire while I see to this."

She gave me no orders, but thinking of the garden I took a wooden spade out to the irrigation channels, which were in predictable choked or broken ruin. While I worked, the storm bellowed off southward and the light cleared to that still sweet aftermath of dry-land rain, leaving a tender cerulean blue sky to the north, and overhead, a sunset spectacle to rival Hethria's. The entire side of Eskan Helken turned the color of golden wine, which pools and wet leaves shot with scintillance, all framed in deep, burnt-gold rock, and overhung first in lurid scarlet, then by a purple gloaming shot with lights of silver and royal crimson. As splendid but less transient than the meteors in Maerdrigg's maerian.

As the image came to mind I straightened up, content with my labors, and turned: and Maerdrigg was at my back.

I do not think I thought. There was no time. One flash of recognition, one paralyzed reflex to cry aloud, and I had been sucked into the depths of that milky, gold-shot fire.

A voice was speaking overhead: clear, ringing as a trumpet's does, as did Beryx's spoken voice, but not his mental one. "Helve," it was saying, with soft, impersonal, dispassionate power. "Helve, Maerdrigg. Imsar math." It did not pronounce the words with Fengthira's impulsion, but gravely, almost sadly, like the unanswerable decree of a Sky-lord himself.

I opened my eyes. Beryx stood over me, looking across me to something else. I knew what it was. I kept my eyes on him until his stance eased imperceptibly, and I knew Maerdrigg was gone.

As I got up his eyes shot wide in relief. "Thank the Four! You're all right! I thought—"

Then we both gasped. I said stupidly, "You said it aloud."

He did not answer, but looked past me, and I saw Fengthira standing among the sodden corn.

"Ah," she said. This time the quiet in her voice was a farewell. "Hast broken the Command. And I laid it on thee in Phare. T'would have held against all but this." She came slowly forward. "I thought t'was safe for him alone. Then I heard him cry. But tha wast quicker. Wilt often be quicker, now."

Beryx did not speak. She nodded at him.

"Hast the strength. Knowst the arts—all save a couple tha'lt find at need, and some that are no use now. Hast missed the aedric snare. Art a good lad, Everran. Th'art strong, and I pushed thee to tha limits, and tha never showed an ounce of vice. If tha kicks, tha dost not strike or bite." A curious compassion showed in her eyes. "Everran will be lucky in thee. No, no Yxphare. Tha'lt manage for thaself."

Beryx moved his left hand quickly, opened his mouth. She shook her head and walked away.

When we came down the cleft for the last time, she glanced up at the sword on its ledge, then at Beryx, and shook her head. "Ah. Wilt not need that again. Art thine own weapon now."

She rode with us to the valley's end, and as we reined in she turned to Beryx, saying, "I little thought to use this again, but . . ." She held out her left hand.

Hesitantly, his came to meet it, and she turned it so her thumb pressed the vein inside his wrist. "T'is the aedric way."

Beryx drew a breath. "There's nothing you'd take," he said, "if I had it to give. But I told you once, you'd find a welcome in Everran. This time, it's true."

Fengthira laughed at him with one of those quicksilver transformations into gaiety. "Guard tha harper well," she said, "if tha'lt make truth of that. Luck!" She waved. Then the gray mare came round on her hocks and cantered away, the rider not looking back.

VIII

Leaving Eskan Helken, we struck south-west in as direct a line for southern Everran as is possible in Hethria. When Beryx turned that way I had gulped, which earned me one quietly ironic look. "Don't worry, Harran," he said. "I know where I'm going."

Hethria was in full bloom, fields of unknown, exotic flowers. Water often lay on bare claypans, and beasts ran from our very feet. We were so short of food that in a day or two we had to hunt. Beryx said, "I don't like this, but . . . So we'll make it a gambler's shot." He summoned a wyresparyx in bowshot, then let it go, and I managed, with some help I think, to put an arrow in its skull. The skinning was gruesome, but the flesh tasted a little like fish.

Our next camp was a permanent water which we shared with huge flocks of gweldryx, jewels of lime-green and gold, crimson and azure, gold and azure, or emerald, crimson and gold together, their only blemish an unfailingly raucous voice. As I yearned for a closer look, one splendid crimson and cobalt-winged specimen swooped across the water to my very feet. A lime and scarlet followed, an emerald and azure stipple-winged, a violet-cheeked . . . they stood in a row, lifting their wings, turning their heads from side to side. Then they exploded into a cloud of wings, a shattered rainbow in flight.

Restored to myself at last, I turned to find Beryx with amusement in his look. "Yes," he said. "The only trouble with birds is that they see one eye at a time." He crossed his eyes and moved one each way so comically that my dawning comprehension turned from fear to mirth.

After that a bird or beast which took my interest would often come closer, even put itself on display. I did not think, or rather, I hid from thinking, what the prelude to these kindnesses would have to be.

In Eskan Helken, Everran had seemed a mere premise, like zero in figures, accepted by the mind, not physically real. But as those red towers sank in thought as they had on the horizon, Everran rose in their place. I wondered what the dragon had done. I counted the months: three now since we left. It would be winter, we should have to find warm clothes if we were going, as it seemed, into the hills of the south.

Tirs made me think of Sellithar. I had forgotten Fengthira ever gave me a command, I had even forgotten why. I saw our farewell in Maer Selloth, when she kissed me with stoic composure and said, "Take care of yourself." And then I found myself thinking of Sellithar when she shared my bed, as a man thinks of a lover and not his love, with a hot pang of longing imaging her body, her limbs, her breasts—

I glanced up across the fire to find Beryx watching me and did not have to wonder what had lightened and crystallized those green eyes. I knew my thoughts had been shared.

Could I have run into the sand like water, I would have run. Horrified, shamed to my soul, terrified, I tore away my eyes.

There was a dreadful pause. Then Beryx said in a rush with a shame that seared deeper than my own, "I'm sorry, Harran, I didn't mean to do that . . . It was—when someone thinks with, with—loudly—you can listen before you know, and I—" he turned away.

I knew his shame at eavesdropping would dwarf mine at what he had read. That he would absolve me, and probably never forgive himself. Never had I missed my harp with such a pang. Bitterly I recalled Fengthira's, "Horses' morals are simpler than men's."

He stood up, his back to me. Over his shoulder, muffled, he said, "I can't bear that you should be—afraid."

In that moment I plumbed the depths of an aedr's isolation as well as the lure of the aedric vice. So easy to take a fearsome revenge. So impossible to live as a man among men whom your smallest art can reduce to terror, drive away.

"It doesn't matter," I gabbled, snatching at the nearest banality. "Don't blame yourself—it was my own fault. I shouldn't have 'thought so loud.' "

The sally was as pathetic as his laugh. "Well, in future," he said, turning, "when you mean to do it, put up a sign." And I knew with grief that if our comradeship had been salved, it would never be quite the same again.

When Everran next came to my mind I diverted it by asking Beryx what had happened there. If it pained him, I felt it would be the lesser hurt.

"Hawge has finished up . . . Saphar Resh." He was staring into the fire. It made his face seem chipped from hard red stone. "It had a turn round Meldene too." I saw ancient hethel groves blazing: the knife turned in my own wound. "Then it went back to Tirs. Tenevel was very pleased about that." The irony in his mouth's twist deepened. "My uncle got out of Askath with singed heels, and now he's down in Maer Selloth too. My 'government.' " That was black bitterness. "Morran managed to survive being left behind. The Guard have drilled so much they wish he'd gone."

Two impossible alternatives lay before me. I was thankful when he chose the lesser one.

"The maerian thief is hiding in Estar. Perhaps he thinks, among so many, Hawge won't recognize one." The irony muted. "Odd that dragons know Letharthir, yet not Pharaone . . . But Maerdrigg will have to wait till I have time to fetch him back." As I swallowed, his mouth-corner spoke Fengthira's mockery. "Oh, yes, I can bring him back. Like a fish on a line."

Skirting the other pit, I asked tentatively, "And Hawge? How will you—?"

"We'll cross the Gebros at Gebasterne. It still has an open gate." Remembering the road west to Astil I thought he meant to move with speed, but he shook his head. "I'm going to deal with Hawge as soon and as safely as I can. Out in Gebria on some nice . . . flat . . . barren plain."

His brows were down. His mouth had straightened. What looked into the fire was cold, sure, implacable, fuelled but not commanded by revenge. I said, "But if Hawge is in Tirs . . ." And he glanced up: I caught one glimpse of his eyes before I averted mine.

"King-summoned," he said. "I understand part of that, now. When I'm ready, I'll call it. And it'll come."

Gebasterne lies at the point of the V where the Gebros meets the Helkents' last northern elbow, before they vanish into Hethria. We came there just before sunset on a bitter afternoon, riding for miles over a plain of stones no bigger but harder than a fist, with a few silver-green istarel bushes scattered on its breadth. The wind was behind us with all the cold of Hethria's wastes. Low, mean clouds broke the sun, so the Helkent glowered, the Gebros looked decrepit, and homecoming was robbed of joy.

Beryx had ridden slowly, partly for the stones, partly to reach the gate when the token guard would be so thoroughly bored two desert travelers would earn no more than a glance that missed the phenomenon of his eyes. For some reason he meant to remain anonymous.

In the event it was quite easy. I said we had come from Phengis' garrison, on a hunting trip. Agreed that it was wretched weather. Wished them goodnight, and beyond the echoing arch Gebasterne's cluster of adobe houses lay behind the spike-topped mud wall, all dim in a dusk already starred with lamps. As I looked longingly, ashiver in my thin desert robe, Beryx reined in.

"Harran," he said, "could you buy us some supplies? A couple of coats?" He dragged out the pouch so long unused and tipped the last three rhodellin into my hand. "I'll water the horses while I wait."

The travelers' well is outside the gate. When I arrived he had hobbled the horses and made a fire of prickly bush. We ate some of the nauseous dried Gebrian cheese and a few flourcakes, shivered through the night, and before dawn were riding north-west into Gebria's flat, monotonous red wastes.

Before I went there I wondered how people lived in Gebria, and I am no wiser for having been. The truth is that they are only born there and depart as soon as possible, to be replaced by those with no money or no sense or no choice, who take up the little wretched holdings east of Saeverran Slief, work them a year or five if they have good seasons, then go bankrupt and leave. Or those who come on east to the deep gold mines at Deltyr or Gevdelyn and work a season or two before moving on, or being killed in the drives. Or those who are posted to the Gebros. Survive a season of garrison feuds, Hethrian hunting and Gebros boredom, say the Guard, and you are safe in war.

We, however, were riding into the real desert, south of the mines, east of the farms, west of the wall, stony red flatland stretching to the horizon, with desert herbage too meager to make a show. It would have been impossible, except in autumn, and with an aedr. But storms had left some pools, and Beryx found them where no native Gebrian would have dared to go.

What he was seeking I have no idea. What he chose was another stretch of rusty stones running north from a semi-permanent water in a weathered outcrop that I suspect would interest a miner far more than it did me. A few of the rare Gebrian desert trees stood on the northern side. We arrived in late afternoon, icy cold, and Beryx insisted on a bath as well as a shave, which I thought lunacy, until I realized: tomorrow was battle-day.

I was knee-hobbling the horses out on the apology for feed when a more pressing point arose. How was I supposed to 'appraise the men of valor' on a plain that would not hide a half-grown mouse?

I walked back to the saddlebags. Beryx was shaving, carefully as a bridegroom. This time there was none of that crazy gaiety he had shared at Coed Wrock: he was composed, contained, entirely self-assured. Looking round, he gave me a little grin and answered my unvoiced question.

"With me," he said. I hardly noticed, Fengthira had made me so used to it. "You're too valuable to leave anywhere else."

Nothing I could see made me the least valuable, until I recalled Fengthira's parting words. Taking it for some odd aedric superstition, like Sellithar's talisman, I said no more.

Dawn came in a slow wide golden-red glow and a bitter

wind, to find Beryx whistling softly as he piled up sticks, broke off to light them with one quick green flash, put on the tiny traveling kettle, smiled at me, and said, "Mustn't make Hawge wait."

Groaning, I clambered from my blankets into the new sheepskin jacket. Before the sun had risen a hand span we were walking out into the north.

"Have to leave the horses." Yet again he answered my thought. "They'd go crazy. If Hawge tries to take them . . . I'll see what I can do."

I did not answer. My stomach was turning hoops; my heart was trying to climb out of my suddenly arid throat. Beryx looked up into the cloudless blue and lemon-tinged sky and said, "This'll do."

After a while I sat down, which did help to warm my legs. He went on standing, occasionally scanning the sky, patient, utterly unperturbed. The wind tried to make noises in the stones and failed.

The sky turned entirely blue. Not moving, stiffening, betraying any sort of emotion, Beryx said, "There."

I had been looking too high, too far, and the wrong way. As I jumped up, Beryx stepped round in front of me, and past his shoulder I saw Hawge.

It had made a circuit to come in from the east with the sun behind it, and it was gliding down along the sunbeams' angle, no more than three hundred yards away, barely fifty feet up, the huge black wings held out horizontal, motionless, the sun making gold on the impenetrable mail. It must have been stalking us. When Beryx turned, seeing it had failed, it backwatered and dropped heavily to earth.

Then it advanced. Gradually the shoulders sank, the back arched, and the tremendous body seemed to vanish behind the eyes, which did not revolve but were steady and glowing and wide as a stalking cat's.

Beryx's shoulder nudged me. I took a step back.

The dragon spoke, in its vast grating whisper which after aedric speech made me suspect it had no voice at all, but thought directly into your mind.

<Aedr,> it said.

Beryx responded in a soft, carrying, expressionless voice. "Hawge."

When he did not go on, the dragon said, <It is long since I saw . . . one of thy kind.>

Beryx said nothing. After a moment Hawge mused, <But now I remember. I have seen thee before. With the soldiers. It was thee,> slowly, obscenely, it licked its lips, <who had the horse.>

Beryx still did not reply. The dragon sank its chin toward the ground. Its vast nostrils dilated, but blew no fire. The wind tried to blow again, and failed. Yet some sort of duel was going on, too subtle for senses' perception, a preliminary crossing of swords.

Then Hawge said, <What dost thou want with me?>

Beryx's voice was soft, empty, remote. He said, "Thou knowst."

Hawge's eyes revolved slowly, once. When it spoke again its whisper was a suave, ingratiating purr.

<Why should we quarrel, thou and I? There is plenty of room for us both. I will give thee this part north of the mountains. I will go into the south. There should be no warfare between—kin.>

Its eyes cocked, to judge the efficacy of the thrust. Then it went on, softer still.

<Didst not know that we were kin? Why dost think thou canst look into my eyes? And I can read men's thoughts? And we are both destroyers? I, of the flesh. Thou, of the

mind. I will leave these people for thy . . . games. Perhaps I will rid thee of some enemies.>

When Beryx did not reply, it began to straighten from its crouch. The great wings flexed, drawing forward along the ground, the hind claws shifted a little, gaining purchase to launch its flight.

Beryx still sounded soft, almost gentle. He said, "I will follow thee."

Hawge dropped back into a crouch. Its eyes spun rapidly, then grew crystalline and fixed. It said, <Thou knowst why I came? Why thy folk are homeless? Thy city fallen? Thy land in ruin? The lore is true. It is thou, not I, who art Everran's bane.>

Beryx answered softly, "I know."

Hawge's nostrils flared. This time they shot a puff of black oily smoke.

<And knowst how thou called me? Art aedric blood. Hast seen, then, thy ancestors wailing for their ended line? Because thou art a king with a barren queen? And knowst that the barrenness is in thee?>

I flinched. Beryx did not. His voice was soft as ever. "I know."

Hawge breathed a short, sharp gout of flame.

<And dost thou know,> now the whisper grated, <that the one at thy back is thy betrayer? That thy queen has lain in his bed, in his arms, and wished to be rid of thee?>

Through a black wave of horror I heard Beryx answer, soft, steady, quite unflinching, "I know."

Hawge's breath came in pants. Its tail lashed. The whisper went shrill.

<And thou *also* knowst who holds my firestone!>

Beryx moved. His shoulder pushed me sideways and I woke with a shock to find the sun behind me and realize in hair-crisping fright that all the time it spoke Hawge had been creeping forward, and Beryx had been edging side-long, keeping his distance and forcing it to pivot to maintain its own. As the sun centered behind us he answered, softly as ever, "I know." And then he smiled.

Hawge reared right up on its hind legs with a scream that stunned my ears and blasted a huge gout of fire at the sky. The tail lashed round with the sting flying foremost and Beryx bent his knees, arched his back, his eyes shot a blinding green flash and the tail flew harmlessly over our heads while Hawge turned turtle as the force of the stroke upset its balance and rolled it over and over, hurling stones like a horizontal avalanche.

It came up with a plunge, gravel flying from the monstrous claws, and the wing-blast battered us as it flung itself into the air. It screamed again. Beryx tilted his head back as it climbed, shooting itself up in huge rocketing thrusts, then whipped over with folded wings as the head came out in that arrow-like dive. I cowered, Beryx took a quick fierce breath.

Down it came, those eyes skewered me, the nostrils were open furnaces, big as caves, full of leaping flame—Beryx clenched his hand and went up on his toes as if launching a missile with all his bodily strength. Hawge shrieked hideously and botched its dive in a tangle of head and claws and floundering wings, hit the ground, ran a few ungainly strides like a pelican that has misjudged its landing, and thrust itself back aloft.

Beryx stood rigid, panting, huge hungry breaths. Hawge whipped round again. Dived. Beryx arched his back. And the dragon's nerve broke.

It could have been nothing else. It swerved out of the dive, planed round in a long furious circle, and thumped

216

back to earth. Then it came forward, stalking once more, but this time the tail lashed behind it, and the lips were drawn up in a grin of bloodcurdling rage.

Beryx had caught his breath. Now he shifted a little and his whole body seemed to loosen, with the hair-trigger suppleness of a snake prepared to strike. As he moved I caught a glimpse of his eyes. They were dazzling, blinding, pits of green-white flame.

Hawge was hissing: flame and smoke spurted with each breath. Beryx moved a hand. It was very nearly a drawl, gentle, silky, and quite terrifying. He said, "Stop."

And Hawge stopped. Its tremendous thighs and shoulders bulged, its neck arched over, its spines rose as the back doubled like a hairpin. I saw every muscle in the mailed flanks stand out in ridges high as a man's forearm and wider than his chest. Its head came down, down, tucking back and under, the monstrous dilated nostrils leveled right at us, the eyes starting from the nightmare head. Its breath turned to gigantic, straining grunts.

Beryx did not breathe. His body was like an iron bar and his face had contorted into a copy of the dragon's grimace, and the air between them shuddered like an over-weighted wall.

With the kick of a parted hawser, something snapped. Hawge fell flat on its belly, all four legs straight out. Beryx's body whiplashed and shot straight. Hawge got up, and stood unsteadily. I would not have believed those trunks of legs could shake.

Beryx said, sounding as if he had barely exerted himself, "Hast played with words, and with muscles. Now wilt thou fight?"

Hawge reared its head to the sky. Beryx smiled. It was cold and passionless and deadly as his voice.

Hawge's head sank again. The eyes, which had been re-
volving, came to a stop. A green fire shot through them,
splintering into a thousand facets, and Beryx said quietly,
"Harran, look away."

My head turned as if on a peg. I dropped my eyes, and
they came to rest on the dragon's forefoot. It was so close I
could see the horn-like graining of the claws, black blended
into streaky grays, then a dirty yellow at the tip.

Beryx's breathing grew audible. Time bent to the pattern
of his respiration, long, slow, metronomically regular
breaths, hardly abnormal, with no indication of strain. It
was perhaps a hundred of them before I realized he had an
accompaniment. A vast, grating, throaty inhalation, exhala-
tion, was keeping perfect time with him, like a choir singing
behind the soloist. Hawge was breathing too.

Little by little the rhythm grew labored. Slower. Each inhalation became effortful, strenuous. Slower still. Now
heartbeats passed between release and inhalation, still more
between inhalation and release. The sounds grew louder,
less like breathing than long-drawn groans. Louder. Then
something like a huge death-rattle made me leap out of my
skin and the rhythm broke in a flurry of grunts and gasps
and coughs and clatters like stone flung on a roof; I caught
one glimpse of Hawge crouched with all four feet thrust out
and braced and head stretched like a horse at full gallop,
black and searingly vivid on a ground of flame; then something like an explosion in the sun's heart quite blinded me.
Only my eyelids retained the after-image, a blast like the
clash of lightning bolts, a starburst of green-white, scalding,
incandescent light.

By the time my vision returned the mêlée was over, but
now the sounds were so dreadful I wanted to block my ears.
Hawge was the worse. Its frightful furnace roars began with

a rattle and ended with a gagging retch, then resumed after
such a lapse that each time I thought it had died. Beryx was
harder to hear. They were out of time now: all I caught was
an occasional thin, whooping crow, like a man in lung-fever
unable to take his breath.

It went on, and on, and on. My own lungs started to
strain, to founder, there was no air left in the world. Red
spots swarmed across my sight. The air around me was
shivering, as it had when Beryx and Fengthira fought, but
this was no mere tension, this was a stress that would rend
the very earth. I heard myself panting. My eyes swam. It
was unbearable. It had to end. Since I dared not look at
Beryx, I looked at the dragon's foot.

Hawge was standing on the claws. The pad was three
feet off the ground and the claws were driven half their
length into the ground, the spur was bowed clean under the
pad and was grinding down, then up, then down, in time
with each gargantuan struggle for breath. Something glistened in the muscle grooves of the foreleg: drops, rivulets,
that dripped down to darken the torn-up soil. It took me
some time to believe it must be sweat.

Caution went to the winds. Unable to help myself, I
looked up.

Though it was broad day, I still see that image on a
background of red-shot, firelit black. I must have moved, or
they had, for they are in profile, the vast body of the
dragon, arched almost double, drawn up on its claws as if
convulsed, the muscles trembling so the mail spangled like
reflections on a gold-shot morning lake, the head strained
right back into the shoulder spines, the jaws wide open, and
the eyes—I could not look at those. And opposite it the
man, so small and fragile in contrast you wondered why
Hawge had not pulped him into the dust. Until you realized

he was not a small mass but a sliver of compacted energy, the sort of power that detonates volcanoes and makes earthquakes rip whole mountain chains apart.

Next moment both image and battle shattered. Hawge leapt forty feet backward in one spasmodic plunge whose recoil fired it high into the air, Beryx went down as if pile-driven full on his back and rebounded like steel instead of flesh. I was still trying to believe my eyes and wondering when I would be incinerated when it dawned on me. The dragon had not been attacking. In both senses, it was in flight.

I was too stunned for reaction: disbelief, triumph, anything at all. I looked at Beryx instead.

He was drenched from head to toe in sweat, but he showed no distress. I could not see him breathe. His eyes were indescribable. He looked up into the air after Hawge's dwindling shape, and then his lips drew back in something that might have been a smile, if volcanoes smile, before the eyes quite obliterated his face. I heard him speak, though: a thin, fine, vibrant articulation that was the conveyance of naked thought.

He said, <Fly.>

Hawge's head tilted up. It began to climb, the angle growing steeper and steeper and the forward motion less until it was rising almost vertically, as hawks do up a shaft of wind. Higher and higher it lifted, clear into the zenith, a minute black insect shape.

Beryx addressed it again then, in that blood-chilling speech. This time he commanded, <Stop.>

My eyes were dazzled by distance and light. Through sliding beads of tears I saw the tiny wings falter, beat wildly, go limp. Then, with a scream that seemed to rend the firmament to its foundations, Hawge began to fall.

At some stage it must have turned over, in response to Beryx's will or in an attempt to escape. It hit on its back, its body almost horizontal, and it landed fairly athwart the outcrop by the waterhole with an impact that shivered every rock for yards, split the mailed body like a melon, and threw black blood and dust so high that I felt it descending, like rain upon my face.

Beryx may or may not have watched it all the way to the ground. When I came to myself, drew breath, looked round, it was just in time to see him silently, bonelessly, collapse.

My limbs untied. I flew to him. He was not breathing. I jammed my head to his chest. Nothing. I think I knelt up and screamed to the unforgiving heavens at the injustice of it, that having paid such a price, having sacrificed and lost so much, he should fall dead with victory in his very grasp. I know I tore my hair. And then an insane fury took possession of me. He should not be dead, I would not let him be dead, he should live whether the heavens decreed it or not.

I yanked him on his back. I know nothing of medicine. Some instinct dictated it, perhaps: he was not breathing, so he should breathe. I could almost hear Fengthira acidly commanding, <Make him breathe, tha dolt!>

I thumped him in the chest. He gasped. But thumping his chest would only drive breath out. I had to drive it in.

I scrambled frenziedly to his head, pried his mouth open, and forced my own breath into it with all the pressure of my lungs. His chest moved. Now, said instinct, he is not a balloon: it must come out. I drove both hands under his rib cage and he gasped again. His lips were blue. I shot back to his head, forced another breath in, drove it out. Pump, I screamed silently, ramming the heel of my palm over his heart, and flew to drive in another breath.

His face was whiter than Maerdrigg's. No use, sobbed reason: he is dead. You are mishandling a corpse. Four rot you, screamed unreason. He is not dead. He is not!

I drove another breath into him, forced it out. Another. My own heart was pounding madly, my muscles shook, I could hardly find wind to breathe for myself. But a harper learns young to stretch his lungs beyond the compass of other men's. Pump, damn you, pump, I swore at his heart with tears running down my cheeks, and gave it a furious rub as I caught my next breath.

Another. Another. I do not know how many it was before I sat back on my heels, weeping outright now with rage and despair and grief, ready to give up: looked at his face, and saw the blue was gone from his lips.

Not daring to believe it, I set an ear, more gently than a feather landing, to his chest. My own blood was in such a thunder I was slow to hear. But what I heard sent me back to breathing for him as if I had an aedr's endurance myself.

Eventually, after driving out a breath, I dared sit back, my own heart in my mouth. And when his chest lifted, so faintly I could barely feel it against my lightly resting fingers, I felt as if I had beaten Hawge with my own hands.

For a good while longer I watched, every now and then wetting a finger to hold before his lips lest the Sky-lords should have betrayed me at the last. Finally, when it seemed credible, I sat on, looking down into his face, spattered with black drops of dragon blood, caked with dust that had rained down upon his own sweat, blotched an ugly yellow by the great scar under all. His eyes were closed now, normally, so it was safe to look.

With all conscious control and feeling removed, his face recorded every ravage of the war: those two upright furrows

above the nose had come at Eskan Helken. The Confederacy had etched the bitter, finely traced brackets about the
mouth, the deep horizontal scores across the forehead were
from Coed Wrock. The gauntness, the look of chronic suffering might have come from Tirs, or Saphar, or Inyx's
death, or his own inner burden. Or from Sellithar. Or me.
Yet I found myself recalling Fengthira's words: suffering
there was, wounds there had been, but even in that naked-
ness of the asleep or the unconscious, he did not show an
ounce of vice.

I was still looking when he drew an audible breath and
moved his head. Woken to sense, I doffed my jacket and
eased it under for a pillow. Then I thought of water, the
only other help I had, but was too convinced of my work's
frailty to leave him, or dare to move him, until it had drawn
toward noon, and his breathing had the relaxed sound of
natural sleep.

Then, rather doubtfully, I tried him in my arms. But at
Coed Wrock he had been a tall healthy man in the flower of
a soldier's strength, and now I could lift him quite ade-
quately. With wry memories of Eskan Helken I tied his
wrists together and slipped them round my neck, got an
arm where it would support his head, and tottered up.

His eyes opened halfway across the plain. He looked
sleepy, bewildered, not at all like an aedr. He studied me,
then the sky. Then I saw memory and understanding blend
with consciousness, and gradually become a drowsy content.

Presently he remarked, <We seem to make a habit of this.>

I was too busy to reply aloud. In the same serene lassi-
tude he answered my thought.

<You carrying me off battlefields, I mean.> I stumbled
on a stone, and with the faintest trace of a grin he added,
<I'll keep quiet now.>

How morvallin communicate or how they live in Gebria I do not know, but as we neared the waterhole and Hawge's massive wreck rose like a new-made hill above us, a cloud of black scavengers whirled up with irate yarks. Glancing down, I saw that though Beryx's eyes were closed, he wore a small, tired, triumphant smile. Then I understood that Inyx had been finally and fittingly avenged.

While I brewed mint-tea he sat propped on a pack and began, as all soldiers do, to fight the battle over again.

"It was quite easy, really. No, I mean it." A grin at my look. "Those word-games at the start. Misleading. All the time I was using Scarthe . . . knew every word it would say. The tail—used axynbr'arve for that. The fire . . . I don't know what that was. Something with its eyes. But then I had it sorted. So I made it stop. Just to upset it. Calke, that was. And then challenged it. Very strong, of course. But stupid. No finesse." He sounded quite regretful. "When it flew . . . Silliest thing it could have done. If it had stayed on the ground, I could never have killed it. It just had to wait till I wore out." He smiled reflectively toward the massive corpse. "I doubt we'll get so much as a trophy out of that."

Indeed, all we got was the stench, which was supernatural as Hawge, and it was two full days before Beryx was fit to ride. I gratefully used the second one to find the horses, which when Hawge came down beside them had found they could gallop in hobbles after all.

The third morning we saddled up. By then the morvallin had made sizeable inroads even on that mighty carcass, and Beryx looked longingly at a half-picked rib-bone thick as a ship's. But then he shrugged, and turned his horse, and did not glance back.

Six days later we rode across the Gebasterne road upon a

mirror-signal unit and four frustrated needle-eyed boys who were Morran's idea of a dragon watch and had trailed their quarry clean from Tirs, only to be baulked by Gebria's wastes. At sight of them Beryx pulled up his horse. "Tell them, Harran," he said, rather awkwardly. "I'll wait here."

It was difficult to tell them, and harder to win belief. When they did flash out a signal to Lynglos I think they were still inclined to put, "Unconfirmed," on the end. But when one of them nodded to Beryx, asking, "Who's he?" and I said, "The king," his face cleared in a flash.

"The king! King-slain! It must be right!" He was a wiry, freckly, carroty young Tiriann with as much bounce as his unruly hair, and he promptly went rushing up to Beryx's horse. "Lord! Lord! You did it, you killed it! Tell me, show me, it was the weapon, wasn't it?" Evidently Phengis' message had traveled as far as Tirs. "Where is it? What is it? Ouh, it must be, must be . . ."

His eye took the empty scabbard, and filled with disbelief. It lifted, and Beryx looked silently down from his horse.

With his sheepskin jacket, the filthy sling, battered trousers, and what remained of his black turban, he did not look a king. He might have been an outlaw, a desert vagabond. But one glance into those fathomless, steadfast, yet constantly fluxing green eyes would teach you your mistake.

I saw the boy's own eyes widen. His jaw sank. His jubilation died in uncomprehending fear that went deep as consciousness itself. Then, still mute, still staring, he began to back away.

Beryx smiled a little, sad, tired smile. "That's the weapon, Skith." Now I listened, I could hear the aedric intonation, the soft, impersonal, menacing sound of dormant power. "To kill a dragon, that's all you need."

★ ★ ★ ★ ★

Lynglos took the quick way to verify the signal by coming out to meet us on the road. When we topped the last long ridge and saw its untidy outskirts spreading their vegetable patches and stunted trees and clotheslines about the seething human mass, Beryx pulled off his turban, observing, <Better show them it's me.> Our youthful honor guard, all personal qualms lost in the glory of their role, were already chanting, "It's the king! The dragon's dead! It's the king!"

Lynglos was not so sure. It is a Gebrian town, and Gebrians are as skeptical as they are dour. I saw a large man with the stomach of office reserving judgment, a band with instruments tucked under their arms, a banner not yet unrolled. Then a broad lame person with Phalanx written all over him reached the front. I heard him grunt, "That's Beryx all right!" He hobbled forward, demanding, "You've done it, sir? It's dead?"

When Beryx nodded, he drew a long, long breath. Then he flung back his head and let out an ear-splitting triumph yell.

Next moment the band was thumping, the banner waving, the stomach had surged forward with an effulgent smile, and Lynglos had lined the road, laughing, weeping, cheering, patting our knees or feet or horses' shoulders, shouting whatever came into their heads. I heard two ancients disputing fiercely over what weapon would suit a one-handed man. A girl threw me the keerphar flower from behind her ear, the veteran was fighting the stomach for the honor of housing us. Ahead of me all was tearful rapture: behind me, I could hear the moment when Beryx passed.

He had been looking straight ahead, but no king like Beryx could bear to greet such a welcome with indifference.

I knew he would begin to smile, to glance about in search of known faces or in answer to some particularly pressing call, and I knew what happened when he did. I had seen it with Skith. My heart bled for him as the wave of silence passed and the valiant, uncertain rejoicing broke out again in its wake.

The veteran won the battle of the beds on condition that the stomach, who was council Ruand, had us to dine with them. It was a poor meal, for if Lynglos had escaped Hawge's personal attentions it was still part of Everran, and worsted the stomach's eagerness to give us what we deserved. When the watered wine stood alone on the table, he said, "And now, lord, tell us. How was it done?"

Four! I thought. I could almost hear Fengthira's, "Dost not know what tha askst." Then I glanced at the council, leaning forward with every appearance of avidity and not an eye on his face, and thought, How can he tell you, when you dare not even admit what he is?

Beryx too had mostly kept his eyes on his plate. Now he smiled quickly, a man not wanting to seem aloof and unable to be otherwise. A mere shadow of his old charm, but enough.

"Harran's making a song," he said. "If I steal his audience, I dread to think what he'll do." He told the tale of our slander-bout in Estar, and rose on the laugh. "I beg your pardon, Tarmel, but after so much Hethrian water I daren't tackle a night on our own wine."

The veteran made a better fist of meeting his eyes, but I could feel the effort in every glance. When the abbreviated reminiscences were over and we were left in the tiny best bedroom, with horses feeding under the window and Everran's helliens masking a star, Beryx sank down on the nearer bed. And when I saw the way his shoulders bent, the pain became too much.

227

"Dost thou wish," I said, "thee"ing him for the first time, partly out of love, partly from my own distress, "that I had never carried thee from a field?"

After a moment he shook his head.

"No," he said. It came with conviction. He was looking eastward through the hellien, and I knew he saw those half-stripped bones in the desert sun. "It was worth it. All of it. Even this."

It was the same all the way west, through ever more elaborate, better prepared welcomes, more hectic rejoicing, more determined attempts to confront him normally. But always that silence would run along the crowds as they sought for a weapon and found it, always there was that reluctance to meet or too-quick aversion from his eyes.

Or not always. What was worse was the ones who looked and then stood entranced, who would sometimes follow us to the next town and beyond, and when asked why, would answer in bewilderment, "I don't know. I just . . . had to come."

The people of Saphar had been returning before Phengis's message arrived. We rode up on a wet gray winter morning to a city with sodden banners strung across gaps whence rubble had been cleared, with a wall of fully furbished Guardsmen restraining a thin, patched but spirited populace, and to my infuriated amazement, a Regent posted at the bridgehead under an umbrella to protect his official robes.

Beryx's eyes slitted. "My uncle," he murmured, with that new, fearful intonation, "never learns." Then he choked. "And," the gurgle was suppressed laughter, "he'll be *so* happy with this!"

The Regent, however, had evidently been warned, for if

his welcome was forced it did not break. "We've worked on the palace for you, m'boy . . . Ah, here's Kyvan—" And out popped Kyvan, complete with prayers and crimson cloak, which had to be girded on then and there. Beryx submitted, with the first softening of his braced composure since Lynglos: but as he walked forward into the roar of cheering it became a smile of genuine delight.

"Morran!" he said. "Well done!"

I saw the young face under the helmet flush. I also saw he was one of the rare few who could manage, quite naturally, to hold Beryx's eye. "Sir," he said stiffly. Then, more easily, "I've left a terrible lot for you."

For the next three weeks Beryx did it, at more than his old pace. This I can vouch for, since I had to share the task. It was, "Harran, what do you think of this? Harran, what shall we do about that? Harran, will you see so-and-so, fix something-or-other, decide such-and-such," so in those three weeks I never touched a harp. I thought he wanted to keep out of view, I feared a loss of his inherent decisiveness, and was too busy to ponder the cause. I was finding a new Treasurer, blazoning Everran's redemption round the Confederacy, even arranging a new audience hall and rooms for Sellithar.

It was raining hard that morning, so we had drawn the panels at the roofed end of the old hall, lit the fire, put hangings for the drafts and buckets under the drips. There was little business. More and more often it was, "Harran, will you ask the king this? See if he wants that?" It hurt me, if I understood why. But at the very end a thin, furtive man with an Estarian face and fixed, blank eye emerged from the departing crowd. He did not speak. He merely stood before the high seat and looked up at the king.

That disquieting aedric smile began to weave in Beryx's eyes. He held out his hand.

Still with a tranced stare, the man slid his own hand into his cloak, and Beryx's palm filled with the cataracted, golden-shot white fire of Maerdrigg's maerian.

Beryx looked into the man's eyes. Slowly they woke, showed bewilderment, panic; he gave a wild start. Beryx shook his head. The man stood still.

Beryx said softly, "For the nerve, I admire you. For what you cost Everran, I should roast you alive. I won't. But if I were you, I should be in Quarred tomorrow night."

The man fled like a lydyr with ulfann on its track. Beryx tilted the great maerian. Then he said without looking up, "Harran, will you ride with me, one more time?"

We wore our old traveler's clothes and took the horses we had ridden so very far. As they led up Beryx's big dark-brown, one of the blood horses he had so loved in earlier days, he slapped its neck lightly and clicked his tongue. And did not tighten the reins, I noticed, when he swung up.

We rode south into the dark winter rain that would heal Everran's scars, always cold, more often wet than dry. I wondered why Beryx did not use wryvurx to shield us, and he shook his head at me. "It's better not to meddle," he said, "unless you must."

Before we reached Saphar I had noticed how little he used a bridle to manage his horse. That night, as we sat in an upstairs room of the inn at Asleax, I watched him reach over the wine jug without moving a hand. A shamefaced grin came as he caught my eye.

"Well," he said, "it is easier." And thinking it little enough compensation for all the sorrow his arts had brought, I nodded and reached for my new harp.

Next day we struck off from the Azilien into central Tirs, traveling now as Inyx had once led us, as the morvallin fly. That night Beryx found a huge old burnt-out khanel to shelter us. Next day we were high in the hills, the Helkent looming over us, slashed white with waterfalls, dark meat-red from the rain. Beryx murmured, "It will be a good season this year."

I did not ask our destination. I had already guessed. We found it next day, a narrow black valley running up into the mountains' gut, stony, deserted, pathless, oddly eerie in the unbroken rain. At the mouth Beryx reined in, narrowed his eyes, and nodded. "Ker Eygjafell," he said. "Shadows' Home."

We rode in, our horses slipping and stumbling on the stones. The valley turned, showing its true head was still some way off, a black cliff with the blind mouth of a cave at its base. Something in the very atmosphere made me half rein in, and Beryx gave me a quick, warm smile. "You'll be with me," he said.

The horses would not enter the cave, even in the rain, and we did not force them. We walked through what had once been a tall double doorway, into a black, dank, echoing space whose frigid air made me gasp.

"I suppose," Beryx remarked absently, "he expects me to see in the dark. But I can't. Harran, did we put any wood in those saddlebags?"

I brought him a piece of twine and five or six sticks, and he lit the torch with one quick flash. "May as well announce ourselves," he said. "Now. The Ilam." It is the old Everran word for a high chamber. "It'll be up here."

We climbed some broken, hollowed steps, Beryx walking steadily, me treading on his heels. The high chamber was empty and cheerless as the rest. I saw Beryx's eye alter, and knew that at some time he had seen it differently.

"There should have been a coffer," he said, "but I suppose that's gone with the rest. We'll have to do the best we can."

He slid a hand into his sheepskin jacket. The maerian answered the torch with a royal crimson meteor, and on its flare, in the darkness beyond us, shone two white, glowing, phantom gems.

My blood curdled. Beryx, unperturbed, looked at the Dead and asked simply, "Where?"

Maerdrigg retreated, or rather receded. Beryx followed. On the far side of the chamber a niche had been delved, high in the stone. He slid the maerian in. With a last flare it vanished, and Maerdrigg vanished with it. Beryx stood a moment looking into the dark, before he murmured, in pity and sadness, "Sleep well."

I left the Ilam backward, and the cave the same way. Only when we were clear of the valley did Beryx's shoulders relax and he let out a long, heartfelt, "Whew!"

"No wonder the horses wouldn't go in," he said, when I looked at him. "They're all there. Darrhan, Maersal, Maerond, Darven. The whole Maerheage clan. Worse than the Quarred Tingrith. Ugh!" Then he began to whistle, my catch for the Eskan Helken saeveryr, and we rode off thankfully through the rain.

It had broken when we came down toward Asleax, so Everran lay out beneath us with that vividness only winter sunshine can bestow, azure and pigeon's breast purple and iridescent emerald. South of Asleax they were flying the kites for Air, specks of color that ducked and towered on the shrewd, gay wind.

As the road appeared Beryx reined in, and took a breath.

"Well, Harran," he said, matter-of-fact as if it had long been agreed to, "this is where we say goodbye."

The best I could do was, "G-g-g?"

"Goodbye, yes." His eyes danced with that disconcerting aedric mirth. "Maerdrigg's asleep. Hawge is dead. There's only one ghost left to lay. And if you're going to Maer Selloth and I'm going to—where I'm going—this is where our roads divide."

"M-Maer Selloth?" None of it made sense.

"Maer Selloth." He was still smiling, eyes green and scintillant against his damp black hair and scruffy jacket and stubbled face. "Saphar may not look much, but I think it's fit for a queen—don't you?"

I thought he had lost his wits. Did he think Sellithar, who had lost him for a scar, would take an aedr back? Horrific images filled my eyes: the old life in Saphar, shameful secrecy, furtive lust, more horrific images of Tenevel when I announced that the king refused to accept a divorce, the reply I should have to relay to Beryx, agonizing images of Sellithar, lost before she was found, brought back to someone else . . .

I caught for a straw, any straw. "But—but—where are you going yourself?"

His eyes took on a distance that made them wells of emerald.

"I . . . don't know yet. Eskan Helken first. There were a lot of things I didn't learn. Then . . . they say there's another ocean beyond Hethria. I haven't used Pharaone. Some things should be seen with eyes. But an aedr could do things in Hethria too. Dam Kemreswash. Send the water south. Fengthira might be interested. Or she might travel with me . . ."

It had taken me this long to reach comprehension, let be

speech. Even after aedryx, some things exceed the compass of the mind.

"You're going—away?" He nodded. "Right away?" He nodded again. "Leaving Everran?" He nodded once more. I was too dazed to see that every question would hit him harder than Fengthira's that first day. "Leaving Everran?" He nodded yet again. His face was set now, stripped of its smile. "But, but, you can't! It's what you fought for—what you went through all that for—it's, it's—it's your whole life!"

I must have bared nerves with every phrase. He looked steadily back at me. Fengthira was right: he never had an ounce of vice.

"Everything I fought for," he agreed. "But the fighting's done."

"But, but, but, the rebuilding!" I yelled. "Saphar, Everran, the Confederacy, the—" Now I glimpsed a catastrophe wider than his own. "You can't, you can't! We have to have a king!"

At that he grinned in genuine amusement. "Of course they do. Why do you think you've been schooled these last three weeks? Why do you think Fengthira told me, if I'd make her welcome in Everran, to guard my harper well?"

That winded me altogether. I could not so much as gasp. He surveyed the shimmering lowlands and spoke as if selecting a new town governor.

"Morran's too young, and a soldier anyway. My uncle's a clot. The Council needs a leader. Any lord or Resh-lord would make the others revolt. Tenevel's only a Resh-lord too. But you know the Confederacy. And kingship. You've traveled with me, you've done things yourself. The people will accept you. It's the only choice."

This time speech came without any travail.

"No!"

"Now, Harran," he began reprovingly, "don't be foolish—"

But I was beyond considering foolishness. "No, no, no! I won't do it! You can't lose all—give all—suffer all you've done and then—not to me! I won't!" I could not even voice the ultimate shame. If I had been his savior, I was also his betrayer. That he should gift me with Everran as well as Sellithar was such injustice as the heavens would not countenance.

"Harran," he said gently. He waited till I looked round. His eyes were withdrawn, the marks of old suffering clear in his face. "You know better. You've seen how they look at me. Do you think I could bear to rule . . . like that?"

I could not speak.

"And do you think Tenevel would stomach an aedric king?" He shook his head. "More to the point: every line has its ending. I am the end of mine."

"Hawge said that!" I exploded. "It's a lie!"

He shook his head. Very gently he said, "I already knew."

I could only gape.

"When it first came," he went on in that voice like falling water, gentle, irrecoverable, "Hawge made me suspect. After Phare, I knew."

It was more than I could bear to contemplate, that he should find he was himself Everran's bane. And atop that, I had betrayed him. So long it had lain between us, and it lay there still. But it could lie no longer.

I turned my head away. Then I got out, "Sellithar—and I—"

He answered softly, "I knew that too."

"If only," I burst out in bitter, futile retrospect, "I had not 'thought so loud'—"

"No," he replied quietly. "I knew in Saphar. Phare made me know I knew."

A pit yawned under me. When I came to him on the hill he had been raw with these manifold wounds, and it was I who reached him first. He had not only to confront Fengthira, but to look at me, speak to me, as if I were in truth a friend . . .

His voice was not bitter, only sad. "I couldn't blame you—or Sellithar. What did Fengthira tell you? 'Horses' morals are simpler than men's.' After Phare . . . I had to use them. So it didn't come between us then. It doesn't now."

There must, there had to be, some recompense. "We'll go away," I burst out. "Out of Everran. You can be king until—the new line can begin after you!"

When he did not speak, I looked around. There was a kind of laughter in his face, the laughter with which some men meet the deepest hurts of all. He started to speak, and shook his head.

Then he said, "Harran . . . Hawge didn't lie, you know. Aedryx and dragons are—kin."

My hair rose. I choked.

"You saw it," he insisted softly. "When we did Letharthir, you thought I was Hawge. Fengthira warned me, 'And dragons have green eyes.' When you fought me, I felt it for myself."

He turned his eyes to Everran. "She lives in Eskan Helken, to avoid temptation. But I would be a king. It would be so easy. Lose your patience with one incompetent, coerce one balky council—" His eyes were still and steadfast and irredeemably sad. "I made myself an aedr. I can't go back. Unless I leave it . . . I am still Everran's bane."

I tore the reins through and through my fingers. The

pity, the injustice, the sorrow of it was too much. Everran lay below us, scars masked by the falling sun, the thing he loved best in life, for which he had given his health, his manhood, his very humanity. And now was going, of his own will, to give the thing itself.

"You mustn't think I'm so unselfish," he said softly. "Fengthira said once, 'If tha walkst, t'will not be for any trumpery maerian.' Maerdrigg taught me such a lesson. To waste your life, your inheritance, your very death, for a stone. If you must have an obsession, it should be worth the price. Like Everran. It will be easier leaving than you think. Everran's still—my whole life. And I know Everran will be safer without me."

I thought of the Quarred clans, the Estar guild leaders, the lords like Vellan, the myriad small daily choices upon which Everran rested, as upon the harp's firm arms the fragile strings. I think I howled aloud.

"Of course you can do it." His crispness told me the smile had revived. "You'll have Morran. A reasonable Council. Tenevel to second you." I tore my head away. He chuckled. "Four, man, if you can get me off Coed Wrock and bring me back this last time, you can do anything!"

I looked round. He was grinning, those green eyes full of simple human mirth. Swinging down from his horse he said gravely, but with a twinkle, "Do you think you could bring yourself, without shrinking, to—er—give me a farewell?"

When we embraced, I found I did not want to let him go. Not only for the injustice, the terror of the future, our broken comradeship, the loss of the man himself, but because I knew now why those he tranced had followed him. He was an aedr. If his going would free me of something fearsome, beyond nature, it would also leave life empty, robbed of a glamour, a savor, that only imminent peril can bestow.

It was he who stood back first. "And," he said, more gravely, "you really should call me Beryx now."

He clicked his tongue to summon the horse. Swung astride. Then he looked back, and there was no laughter in his eyes.

"Harran?" he sounded tentative, almost appealing. "When everything's healed . . . if I'm to be known hereafter as the king who forsook his kingdom, I'd like them to—understand why?"

Now, with Saphar rebuilt, Everran re-united, back in tune with the Confederacy, with Morran for my general, Zarrar for a hearthbard, and the queen to rescue this song from the jaws of our small but terrible son, I can say to him as truth what I said then as promise, there on the hill above Asleax before he rode away.

"Wherever you are, lord, rest easy. I am still your harper. The songs will be sung."

About the Author

SYLVIA KELSO lives in North Queensland, Australia, and has been writing or telling stories for as long as she remembers. *Everran's Bane* is her first published fantasy novel, but she has published poetry in Australian literary magazines, and has a Creative Writing MA for an alternate history/SF novel set in alternate North Queenslands. She lives in a house with a lot of trees in the garden, but no cats or dogs. She makes up for this by playing an Irish whistle. In public she plays Celtic music with a group of friends in a group called Kilbeggan, or with the local bush band, Wattle'n'Gum.